THE
FALL
OF THE
TEMPLAR

GREY
GRIFFINS

BOOK
3

THE FALL OF THE

TEMPLAR

Derek Benz
& J. S. Lewis

SCHOLASTIC INC.
NEW YORK TORONTO LONDON AUCKLAND SYDNEY
MEXICO CITY NEW DELHI HONG KONG BUENOS AIRES

ISBN-13: 978-0-545-10884-3
ISBN-10: 0-545-10884-5

12 11 10 9 8 7 6 5 4 3 2 1   9 10 11 12 13 14/0

Printed in the U.S.A.   40

First Scholastic paperback printing, January 2009

For Noah: Welcome to the world! Your mom and I are so glad to see you!
And for Ioulia, my wife, bless you and your kind, wonderful heart.

— Derek

For Joshua and Jesse. Brothers and Griffins for life.

— Jon

Acknowledgments

I'd like to thank my family. You mean the world to me and always will. Thanks also to Roger Lane for saving my life from the hungry tractor! Thanks to all my teachers, and especially Mrs. Merical, who inspired me and encouraged my dreams. And thank you as well to all my friends over the years and the countless things we shared: sack lunches, school dances, one hundred meter dashes, intricately folded notes, turtle hunting, leaf burning, ninja stalking, monkey bar swinging, rainy nights, video games, Lord of the Rings, and trips down the gravel road in an old Impala.   — D. B.

Though Derek and I are the lucky ones who get our names on the cover, writing a book truly takes a village. I'd like to thank my wife, Kelly, for her support — when that creative storm hits, she gives me the freedom to ride it to the last wind. Whenever I get stuck in a rut, my daughters, Bailey and Olivia, are there to inspire me with their laughter and love. I'd like to thank my parents, Brian and Annette, for encouraging me to reach for the stars. Thanks to the Crawford family, who has always been there for me. Thank you as well to Mike Reynolds for your selfless support.   — J. S. L.

Very special thanks to Nancy Coffey for continually shepherding us down this wild path. We wouldn't be here without you. Thank you to our friends at Scholastic. Lisa Sandell, you are the best editor in the business! Thank you for pushing us to greater heights. Thank you to Melissa Bloomfield for your patience and hard work.

Thanks as well to Rachel Coun, Stephanie Nooney, Suzanne Murphy, Tracy van Straaten, Richard Amari, Marijka Kostiw, Ken Geist, and the entire Scholastic family. We're so blessed to be working with you. We'd also like to thank Scholastic Book Fairs, and in particular, Stacey Phelan, for the amazing support you've given to us. Thank you as well to Yvette Roeder, Faith Horlacher, Donna Powers, Kendra Lux, Amy Black, Sarah Bolger, and all the incredible booksellers who have adopted us. We've also received the most amazing support from teachers and librarians across the country. We appreciate it more than you know. And to our readers, we give you our thanks. The letters, e-mails, and drawings have been a blast. Keep 'em coming! — D. B. & J. S. L.

Contents

PROLOGUE

CLOUDS OBSCURED a full moon, bringing rolling thunder and jagged lightning over Avalon's only cemetery far below. The graveyard was set inside a wooded hollow, lined with crumbling headstones, like a mouth of broken teeth waiting to devour unwary visitors. Just as the rain began to fall, the gates shuddered violently, and the chains twisted and fractured. With a heavy gust the doorway blew apart, and long shadows appeared through the opening. Teeth flashed in the moonlight, accompanied by the disquieting sound of sniffing. The hunt was on. . . .

At that same moment, on the far side of the cemetery, a light flickered weakly to life. The portal appeared. Limping out onto the damp earth was the tiny form of a spriggan. Her furtive eyes looked about as the faerie's spiky fur stood on end. With her scaly tail twitching nervously, she skulked from the shadow of one headstone to the next.

Though the spriggan's leg was wounded, she moved like a phantom through the graveyard, never once making a sound — she couldn't risk it. The werewolves were on her trail, and she knew they were near. They'd been following her through an endless network of portals. With trepidation, the spriggan looked down at her hands where a golden amulet lay. She drew her breath, losing herself for a moment in its beauty, but when her ears caught the faint padding of wolf paws, she tucked it away and doubled her speed. They'd found her!

The sound of the werewolves approaching grew steadily closer. No matter which way she ran, they seemed to be on every side. Wounded, she didn't have the strength to open another portal, let alone shape-shift into a bird and fly away. With her heart beating rapidly, the spriggan raced down a row of headstones, where the slabs of marble and granite seemed to close in on either side, forcing her straight ahead.

A wolf howled. They were almost on top of her!

The injured spriggan soon found herself at a dead end, backed against a gravestone. Lightning flashed, illuminating the chiseled text:

HERE LIES OLAF "IVER" IVERSON

TEMPLAR & FRIEND

REST IN PEACE

Another flash of lightning. New shadows slowly rose over the spriggan's trembling form. Slowly, she turned back to Iver's grave as she faced the hunters. Their eyes were red and their teeth were bared. The spriggan's flight was over. There was nowhere to run.

"Sprig!" Max Sumner called out, his own heart pounding as he sat up in his bed, breaking free of the terrible nightmare.

1

Iceland . . .

"WE CAN'T last much longer in this storm," a soldier shouted above howling mountain winds. His beard and brows were thick with ice. Like his six comrades, he was dressed in arctic gear, standing on a narrow ledge. Above towered the high peak of a frozen volcano. Thousands of feet below lay swirling mists.

"We leave when I say we leave," the unit leader yelled back. Dark sunglasses shielded his piercing eyes, and his grim face was covered in stubble. His name was Logan, and he was one of the most dangerous men alive. Standing like an immovable stone amidst the raging winds, the Scotsman studied the rock face, deep in thought. He'd been there for almost an hour, silent as death as the temperature continued to drop.

"You sure this is the place?" shouted another soldier, before clearing the frost from his goggles.

"How 'bout a bit of quiet, eh?" Logan requested. Without further question, the soldier returned to his post. Besides, even if they were wrong, it was too late to go back and they knew it. Either the map was right, or soon they'd become a frozen part of the landscape themselves.

Soon, as if the answer had suddenly become clear, Logan pulled out his ice ax and drove it into the wall with an explosion

3

of frost and rime. As he stared silently at the newly exposed rock, a knowing smile crept across his face. The Scotsman brought out a tattered map from his parka and checked it twice, comparing it with what he saw on the wall. He reached out to where the three concentric circles lay inscribed on the rock, then he made several signs in the air. Almost immediately, shimmering light pooled in the circles like molten lava, and the rock face swung open, revealing a long tunnel that led down into the volcano. He waved to his men, and the adventurers ditched their climbing gear and ducked into the mysterious tunnel, leaving the howling wind far behind.

"So this is it," Logan murmured to himself, throwing back his hood. The trail had led them to a stony chamber layered in shadow.

One of the soldiers lit a torch, holding it aloft as they all looked around. The room was perfectly square, with a stone sarcophagus positioned in the center, strange runes etched across its surface.

"Looks like the competition got here first," noted Søren, Logan's second-in-command. A ski mask covering all but his wary eyes, Søren was a lean man with a cold, calculating voice that made him sound more like a machine than a man. He was pointing toward the base of the tomb, where several bodies dressed in black leather lay scattered. They were frozen solid. At first glance they might have appeared human, but their faces were covered in bristling fur and their canine jaws were lined with yellow teeth. "Werewolves," he confirmed.

"But they didn't come in through the front door," Logan noted, looking back up the long passage from where they'd come. "We'd have picked up their trail before now. Must have used portals." Logan signaled for everyone to stay where he was. Whatever had finished off the werewolves was probably still around.

"How'd the Black Wolf Society know where to find Lord Saxon's tomb?" asked another soldier. Like the famed Lord Saxon, Logan and his men were adventurers. The difference was that Lord Saxon had come to protect the secret that lay in this cave, while Logan and his men had come to steal it.

"Don't know," Logan replied, his eyes skittering about the room, looking for traps or trick doors. "Just keep sharp. This is a hit and run. I want out of here quick as can be, understand?"

Søren nodded and slid on a pair of strange goggles, hitting a few buttons on the side before sweeping the room with a visual scan. "Low-level magic signature on the floor," he explained. "Looks like a trap was triggered by some kind of motion detector that picked up activity near the tomb."

"Tundra Trolls . . . ," Logan said with a half smile. It made all the sense in the world. Not many creatures, even from the faerie world, could survive a godforsaken hell like this. "The Black Wolves portal'd in and landed themselves in a nasty nest of trolls, eh? Serves those dogs right." The other soldiers nodded. Werewolves were nasty business, but they were no match for a Tundra Troll.

"Looks like they didn't make it to the tomb," Søren noted.

Logan shook his head and grinned. "That they didn't.

Which means we're in luck. That the only trap your scanner picked up?"

Søren nodded. "You're clear to move in."

"Good," Logan replied, taking off his sunglasses to brush away the frost. "I want you to fan out . . . secure the room. And stay clear of that trap if you'd be so kind, gents. I don't want any trolls dropping on my head."

The soldiers moved briskly through the tomb. In the blink of an eye, all entrances were secured. If any more werewolves were on the way, they'd regret it. No Tundra Troll would be making a surprise attack, either. These men were agents of T.H.O.R., the vaunted Special Forces of the Templar. They'd seen everything, done everything, and survived the impossible. It would take more than a creepy tomb or an oversized yeti to stop them. . . .

Logan walked across the room and stopped just short of the trap, the toe of his boot only millimeters from the trip line. He turned to Søren. "What level of trap?"

"Level six, sir."

Logan nodded and turned back to the tomb. Reaching into his jacket, he pulled out a metal cylinder, hollow in the middle. Then the Scotsman placed his right arm inside and tapped a button six times. It tightened around his forearm, and a humming sound filled the room. "See you blokes in a bit." He nodded curtly toward Søren, who saluted in return. A second later, the light around Logan seemed to flicker; then he dimmed from view, leaving an empty floor where the knight had once stood.

"Everybody out! Now!" Logan shouted as he suddenly reappeared in a flash of light. He was standing on top of the sarcophagus, its lid thrown to one side. From inside, a skeletal hand reached hungrily toward him. The Scotsman was carrying an ancient box as he leapt into the air, narrowly avoiding the bony fingers of the undead monster. "Cripes!" Logan shouted, as he hit the ground. Mistiming his landing, he didn't quite clear the trap. At the same moment, there was a terrible roar as three massive Tundra Trolls materialized in the room, leaving little space for the T.H.O.R. agents to maneuver. Huge, white, and covered in a shaggy coat of fur, the arctic beasts had massive horns that jutted from their heads and arms the size of bridge cables. With ear-shattering bellows, they launched at the Templar, who were now in a fight for their lives.

"You're a nasty one," Logan growled through clenched teeth as he fought off the fanatical skeleton, while trying to avoid the trolls. "Søren!" the Scotsman yelled over the roar of battle. "We need a way out. Now!"

Søren ducked beneath the arm of one of the trolls before leaping over another and finally somersaulting to the exit where their abandoned packs lay. Reaching in, he grabbed a handful of canisters, pulled the pins, and rolled them toward the trolls. Instantly, the room was awash in thick smoke.

The trolls roared and swung blindly at the air. With aid from their high-tech goggles, the knights quickly disengaged and made their way back to the exit. All that remained was Logan, who continued his struggle against his undead assailant. It pressed wildly with bony claws, looking for any opening. With a sweeping kick, Logan managed to break off the skeleton's legs at the knees, and the crypt sentinel was sent crashing to the ground.

Wasting no time, Logan shot through the exit, racing up the tunnel until he caught up with his men. Below, the Tundra Trolls were bellowing, blinded by the smoke. "We're safe . . . at least for the moment," he said, turning to his men as they stood in the narrow passage a safe distance from the trolls. "Those nasties are too big to fit through their own front door. They're stuck like sardines in a can."

Logan checked the box he'd taken from the crypt, but not before taking a visual roll call. Luckily, all knights were present and accounted for. They'd survived their encounter with only a few scratches, though all the treasure hunters before them had perished in their attempts to secure Lord Saxon's diary.

"So what went wrong back there?" Søren asked, looking over at Logan.

"The trap was a level six," replied Logan, brushing dust from his shoulder in irritation. "But the Skeleton Keeper was a level eight. You might have told me about that."

Søren nodded. "The sarcophagus must have been lined with iron. The MQH goggles can't see through that particular metal. Not yet anyway."

"Now you tell me," Logan said with a half smile. Then he looked down at the box he'd pilfered with grim satisfaction. The smile didn't remain for long, though. "Am I the only one who noticed it got very quiet all of a sudden?"

The T.H.O.R. agents looked around suspiciously until Logan turned and spied the skeletal Crypt Sentinel clawing its legless body toward them. The monster let out a terrible cry as its body started to flicker and spark, as if the enchantment that had held it together was about to unravel.

"It's gonna blow!" Logan shouted in horror. Like the wind, the Templar turned and raced up the passage. They were nearly halfway up when the explosion finally hit, sending a shower of dust and rock everywhere. Then came the fireball. It started as only a glimmer in the distance, but it grew ... and grew ... shaking the mountain as a deafening roar rocketed through the passage. When it hit, everything seemed to fall apart all at once. First, the ceiling. Then, the walls. Finally, the floor began to fall away.

"That's bad news, it is," Logan muttered, sarcasm lacing his voice as he watched their only exit disappear under the weight of the mountain. Everything went dark, and after a few more moments, it grew deathly quiet.

"At least we have what we came for," noted Søren. The wind was bitter as he and Logan scanned the entrance to Lord Saxon's tomb, which was now nothing more than a pile of impassable destruction. It had taken them hours to dig their way out, but somehow their entire party had managed to claw their way to freedom.

Logan looked down at the box in his hands. It was seemingly no worse for the wear. He clicked open the latch. Inside lay a book, bound in tattered leather. "This diary had better be worth it," he growled.

Søren wrapped three of his broken fingers together, but if he felt any pain, he never made a sign. "So, you never told me . . ."

"Told you what?" replied Logan, snapping the lid shut.

"What the devil is so important about that diary that we'd travel halfway across the world to find it?"

Logan turned back to Søren and smiled.

"Ever heard of the Eye of Odin?"

2   A Most Uncertain Prognosis

Beep . . . Beep . . . Beep . . .

THE LONELY sound of a heart monitor rang through the hospital room, its somber staccato reminding the Grey Griffins that it could have been any one of them lying in that bed instead of Ernie Tweeny. The other three members of their secret club had been lucky. At least they'd survived the dark adventure to Scotland and back without a scratch. How long would that good fortune hold out, though?

It had been two dreadful months since Ernie had been admitted to the hospital under the pretense of a tragic skiing accident. That couldn't have been further from the truth. The problem is that honesty would have landed them all in an insane asylum. Who would have believed that Ernie had been caught in the explosion of an ancient witch's secret Antarctic lair? Luckily, no one had questioned the Griffins too closely. Hardly a day went by when the three friends didn't visit their fallen companion. Sometimes they'd spend the entire weekend with him. Like strands from the same piece of rope, they'd become so intertwined that each felt lost when even one of their members was missing.

"He looks so peaceful," Natalia Romanov commented. Her auburn hair, darkened by winter, was tied back into thick braids, and as she watched over Ernie, her green eyes grew misty. Natalia's face was ivory, with a light dusting of freckles that collected tenaciously about the bridge of her nose — especially during the sunny months of summer, which now seemed so far away.

"He's probably dreaming about being a superhero," chuckled Harley Davidson Eisenstein, the largest of the four Griffins. Hair the color and texture of wheat (that probably hadn't been washed in a week) hung down over blue eyes. Sometimes it felt as if Harley's good nature and easygoing humor were all the Griffins had to hold them on course. It'd been that way since kindergarten, when Harley, Natalia, and Max banded together to save Ernie from the schoolyard bully. Harley was definitely the muscle of their team, streetwise and tough as a bull.

Max, or more formally, Grayson Maximillian Sumner III, was the official leader of the Grey Griffins. His family was wealthy, powerful, and broken. The carefree days of the Sumner family lounging around the house playing board games and watching movies were long gone. His parents' divorce had wrecked everything.

On top of everything else, the guilt of pulling his friends into this whole mess weighed heavily on his heart. The trip to Scotland was just supposed to be a Christmas holiday spent on his father's estate. Instead, Max and his friends had landed in the middle of a war between the Templar Knights and Morgan LaFey's army of werewolves — a war where Max had handed victory over to the claws of the enemy. The Black Wolf Society and their witch queen had played Max for a fool, using his own father against him. Now, after Max had unwittingly given them the dreaded Spear of Ragnarok, the Black Wolves were growing more powerful every day.

"I miss Ernie so much," Natalia murmured with a trembling smile that hinted of some fond memory. They all had wonderful memories of the bespectacled, comical, rail-thin, munch-o-holic, asthmatic, and reluctant hero. Ernie was a complex ball of tangled absurdities that had bound the four of them together like glue. Without him, it would never be the same.

"We all do," agreed Max, wishing he could switch places with Ernie. He would have given up all his family's wealth, his grandfather's legacy as the Guardian of the *Codex*, and the connection with the Knights Templar to get Ernie back.

"You thought about how we're gonna get back at them for this?" Harley asked, spinning a thick iron ring on his index finger — the same ring that he'd chanced upon at a Freemason's garage sale. It wasn't until later that he discovered it was as an ideal weapon against evil faeries. They're all allergic to Faerie's Bane, or iron.

"Every day," Max said grimly.

"So what's the plan?"

"That's the problem. I just don't know," Max said, shrugging. "If the Templar Knights can't stop the Black Wolves, how are we supposed to do it? Besides, even if we wanted to get the Spear of Ragnarok back, Iver won't tell me where it is. It's like he doesn't trust me."

"Can you blame him?" Natalia asked.

"I guess not," answered Max. "I should have listened to him to begin with."

"What about Logan?" Harley wondered. "I bet he knows where the Spear is."

"I already tried, and he's not talking either," answered Max. "Most of the time he's out with the T.H.O.R. agents trying to hunt down werewolves."

"So do you think your dad is in charge of the Black Wolves?" Harley asked cautiously. "I heard a couple of knights talking, and nobody has seen the Black Witch since she fought Dracula."

Max shook his head. His dad, after betraying Max and stealing the Spear of Ragnarok, had left Max feeling empty and alone. It was even worse than the day his mom told him about the divorce. Finding out your dad was moving out forever was one thing, but discovering he was an evil overlord who wanted to destroy the planet was an entirely different level of depression.

"I'm sorry, Max," offered Natalia, patting him on the shoulder. "I know this isn't easy, but Harley's right, you know. The problem is, as difficult as it may be, we need to do *something* before it's too late. We can't just sit here and feel sorry for ourselves forever. It's called the Spear of Ragnarok for a reason. *Ragnarok* means the end of the world! Unless we want Fire Giants and armies of skeleton soldiers marching down Main Street, we'd better get a move on."

No one questioned Natalia's facts. She was voracious in her research, as any good detective should be. Rarely did a clue get overlooked when she was on the job, whether it dealt with tracking down a stolen bicycle, or investigating events surrounding the end of the world. As tenacious as they came, Natalia took her detective work very seriously. Unfortunately, these and other eccentricities didn't do much for her popularity at school — particularly with the other girls. Natalia tended to find them boring and a bit silly. In turn, they avoided her like last week's moldy lunch.

The room fell into silence as the three friends looked out the window, lost in their own cloudy thoughts.

"I've been meaning to tell you guys something," Max said hesitantly after a bit. With a quick glance to ensure the door was closed, Max rolled up his sleeve and placed his arm, palm up, on the table before them. "Well, I don't know if this can help us very much or not. I'm not even sure how it happens, but I've been kinda practicing something. Watch this. . . ."

Harley and Natalia watched patiently as Max furrowed his brow in concentration. Then it happened. At first it was only a pale ripple. Then, with a sudden whoosh, blue fire sparked to life, racing up and down his arm and rolling across his fingertips.

Harley's eyes grew wide and Natalia gasped. "Why didn't you tell us?" she asked. The other Griffins had seen Max's mysterious blue fire in the past, but until now, he'd never been able to turn it on and off like a switch. Natalia reached a curious hand toward the fire, then jerked it back suddenly.

"What'd it feel like?" Harley asked, anxious to try it himself.

"I . . . I don't know," mused Natalia. "Kind of like an electrical shock, I guess."

Max nodded, a smile flirting with the corners of his mouth. "I've been able to do it for a couple of weeks now."

"Does it hurt?" asked Harley.

"It just tingles a bit," Max said, flexing his hand as he made the flames dance. "I mean, it doesn't burn my clothes or anything. I can't even light a candle with it."

Just as Max's cobalt fire disappeared, there was a knock at the door. Without waiting for a response, an attractive young woman dressed in blue medical scrubs walked in. A stethoscope hung about her slender neck, and she held a clipboard in her hands. Not much taller than Harley, she had flowing black hair pulled back into a ponytail, with a forelock of silver that fell across her face. She wore stylish glasses over a pair of eyes that seemed to be aware of everything around her, visible and invisible — and she smelled like fresh flowers.

"Good afternoon," she said, not bothering to look up from her notes. "How's our patient doing?"

"Hey, Athena," Max replied as he rolled down his sleeve. "Same as always, I guess."

Athena, who was actually a Templar Knight and not a doctor at all, sat down beside Ernie's bed and listened to his heartbeat, her face a mask of concern. Only last Christmas, the Griffins had been at her bedside after she'd barely survived a run-in with the Black Wolf Society. Yet despite the gravity of her wounds, Athena pulled through, recovering remarkably quickly.

Now it was her turn to sit at the bedside of a fallen Griffin. They couldn't have wished for a brighter, more competent person to look after Ernie. Through the trials, Natalia and Athena had formed a close friendship, often spending time together in the hospital cafeteria talking about Athena's adventures around the world.

Max and Harley, however, preferred hanging out with Logan, who, like Athena, was a Templar Knight. Normally dressed in black leather and sunglasses, the Scotsman drove fast cars, had been a street fighter in his younger years, and spoke at least a dozen languages. He was no-nonsense, had a stubbly beard, and was equally at home working in the Sumner garage as he was wrestling with a six-armed ogre.

Reaching down into her medical bag, Athena pulled out a strange object that resembled the instrument a doctor might use to look inside your ear. This one, however, was made of brass, with runes etched along the handle. A stream of shifting colors filtered down from prisms inside, racing along Ernie's sleeping form. The Griffins watched Athena's eyes narrow as she placed the instrument back into her bag before quickly rising to her feet. Suddenly an alarm went off, and Ernie's heart monitor started to scream. Athena's face paled and her tone grew urgent. "Everyone out!"

3

Over the Troll Bridge
and into the Inferno

One week later . . .

"I THINK it's time we had that talk, Master Sumner," Olaf
Iverson stated thoughtfully as they cruised down the country
road, gravel and ice crunching beneath the tires of his antique
Plymouth. Although old enough to be Max's grandfather, Iver
moved without the slowness of age, and his mind was as sharp as
steel. He was tall and inclined to stoutness, and his shoulders were
exceedingly broad. With his rosy cheeks, reading glasses, a snowy
beard, and thick eyebrows, Iver's resemblance to Old Saint Nick
would have fooled the most discriminating of reindeer. Iver was
no jolly old elf, though. He was a Templar Knight and Max's mentor. He was also the official Round Table game master, a very
important role. The Grey Griffins had quickly come to realize that
it wasn't safe to play their favorite trading card game without Iver
nearby. One lapse in judgment, and a monster from the Round
Table cards could very well end up in their locker the next day.

Max looked at his old friend with trepidation, certain he was
about to get the lecture of his life. Having recklessly ignored
Iver's advice, Max had gone after the Spear of Ragnarok and
handed it over to his father. Now it appeared that the entire
world was about ready to pay the price for Max's mistake.

"I just received word that another Templar outpost has been

destroyed by the Black Wolves under your father's command," Iver began, as a gust of snow buffeted the car. "They are getting bolder with every attack. With each strike, the Templar Knights are growing weaker. And now the Spear of Ragnarok hangs over our heads. Once they learn how to use it, I'm afraid it will ensure their victory . . . and our extinction. That's why I wanted to talk with you. You see, I've been called before the Grand Council to explain what went wrong — and, more to the point, how the Spear ended up in your father's hands."

Max slunk in his seat. "They hate me, don't they?"

Iver smiled faintly, peering through the pelting sleet before glancing thoughtfully at Max. "You weren't the only one who was fooled, Master Sumner. Morgan LaFey and your father fooled us all, I'm embarrassed to say. Did you know that we actually believed she was working for Oberon all these years, when all along she'd been waiting for *you*?"

"Why?"

"She needed the Spear of Ragnarok to fulfill her dark conspiracies, and according to the prophecy, you're the only person alive who could use it. In fact, she accelerated your discovery of the *Codex Spiritus*. It shouldn't have happened until you were much older."

"The Black Witch sent that Slayer Goblin to chase me into Grandma Caliburn's attic, didn't she?"

"Indubitably."

"And only a Guardian of the *Codex* could fulfill the prophecy and take the Spear?"

"Right again," Iver agreed.

"And she knew I'd give it to my dad. . . ."

Iver nodded. "Of course she did, and why shouldn't she? You acted from love, as any son should. Besides, Morgan knew you'd never *willingly* use the Spear — not once you understood its power. That's where your old classmate Ray Fisher came in. And now that your blood courses through Ray's veins, she believes Ray will be able to unlock the power of the Spear."

"But Vlad destroyed her, right?"

Iver paused. "Perhaps," he mused. "Intelligence reports indicate that her body wasn't discovered after the battle, yet your father now commands the Black Wolf Society. It may mean she is no longer with us, or it could be that she is lying in wait. We don't know for certain."

For a long while, Max remained silent. He watched ice creep across the passenger window as he thought about everything Iver had said. All of this was his fault. That much he knew. The problem was that Iver was about to take the fall for Max's transgressions.

"You're too hard on yourself, Master Sumner," Iver said, chuckling as he watched the storm clouds gather. "Your grandfather made a mistake or two in his day also, you know."

"You're just trying to make me feel better."

"Am I now?" Iver asked, arching one eyebrow. "Well, we weren't much older than you . . . perhaps sixteen or so, when your grandfather and I found ourselves in a regrettable situation." Max was hooked. He listened intently as Iver began to spin his tale. "William and I were still in training. As I recall it was near Shipdham, in the English countryside. Shipdham was a quiet stretch of land in the days before the War. Like Avalon, it could get a touch boring now and again. So, foolishly, we were anxious to get our first taste of battle. Tempestuous fools, we were. So when we heard about an ogre attack at some school where an important artifact had been stolen, we figured it was time to put our training to the test."

"What happened?"

"Stupidity," Iver responded flatly. "One of the ogres had taken refuge close to where we were stationed. Your grandfather and I asked our commander for permission to apprehend the criminal, but he flatly refused. He knew full well that we were too young and inexperienced to handle an ogre — at least by ourselves. He was dead right, of course, but like the mules we were, we didn't listen. Instead, the two of us snuck out under the cover of night, fully expecting to return as heroes."

"Then what?"

"We made short work of tracking down the beast. That was the easy part. The problem arose when we found it. I can't tell you who was more surprised, the ogre or us. He was a sharp one, I confess, and faster than either of us expected. I can't tell you exactly what happened, but before your grandfather could so much as shout a warning, the beast was on top of us. We didn't have time to draw weapons, let alone use the *Codex Spiritus*." Max's eyebrows raised. "Yes, by that time, your grandfather had begun his training with the very book you hold in your backpack."

"Cool."

"Indeed," agreed Iver with a chuckle. "Luckily, we survived, though more through chance than skill. The ogre had sunk his fist into a tree — a fist that was meant for my neck, mind you. It stuck just long enough for your grandfather and me to make our escape."

Max sighed. Iver's story had taken him on a roller-coaster-ride adventure. It was better than a movie. "So everything turned out okay, right?"

"Except one small detail. We had accidentally left the *Codex* behind."

"What?"

"As you can imagine, a book, regardless of its value, was the last thing on our minds," Iver said, smiling at Max's disbelief. "Thankfully, our superiors sent back more qualified reinforcements to retrieve it. I must tell you, though, that given the choice, I'd rather face that ogre barehanded than receive the lecture waiting for us when we returned. It was a long time before any assignments came our way after that." Iver paused thoughtfully, then turned to Max and smiled. "So you see, all of us make mistakes. If we live through them, we learn."

"So how'd Grandpa become a knight?" Max inquired.

"He was born into his position, same as you," explained Iver. "Historically speaking, you cannot simply be born into knighthood, but the special status of the Guardians, and their inheritable talent, made it only logical. I, on the other hand, was recruited."

"Really?"

"It's a rather long story that we can discuss later, but whether it was luck or fate, your grandfather and I were assigned to the T.H.O.R. Agency together."

"The what?"

"Think of the T.H.O.R. as an elite Special Forces unit within the ranks of the Templar. It stands for Tactical Headquarters for Operations and Research.

"The Templar have many divisions specializing in every conceivable discipline," the old man continued. "Specifically, the T.H.O.R. Agency dealt in paranormal affairs — faeries, sorcery, interdimensional invasions — that sort of thing. While all Templar are trained in battle, it's the T.H.O.R. agents that answer the call when things get really bad. Logan's a member, too."

"Really?"

"Of course, though it shouldn't surprise you in the least, Master Sumner. You know him better than any." Max had to agree. "Trust me when I tell you that there are few men who are his equal. Your father picked a very suitable protector for his son, that much I'll give him."

"So how long have you been a T.H.O.R. agent?" asked Max.

"Your grandfather and I were first recruited to that unit during the War, where we worked with British intelligence to deal with the threat of Sigurd the Slayer and his Black Wolf Society. William used to say that when things went bump in the night, we were the ones who brought the fury of Thor's hammer down on them."

"That's cool."

Iver smiled briefly. "Unfortunately, there's little glory in warfare," he began with a sigh. "Those were dark days, and afterward, your grandfather and I were never the same, I'm sorry to say. War does that to a man. But enough musings from an old fool. I'll tell you this much, young man. I miss your grandfather a great deal. He was my best friend, and it's rare to find a man like him. Mighty rare indeed."

"I miss him, too," Max replied thoughtfully. "But when I'm with you . . . I don't know . . . it's almost like I'm with him, too. I suppose that's kind of weird, but in some ways it's like he never really left."

"Well, Master Sumner," Iver started, after clearing his throat. "I couldn't think of higher praise."

Neither said another word, but both were smiling contentedly, oblivious to the storm outside their windows.

The whitewall tires of Iver's car ran onto a covered wooden bridge that spanned a creek long frozen by the harsh winter. Halfway across, the radio died, filling the speakers with the hiss and crackle of static. Passing over to the other side, Iver took his eyes off the road for a moment to change the tuner. That's when Max noticed something enormous move onto the road. "Look out!" he shouted, figuring it was a stray cow. Iver realized their peril too late. He slammed on the brakes just before the old Plymouth plowed into the beast. Metal crunched and the windshield shattered. When they'd finally slid to a stop, Iver was slumped over the steering wheel, his eyes closed. "Iver . . . Iver," Max said, gently nudging the old man as panic welled up inside his chest.

No answer.

Outside, the sleet had turned to snow, and a wet curtain of white obscured the horizon. Wind whistled through the broken windshield and the car started to shake. Max watched in horror as the roof was ripped away, then thrown aside like discarded trash. The Guardian of the *Codex* quickly realized that whatever had done that was no cow, as beastly eyes now looked down at him through the storm. Uselessly, Max yanked at the door handle. It had been destroyed in the wreck. Then he spotted his backpack in the backseat, and the slightest spark of hope flashed. If he could reach the *Codex Spiritus*, he just might be able to trap whatever it was that was attacking them.

The monster roared, and Max knew he didn't have much time. Flipping into the backseat, the Guardian snaked his arm around one of the straps and plunged out the broken rear window and into the open air, just as enormous hands picked up the wreck and studied it with hungry intent. Max staggered backward. The monster was covered with tangled white fur, with two thick horns spiraling from either side of its grizzled head. Well over ten feet tall, its chest and shoulders were as wide as a truck, and it had a spiked collar wrapped around its neck. Then Max noticed a terrible scar on its arm. The beast had been branded with the rune of the Black Wolves.

"A Tundra Troll," he breathed. It was one of his favorite creatures from the *Round Table Creature Compendium*. The monsters ate anything in their path, be it rock, car, or a particularly delicious fifth grader. Like a dog, it sniffed at the car. Then, with a roar of satisfaction, it raised a shaggy arm to peel back the rest of the roof.

"No!" Max shouted as he jumped back onto the road. He couldn't lose Iver. Not again!

Suddenly, the atmosphere filled with a buzzing sound, as a massive stream of cobalt fire shot from Max's trembling fingers and raced across the road before it slammed through the Plymouth and into the monster. The car exploded in a ball of fire. At the same time, the troll let out a tremendous roar as the mysterious flame swept over it like a storm. With a final howl, the monster burst into a cloud of powdery snow that circled several times before disappearing in the wind.

Max stood there for a long moment, staring at the fire that still danced across his fingers. Then he looked at the smoking wreckage of Iver's car. Where was Iver?

"You overdid it a bit, don't you think?" came a weak, though amused, voice from Max's periphery. He turned his head to find Iver actually standing there, one hand upon his umbrella and the other wiping a kerchief across his brow. "I guess we'll have to start teaching you how to control that new power of yours, eh? Perhaps that should be our next lesson." He chuckled, then ruffled Max's hair.

The Guardian of the *Codex* looked up at his tutor in wonder, unable to say anything as the snow continued to fall. Then, through the wailing wind, Max could hear the roar of engines. Moments later, several snowmobiles appeared. All the riders were dressed in arctic battle gear from head to foot, with Templar insignias adorning their shoulders. The foremost rider took off his helmet and approached Iver.

"Car trouble?" Logan asked in his gruff voice.

"It's the mark of the Black Wolf Society, all right," Logan growled as he studied an iron collar as big as a tire.

"Lord Sumner is moving faster than even I had anticipated," Iver noted in concern, pulling out a bag of pipe tobacco and stuffing some of it into his pipe. He was standing on the windswept road with Logan and Max, as a small unit of Templar Knights stalked along the perimeter to ensure they hadn't walked into an ambush. They were dressed in arctic gear, and Max noticed both of them wore two patches, one on each shoulder. The first was a Templar cross. The second was a hammer — the symbol of the elite T.H.O.R. Special Forces Agency. "I fear that this is the result of our Templar forces being spread too thin. It appears we can't even protect our own borders," Iver added.

"Maybe, but Tundra Trolls never travel far from home," Logan pointed out. "My guess is there's a portal nearby — inside our perimeter," the Scotsman continued, his eyes narrowed in dark thought. "Whatever the case, we need to catch up with that troll and 'ask' it some questions before it leaves the same way it came."

"But I destroyed it," argued Max, though he wasn't necessarily proud of the fact. Still, he'd seen it obliterated into a billion flakes of snow.

Logan shook his head as he walked back to a snowmobile that looked like a tricked-out, high-tech spy mobile with rocket boosters and every gadget you could imagine. "Tundra Trolls can't be killed . . . least not without iron. All you did was destroy the body. Get on board, Grasshopper. It's time to do a little troll hunting."

"If you don't mind," Iver began, taking a puff from his pipe before blowing a smoke ring into the air. "I'll sit this one out, Logan. I have an appointment back at the Shoppe of Antiquities for which I cannot be late."

"Is your business to do with Lord Saxon's diary?" asked Logan, his face grim.

"Naturally," the old man answered. "And, thanks to your efforts, we're getting very close to solving the riddle."

"Who's Lord Saxon?" asked Max.

"That's classified, Grasshopper," interrupted Logan.

"But . . ."

Logan nodded back to Iver. "I'll have one of these blokes give you a ride back to town." Moments later, Iver was racing away, just as Logan, Max and the rest of the T.H.O.R. agents sped across the icy field in search of the portal.

According to Logan, there was only one place a portal that size could be hidden: Thistlehaven Wood. A thicket of dead trees on the edge of a lonely cornfield, it wouldn't be easy getting in. Most of the trees had fallen on top of one another, broken stumps stabbing up into the sky like a forest of ship masts.

"Are you sure the troll came through here?" Max asked over the roar of the engine, unsure if he wanted to meet the monster again.

"I'd bet the house," Logan replied, pulling up at the edge of the woods, motioning for the knights to enter the cluster of broken trees on foot. He and Max followed, wisps of steam rising from their mouths. Not a sound was heard as the group moved through the thicket. Logan's men cleared the woods expertly, moving from the cover of one broken tree to the next. There were footprints everywhere, and it didn't take long to realize they weren't just troll prints, either. More than one breed of monster had been patrolling Thistlehaven Wood.

"Be careful," Logan warned Max. "And stay as close to me as you can." Then the Scotsman made another series of signals, and Søren set out into the shadows without a sound. He may have been a knight, but the soldier moved through the thicket like a ghost.

Max held his breath, waiting for the masked Templar to return. Luckily, he didn't have to wait very long. "The portal's just on the other side of a ruined house," Søren soon reported in a dry whisper.

"I know," Max said, sharing a quick glance with Logan. "I can sense it."

"It's surrounded by a small patch of blackened earth and three flags with the Black Wolves' rune on them. No guards are posted," explained Søren. "Your orders?"

"Sounds like a trap to me," Max interjected.

Logan smiled wryly. "Now you're thinking like a Guardian should. Good lad."

"Yes," agreed Søren. "There's a perimeter minefield. It's a low-level signature, but we were able to detect it. All will be disabled soon."

"Are we going to close the portal?" Max wondered.

Logan shook his head. "We don't have that sort of firepower, Grasshopper. We're just gonna take a look and then head back home to report. With luck, they'll never even know we were here."

With uncanny stealth, the T.H.O.R. agents made for the abandoned house, using the debris for cover. The rusted guts of the old building were scattered across the snowy lawn. There was an old washtub, a mangled bicycle, and countless other objects that had been lost to the ravages of time. Max stepped cautiously through the mess, following Logan and the other knights out through the back of the house and onto a charred patch of earth. There were rumors the house was haunted, and Max wanted no part of it.

Sure enough, Max spotted a crimson portal that flickered in the heart of the clearing. Immediately, the white-clad soldiers started taking air-particulate and soil samples, along with snapshots of the footprints and anything else that looked suspicious.

Logan walked over to a shattered link of chain staked next to the portal. "Looks like our troll was just a guard dog. Must've broke free and headed toward town."

"Or somebody let it loose on purpose," Max remarked.

Logan scratched his scruffy chin. "Could be," he agreed. "At any rate, judging from the flicker rate of the portal, it was used just a few minutes ago. That'd be your troll, I'd wager."

A few minutes more, and the group had collected everything they needed and were making ready to depart. Unfortunately, there was to be a change in plans.

The portal suddenly flashed to life as a silhouetted form appeared on the other side. Max watched with trepidation as a diminutive creature with spindly little legs and gigantic yellow eyes stepped out. It had no arms, but instead possessed a long set of bat wings that were folded protectively over its torso.

The monster's skin was crimson, like hot coals, and steam rose from its body into the frosty air. It looked miserable as it stared at the ground.

With a sudden look of urgency, the Scotsman signaled for everyone to clear out. The T.H.O.R. agents were way ahead of him, moving cautiously but steadily away. Max could see the look in their eyes. The soldiers were spooked, and he had no idea why. The pathetic creature was hardly a match for one of them, let alone all of them. "You want me to use the *Codex*?" he whispered, but Logan raised a quick finger to his lips, signaling for Max to shut up. Max obeyed and continued the silent retreat.

Then, just as they neared the abandoned house, the crimson faerie let out a terrible shriek and spread its wings. "Blasted Inferno Imp," Logan hissed. "Run!" With that, he grabbed Max and threw him over his shoulder, racing through the house in a fury of speed. The other knights were right on his heels, and none of them bothered to look back. Except Max. He watched curiously as the Inferno Imp crouched low, clenched its fists, and squinted tightly. Max had read about Inferno Imps before, though he'd never actually seen one. The faeries were meant for one thing and one thing only: exploding.

Just as Max passed out of view, he could see a red glow rise over the trees, followed by an explosive *BOOM*! "Everybody down!" Logan called as he threw himself over Max. A massive wall of fire swept over them, and Max lost consciousness.

4

Bullies Come in All Shapes and Sizes

ONCE UPON a time, Avalon, Minnesota, had been a picturesque backdrop set, miles away from the bustling metropolis of the Twin Cities. Avalon's quiet streets were dotted with lemonade stands on warm days, and parents didn't think twice about letting their children play outside long after the sun went down. The coming of spring usually meant that the land would soon be bursting with corn shoots and the familiar sounds of baseball would be ringing through neighborhood parks. Unfortunately, all that had changed the night Max Sumner found the *Codex Spiritus* in his grandmother's attic. Now, winter seemed to last for an eternity and things could go disastrously wrong in an instant — like the sudden appearance of an Inferno Imp. Once again, Max had been saved by Logan's quick thinking, but he had a bad feeling that his luck was about to run out.

Nestled in a valley surrounded by snow-covered hills, King's Elementary School stood proudly despite the winter gloom, with bright flags snapping in the frosty breeze. The rough-hewn walls of the school gave the impression that King's was an unassailable fortress, with towering ramparts and steep spires that shot into the sky. As she stepped off the bus and onto the school grounds Monday morning, Natalia sighed in relief. If she'd had to endure one more day of her sister's snooping or her

mom's scrapbooking, Natalia felt sure she would have exploded —
just like the Inferno Imp that Max had only narrowly escaped
the day before. So when Max had asked her to start researching
Tundra Trolls and Inferno Imps, she was more than happy to
lock herself in her room, set aside her Sherlock Holmes, and do
some real-life detective work. Unfortunately, there wasn't much
available, except for what she could find in the *Round Table
Creature Compendium*, and all that did was verify everything
Logan had told Max about the monsters. She'd made a note to
have Max look them up in his *Codex Spiritus*, though she had half
a mind to lecture him about hunting after monsters in the
first place — especially at the old Thistlehaven house. He was
lucky to be alive.

Before reaching the front doors of the school, Natalia's smile
faded and she groaned. Blocking her path were Carmela,
Veronica, and Amy, three of the most vicious girls in school.
Natalia simply referred to them as the Triplets. Though they
weren't officially related, Natalia suspected they all shared a
cantankerous wolverine somewhere in their family trees. She
hurried by, hoping to avoid notice. It didn't work.

"Look who's here! It's Detective Dork!" mocked Amy, the
pixie-thin blonde in pink earmuffs. Carmela and Veronica
cackled like a couple of evil mice while Natalia's face flushed.
Natalia simply kept her head down, pretending not to hear as
she tromped past the Triplets. She managed to get about ten
steps farther when a snowball hit her in the head, slopping
down the back of her shirt. With a sigh, Natalia slowly

turned around and glared. Standing with their smug smiles, the Triplets waved innocently.

Natalia had played this game before. "I don't suppose any of you saw who threw that snowball at me?" she inquired, hoping that they'd deny it and then move on to their next victim. The tactic had worked in the past.

"Ah, that would be me," Amy replied, raising her hand while her eyes twinkled maliciously. That snake played the role of teacher's pet perfectly, but in reality Natalia knew that Amy was the sneakiest, most conniving snot in the fifth grade. Worse, there was something that seemed to turn everyone around her into diabolical mimics.

"Then please stop it," Natalia said, batting her eyelashes before she turned away. Ignoring bullies always seemed to be the best policy. Eventually, they would tire of you and move on to a juicier target — like Ernie. Unfortunately, Natalia didn't get far before another snowball hit her in exactly the same spot. Natalia stopped and drew another long breath as the snow leaked down her back. "Can't you find anyone else to torture?" she asked, shaking the snow from her braids.

"Sure," Amy replied. "But we made a rule today. We're only going to pick on the biggest nerd in school. Guess who that is?"

"Your brother?" Natalia answered.

Amy frowned. "You've got a big mouth."

"Compared with what, your brain?" Natalia retorted.

"How'd you like a fat lip?" Carmela threatened as she stepped forward. The biggest member of the Triplets, rumor had it that Carmela had beaten up a seventh-grade boy and made him cry just for the fun of it.

"I'm sorry," Natalia said with a curtsy. "I'm afraid my dance card's already full. Perhaps another time?" With that, she quickly stepped into a parade of students that were walking by and disappeared into the halls of King's Elementary School.

Max, Natalia, and Harley had been unexpectedly excused from class. One minute, Harley had been reading aloud from his book, the next, the classroom door had swung open revealing a very somber Mrs. Speizer, the school nurse. She bustled across the room in pristine orthopedic shoes before whispering something in the ear of their teacher, Mrs. Bone. The next moment, Mrs. Speizer motioned for the Griffins to follow her into the hall. Max was more curious than alarmed, that was, until Ernie was brought up.

"I'm so sorry," she began, pausing so long that the Griffins had an eternity to envision every terrifying possibility. Natalia's eyes watered and Harley's fists clenched.

"Is he . . . ?" Natalia began, unable to finish her sentence.

The nurse shook her head. "He's all right . . . at least for now," she replied slowly, placing a plump hand on Natalia's shoulder. "But he's taken a terrible turn for the worse. That sweet child almost didn't make it through the night."

Max felt numb and couldn't think clearly.

"You're sure he's all right now?" Natalia pressed.

Mrs. Speizer nodded. "Each of your families has excused

you from the rest of your classes today. I believe there's a car waiting to take you to see Ernie now." With that, she turned and walked away, her shoes squeaking as her thick nest of curly hair bounced up and down.

The Griffins turned the corner to go to their lockers, but the hallway was already occupied. It was Dennis Stonebrow, the school bully, who was so enormous he towered over the tallest teacher in school. Dennis was leaning up against one of the lockers with a satisfied smirk on his face. It was obvious that he'd stuffed someone inside again, and now he or she was crying, screaming, and pounding to get out. It was a game Dennis enjoyed immensely.

Already frustrated by the news about Ernie, Max wasn't in the mood, but he couldn't let Dennis get away with it, either. "Why don't you just let 'em go? Then you can get back to whatever trolls do when they cut class."

Dennis sneered. "I don't know what you're talkin' about."

"It's me. Peter!" a weak voice squeaked from inside the locker. Peter Karlsen was a shy farm kid who was known, embarrassingly, as Peter-Peter-Pumpkin-Eater. He really didn't eat pumpkins, but that didn't seem to matter.

"Max told you to let him go, Stonebrow," Harley warned.

Dennis smirked, not bothering to budge. "Well, if you're so tough, Eisenstein, why don't you come over here and let him out yourself."

"Don't you dare," Natalia warned Harley, grabbing him as

he stepped forward. "I don't care how upset you are. Fighting Dennis isn't going to solve anything."

"You better listen to your girlfriend." Dennis laughed. "Otherwise you're gonna end up in the hospital with that nerd, Tweeny."

Harley shook off Natalia's grasp and strode right up to Dennis. "You got one shot, and you better pray I don't get up," Harley growled.

"You've got yourself a death wish," Dennis threatened, moving away from the locker and looking down at Harley, as Peter snuck out and fled down the hall.

Then the bell rang. Soon the hallway was flooded with chattering students. It didn't take long for a crowd to form around Dennis and Harley — they were the toughest kids in school. The air buzzed as they squared off. "Fight!" someone shouted, and soon dozens of students were chanting along: "Fight! Fight! Fight!"

That's when Max saw a dark storm burst through the crowd. "Enough!" It was Dr. Diamonte Blackstone, vice principal, band instructor, and, regrettably, chief disciplinarian of King's Elementary School. Everyone was scared of Blackstone — the students, teachers, Principal Hamm — even Dennis.

"What's the meaning of this?" Blackstone seethed, glaring at each boy in turn. With his thick coif of black hair and a sharp nose, he looked a bit like a raven. Yet Dr. Blackstone was a man who appeared to take great pride in eccentricity. The clamor died down as his authoritative eyes roved across the throng, evoking silence wherever they landed.

"Well?" The vice principal's foot tapped impatiently. Dennis glared back at the man, stone silent. Harley just looked away.

Figuring somebody had to defend her friend's reputation, Natalia tried to explain. "Dennis stuffed Peter in the . . ."

"I was not talking to you, was I, Ms. Romanov?" Blackstone snapped, cutting her off with an icy stare that could have shriveled a forest of leaves. Like the rest of the Griffins, Natalia despised the vice principal. Blackstone had once worked for the Black Witch, and he nearly killed Iver. Why he hadn't been locked up was a mystery. Yet despite the overwhelming evidence against him, the Templar had chosen to let him go.

"Your father is the town preacher, is he not, Mr. Stonebrow?" Blackstone began. Neither boy was talking, which suited Blackstone just fine.

Dennis said nothing.

"No doubt, he's proud of his charming son, but I wonder if he knows you like I do?" Dennis's eyes widened and his jaw clenched. "Oh yes, Mr. Stonebrow. I've been keeping a close eye on you. I know exactly where you go and what you do when you think no one is looking. It would be a shame if . . . well . . . if your little secret were to get out. The local paper would simply have a field day with the story, I'm sure. Then, disgraced, your father would yet again have to search for another town that didn't know his son the way we do." Dennis remained silent, but his face had grown dreadfully pale. Blackstone had struck a nerve.

"And you, Mr. Eisenstein," Blackstone said, turning to the Griffin, his voice dripping with sarcasm. "Such a hero. Oh yes, but you have your secrets as well, don't you?"

"What are you talking about?" Harley asked, folding his arms indignantly. Harley was about as honest as they came. Sure he was a little rough around the edges, and he suffered from a series of calamitous stepfathers, but he didn't keep secrets.

"*That*, Dr. Blackstone, will be enough," a voice called out. It came from a rather tall man dressed in extravagant finery. Despite an ornate cane that offset his limp, the man moved with elegant grace. He had dark hair set with streaks of silver about the temples that matched a distinguished goatee. There was no doubt. It was Dr. Cain Lundgren, Max's next-door neighbor.

When Blackstone's eyes met Lundgren's, the vice principal took a step back, then looked around anxiously, as if he might be set upon by a swarm of secret agents. For the first time in their memory, the Griffins watched Diamonte's dark eyes cloud with uncertainty. "Lundgren. This is a . . . surprise."

"So it would appear," Cain replied, motioning with a gloved hand toward his daughter, who was now standing next to him. "I will need to excuse Brooke from further classes today. A family situation has arisen that cannot be avoided."

Max could see Brooke standing behind her father. The Sumner and Lundgren families had once been close, and he'd spent quite a bit of his childhood with Brooke, exploring the Old Woods, not to mention her father's labyrinthine mansion.

39

All that had come to an abrupt end a few years ago, when their fathers fell into a frightful argument. The families were hastily separated and hadn't spoken since. Given their geographic proximity, that made life a little difficult. Max and Brooke still talked, of course — at least in school — but it wasn't like it used to be.

Blackstone's eyebrows squirmed as he seemed to consider Cain Lundgren's request. "There's nothing more?"

"That is all," Cain Lundgren replied, absently brushing lint from his sleeve. His green eyes lifted, and then fell upon Max, lingering for an uncomfortable moment. Max shivered and took an unintentional step backward.

"Well then," Blackstone began, his voice unraveling. Max wished he knew what was making the vice principal squirm so much. "She's certainly free to go under your care. I assume you have a note of excuse?"

"Of course," Dr. Lundgren said, handing the vice principal a piece of paper that he'd withdrawn from the breast pocket of his coat. "Now as to the boys?"

"I'm sorry?" Blackstone feigned a puzzled look.

"The boys," Doctor Lundgren repeated as he motioned toward Harley and Dennis. "I doubt there'll be any more infractions today. Best to let them be on their way, wouldn't you agree?"

Silence.

Slowly, Diamonte Blackstone waved the children back to class. With a forced smile, he quickly disappeared down the hall.

5

Grandma's Garden Paradise

THEIR TRIP to the hospital had been frantic, but even as they rushed into Ernie's room, Athena met them with a relieved smile. It looked like she hadn't slept in weeks, but with the help of an amazing medical team that had flown up from Rochester, Minnesota, she was able to pull Ernie back from the brink of death. He'd been stabilized, but he still wasn't conscious. Unable to offer any help and too depressed to watch Ernie slip further into his coma, the Griffins didn't stay long.

The rest of the week seemed to crawl by at a snail's pace. Ernie wasn't getting any better, but he wasn't getting any worse, either. At least they had Friday night to look forward to. Grandma Caliburn had invited all of them over for a home-cooked meal to warm their hearts.

Max trudged through the front door of the farmhouse, stomping the snow off his boots. Natalia and Harley were in tow, and all three Griffins took off their coats and hung them in a hallway closet that smelled of mothballs and old cardboard game boxes.

"Max!" a warm voice greeted, as a beautiful older woman with cropped salt-and-pepper hair entered the foyer. Grace Caliburn embraced her grandson warmly.

"Hi, Grandma!" Max smiled, returning the hug. "Thanks for inviting Harley, Natalia, and ..." He paused, catching himself before saying Ernie's name.

Natalia sighed. "I just wish things were like they used to be."

"They will be." Grandma Caliburn smiled, handing Natalia a delicate china cup filled with hot tea, lemon, and honey. "Ernie will be with us soon enough. Just have faith." Whenever the Griffins were near Grace Caliburn, they felt safe — even in a darkening world filled with monsters and witches.

"We're starving, Grandma," Max declared, catching the aroma of homemade potpies and cinnamon applesauce, nice and chunky, just the way Max liked it.

"Then you've come to the right place," she said, nodding with a wink. "I've made enough food for an army."

At that moment the front door opened behind the Griffins, and a tall shadow joined them. Max turned to regard Iver. With careful attentiveness, the old man wiped his shoes, set his umbrella upon a brass rack, and took off his hat. His clear eyes, lined with years, hesitated for a moment, then rose to meet Max's own before passing to Grace Caliburn. The old friends regarded each other in silence. It had been a long time since Iver had last visited. In fact, it hadn't been since Grandpa Caliburn's murder at the hands of the Black Witch. Iver somehow felt responsible for his friend's death, which was why he'd avoided Max's grandmother ever since.

"Hello, Grace," Iver offered, his voice slightly tremulous. Max could see the uncertainty and discomfort in his eyes. He'd invited Iver to the farm at least a hundred times over the past couple years, and though he was relieved that Iver had finally accepted, it was still kind of strange.

"It's good to see you, Olaf," Grandma Caliburn said carefully, using Iver's first name as she wiped her hands absently with her apron. There was restrained warmth in her voice, as if by Iver's presence a thousand memories had come rushing back. "I was beginning to wonder if you'd forgotten your way."

Iver smiled self-consciously, then took in a deep breath and looked around the living room. "It's all as I remember." Though their conversation was awkward at first, as the evening passed, Max's grandma and Iver felt themselves settle back into the familiarity of their old friendship.

After dessert and a few games of gin rummy, Logan came by to take Natalia and Harley back to their homes. Iver, though reluctant to leave, finally waved good-bye as well. Grandma Caliburn had piled the passenger seat of his old pickup to the brim with leftovers, and Iver didn't protest. Finally, with the house to themselves, Grandma Caliburn asked Max to join her on a walk. They bundled up and stepped out into the winter wonderland. She said she had something special to show him in the greenhouse.

"That was awesome, Grandma," Max complimented, still savoring the last taste of dessert as he walked with her across a fresh carpet of powdery snow.

"I'm glad you enjoyed it. And thank *you* for joining me for a walk," Grandma Caliburn returned, patting Max's hand as they walked arm in arm. "It's nice to have the company. Besides, fresh air does me good. And it's such a beautiful night." Max nodded his agreement as he watched steam rise from his mouth like clouds of smoke from a dragon. "And wasn't it wonderful to see Iver? We have such lovely memories."

Max smiled contentedly. He was only now beginning to understand how close Iver and his family had been. Over the last week, Max had spent every free moment he could find at Iver's Shoppe of Antiquities, listening to tales of the vaunted T.H.O.R. Special Forces Agency and their amazing adventures. Max never tired of stories about his grandfather.

"I just wish my dear William were here to join us," she continued, taking in the crisp air as they crunched along the serene path. "He loved freshly fallen snow — always said it reminded him of heaven."

"Do you think we'll ever see Grandpa again?"

"Oh, I think so," Grandma Caliburn replied, walking with her eyes closed, face tilted to the sky. "Though I'm not so sure he'd appreciate the wall that has grown between you and your mother. I think that would've made him very sad."

"I know," answered Max, slowing to a trudge. He'd been hoping to avoid conversation about his mom. Ever since the divorce, Annika Sumner had grown cold, avoiding her own home — and her kids — like the plague. On those rare occasions when she actually was around, all she and Max did was fight. Now he wasn't sure if he was angry that she was gone so much, or that she wasn't gone more often. The Sumners were a mess.

"Have you tried to put yourself in her shoes?" Grandma Caliburn offered as she put her arm around Max's shoulder. "How would you feel if you discovered the person you loved, and the marriage you had dreamed of, all turned out to be a lie?" Max could see his grandmother's greenhouse just a little ways off, its leaded glass glinting in the moonlight.

"Why does she have to take it out on me, though? It's not my fault Dad left her."

"Oh, Grayson, you're being forced to grow up so fast," Grandma Caliburn said, her voice laced with melancholy. "Your mother's just frightened. She's already lost her father, and now her husband. Don't you think she's scared of losing you as well?" Max remained quiet as the doorway to the greenhouse came into view. "You know, it's times like these that I love coming here," she said, reaching for the latch. Then Grandma Caliburn motioned for Max to join her as they stepped over the threshold, warm air rolling over them.

The overflowing jungle within the Victorian greenhouse was a magnificent contrast to the Minnesota winter that waited outside. Within its four walls existed a fairyland of wonder, with the intoxicating aroma of orchids and rolling rose-bushes, the gentle song of the stream running through its sculpted hills, and the school of Japanese koi that darted beneath the shadows of arched bridges. The tropical paradise

45

within the dewy glass walls seemed to wipe away all of Max's worries, and if he closed his eyes, Max could almost imagine he'd traveled to a far-off land.

That was, until a webbed hand with dirty claws grasped him.

Max whirled around, his eyes falling upon a curious hunch-backed creature that looked strikingly similar to a toad dressed for a night on the town. He was positively decrepit, from his threadbare sport coat to the brown rumpled skin that puckered and sagged. Heavy brows framed amphibious eyes, and he wore a tattered tie and stained slacks that hung limply from spindly legs. Where Max was expecting shoes, all he found were long, dirty, wiggling toes.

"Grayson, I'd like you to meet my good friend, Wellington. He's a hobgoblin and one of the caretakers of the green-house," his grandmother announced formally, as if Max had just been introduced to the king of England. Max wrinkled his nose. This creature certainly didn't look like a Wellington. Rock. Lump. Sludge. These would have been more fitting.

"At your service," Wellington offered with a dusty dignity that probably hadn't been practiced in a hundred years. His voice sounded somewhere between a *ribit* and a *croak*, and he bowed in completely the wrong direction.

"Max is over here," Grandma Caliburn corrected with a warm smile.

The hobgoblin cleared his throat. "Yes, of course he is," Wellington replied gruffly, turning in the direction of her voice and bowing. Again, he missed Max by a mile, and the Guardian of the *Codex* tried not to laugh.

"Oh, don't pay that old fool any attention," warned a new character. "He's halfway to senility and back by now. Not to mention, he's blind as a bat." Max spun to see a second hobgoblin standing there, every bit as ugly as the first. The newcomer was a bit taller than his comrade, and his suit was equally dreadful, though he was, perhaps, less gray around the ear hair. Both looked as old as dirt.

"You should talk, Mortimer," Wellington complained, poking an ireful finger in the general direction of the other gnarled faerie. "You look as if you were mugged by a moth. I thought you were going to go change before the boy arrived."

"I did." Mortimer sniffed. "I *changed* my mind." Both hobgoblins began to laugh hard and long, the second one tearing up and blowing his nose into a dirty hanky.

"I'm telling you, Mort," Wellington croaked in admiration, "the more senile I get, the funnier *you* get."

"A faerie doesn't get senile," argued Mortimer.

"Exactly!" Wellington barked. They looked at each other, then immediately howled with laughter, blowing their noses fiercely and wiping their eyes. Max looked up at his grandmother, questions written all over his face.

"These two fine gentlemen keep the greenhouse running shipshape."

"Okay." Max shrugged before turning to the two characters. "Hi, I'm Max."

Mortimer's eyes cleared as he cupped his hand to his pointed ear. "Eh? What'd he say?"

"He was saying," Wellington began loudly as he straightened his worm-chewed tie, "that the funny farm called. Apparently, they want you back."

"Ha!" Mortimer poked a cane at Wellington. "Good one! But they are only looking for me because your expiration date already passed!" The two hobgoblins continued to fire insults for several more minutes until Max began to feel like they'd completely forgotten that his grandmother and he were standing next to them. Hobgoblins were, according to the rules of Round Table, notorious pranksters. Max was just glad they had left him out of the argument. The question was, however, what were two hobgoblins doing in his grandmother's greenhouse? And should Max be reaching for his *Codex* to trap them?

"Max," his grandmother began with a wink. "I think it's time you began to see a different side of the faerie world. Come on out, everyone, it's safe. He won't hurt you." Suddenly, the greenhouse sprung to life with every sort of faerie Max could imagine. There were Bluebell Pixies and Moonglow Sprites fluttering through the air. Garden Gnomes tended mushroom fields, Dragonfly Daisies danced about the fountain, and Lullaby Faeries opened the petals of even the sleepiest flower with a single kiss. Everywhere he glanced, faeries waved back at him, then went about their work in the garden paradise.

"Aren't they wonderful?" his grandmother breathed, drinking

in the view. "To be surrounded by such magnificent creatures is a rare blessing."

"How come you've never told me about this before?" asked Max, watching a strange faerie he originally thought was a rock burrow down into the soft dirt across the path.

"You never asked," she replied, as though that's all it would have taken. "You know, Grayson, being married to your grandfather was quite an adventure. He led a remarkable life, and he often spoke of how he looked forward to sharing it with you."

Then Max decided to brave a question he'd wanted to ask for quite some time. "Does my mom know about the *Codex*?"

"She's your grandfather's daughter, Max. Hiding it would have been impossible, especially from someone as clever as she." His grandmother's voice faded just as Max felt a cool rush of wind from behind. Someone had joined them.

Max turned to find his mother standing there, regarding him with uncertain eyes.

Grandma Caliburn patted Max on the back, offering a reassuring smile as she walked toward the door. "I believe you two have a lot to talk about. Please don't forget to close the door when you leave. If Mortimer and Wellington find frost on the blooms tomorrow, they won't let me forget it." She then turned and winked before disappearing out the door, leaving Max alone with his mom.

The silence was deafening. Even the faeries had scurried away as Max regarded his mother thoughtfully. She was extremely beautiful, even though she frowned more often these days.

Her dark hair was perfect, her figure was perfect, and even her shoes were perfect. She knew exactly what to say and when to smile during important conversations. Annika Sumner was intelligent, gifted, and knew how to run a business just about as well as her ex-husband did. She'd always been a star, but since the divorce, she'd lost it all, and had become a walking train wreck.

"When'd you get back in town?" Max began, clearing his throat. Neither moved toward the other. Though they stood facing each other, no more than a few steps apart, they might as well have been a mile apart.

"I cancelled my meetings and chartered a plane when I heard about your accident. I would have been home earlier, but I had a board meeting. Sales have been slumping a bit with the cosmetic line," she replied. Max couldn't tell if it was worry or anger in her voice. "Are you okay?"

"Why didn't you tell me about Dad?" he asked, ignoring her question entirely. There. He said it. The question *he* most wanted answered was finally out in the open.

His mom looked at him for several long moments. "I tried, Max." Her eyes were downcast. "Lord knows I did. I know you don't want to hear this right now, but the divorce hasn't been easy for me, either. I'm trying to get through it the only way I know how," she answered honestly. "Our house just has too many memories. But . . ."

"But what?" Max exclaimed indignantly. "What about me and Hannah? We can't hop on a jet and fly away whenever we get upset. We're stuck here. I mean, it's like we don't even have parents anymore."

There was nothing Annika Sumner could say to the contrary. "If you'll let me, I want to start over with you . . . ," Annika began, after an awkward silence. "I can cancel my entire calendar. I'll stay right here in Avalon with you and your sister, and we can try to rebuild our family. It's not going to be easy, but I think we can do it."

Another awkward silence.

His mom held out her arms, chin quivering. Max was tempted, but elected to stay right where he was. "Why'd you let me go to Scotland? I mean, if you knew about Dad the whole time. . . ."

Annika shook her head, her arms falling in defeat. "Max, it's . . . it's complicated."

"Complicated?!" Max exclaimed. "He wants to take over the world, and he was willing to kill me to do it. How complicated is that?"

"Your father has a way. . . ." She paused. "Let's just say he has a way of getting whatever he wants. He always has." She seemed to consider saying more, but instead, she pulled out a piece of crumpled paper from her purse. "I've carried this since the day I received it. Do you recognize the letter?"

Max nodded slowly. It was the telegram his father had sent Annika the day she'd suddenly decided to let Max go to Scotland for the winter break. "Read it," his mother urged, pushing it toward him. Hesitantly, Max opened it, though he had no idea what he'd find.

Annika Sumner:

You will allow Maximillian to join his father for the holidays.

If you try, in any way, to defy his will again, you will lose custody of both Grayson and Hannah.

The lawyers have already been notified.

> *Sincerely,*
> *Ursula*
> *Chief Counsel*
> *Sumner Enterprises*

Max's mouth fell open. His father hadn't even signed it himself.

"That's all I've dealt with since your father left us, Max," Annika explained, her voice breaking. "He holds custody of you and your sister over my head like a sledgehammer. If I don't do everything he says, he threatens to rip you away from me. I only wish I ..." Annika's voice crumbled as tears rolled down her face. "Even with half the estate in my name, I can't stand up to his lawyers, Max. Besides, even if I tried, he told me that I'd be endangering people's lives. I have to assume he's talking about your grandmother ... or worse ... maybe you and Hannah." She began to sob. Max softened a bit. With uncertain steps, he approached his mom.

Finally, after months of anguish, they embraced, and for the first time in a very long while, Max felt that he might have a family after all.

6

JUST ABOUT everything had been packed up at the Shoppe of Antiquities. The towering shelves were nearly empty of their dragon tooth necklaces, unicorn horns, and yellowed treasure maps. The glass cases were barren of their knucklebone dice and rare books, and already the window shades were lowered, with the CLOSED sign hung for all to see. The Griffins hadn't expected Iver to pack up his entire life just for a short trip over the Atlantic, and as they stood there looking through the darkness of the empty shop, a pit grew in each of their stomachs.

Cautiously, Max made his way up the creaky staircase in the back of the store, the other Griffins following in his wake. None of them uttered a word. It was just too weird. Then, without knocking, Max pushed his way through the heavy door at the top, revealing the game room that stood above Iver's shop, where they usually played Round Table. Max breathed a sigh of relief to see that the old table and chairs still stood in the center of the room. There was even a deck of Round Table cards lying on the surface, but the rest of the room was picked clean, leaving the floor and walls bare.

"This is getting spooky," Natalia murmured.

"Ah...there you are, my young Griffins," greeted Olaf Iverson, striding into the room from his adjoining apartment across the hall. He was holding an old chipboard suitcase covered with stickers from the dozens of countries he'd visited over the years. Iver paused, looking down at his young friends through his spectacles. "Come for a last game, have you?"

"We just wanted to say good-bye before you left," Max replied, when Iver caught him looking about the empty room. "But we didn't know you were gonna be gone so long."

"Yes," the old man stated solemnly. "This is important business, my dear Griffins, and may take some time. Lord Sumner's Black Wolves have grown increasingly bold and successful in their attacks against the Templar. If we're to stop them, we must strike before they activate the Spear of Ragnarok. If we don't, we will be powerless against them. It's a doomsday weapon meant to bring about one thing: the End of the World. You know this as well as I. And, though I cannot guess your father's motives, Max, we must assume this is his goal. Why else would he go to so much trouble, risking his own life — and yours — to secure the Spear in the first place?"

A sense of foreboding fell over the Griffins, who had tried to forget this depressing fact, but Iver offered an encouraging smile. "But as in Round Table, though we may have lost one round, we have not lost the game — and there are still many cards in our deck that the Black Wolves are not yet privy to. This is our advantage. And it's why my trip to the Grand Council is so important."

"So where are you going?" Natalia inquired.

"Unfortunately, that information has been classified, even for the Guardian of the *Codex*," Iver said, pausing as he turned to

Max with a wink. Natalia groaned in disappointment. "But," he continued as he set his suitcase down near the door, "keep in mind that the secrecy *and* the success of this Grand Council meeting is of the utmost importance. The decisions made could quite possibly change all of our lives."

"I understand." Max hated the idea of Iver having to answer for his stupid mistakes.

"I'm sure you do," Iver said solemnly as he studied Max. "But while I am gone, you'll continue your physical training sessions with Logan. I've gotten excellent reports from him, you know." Max had been training with his Scottish bodyguard for a long time now, and Logan regularly drilled Max in both the finer nuances of kung fu and an exercise regimen that left Max in a continual state of lung-rattling exhaustion. Unfortunately, Iver had been so busy preparing for the Grand Council meeting that he'd cancelled all of Max's other training until further notice. There'd be no more history of the Knights Templar, their terrible betrayal, or their undercover life through the ages. No more expeditions into the Old Woods with the *Codex*, and more important, not a single mention of Max's newly emerging power that had wiped out the Tundra Troll. Max was burning with questions, but it looked like he'd have to wait.

Iver patted Max on the shoulder before clapping his hands together. "Ah yes, I'd nearly forgotten. I have something for each of you: a token of our friendship, if you would."

"Really?" Natalia asked as her eyes filled with excitement, then quickly dimmed. "But we didn't bring *you* anything."

"One never gives a gift in order to receive something in kind," Iver replied with a wave of his hand as he strode over to an old steamer trunk and pulled out a delicate package wrapped in pink paper. "Here you are, my dear." He smiled, handing her the present. "Ladies first."

Natalia gasped as she unwrapped her gift. It was a magnifying glass just like the one Athena had used to investigate Max's infection when they were in Scotland. Slightly tarnished, it had multiple arms and lenses that flipped out from the handle like a Swiss Army knife. "What does it do?" she asked with wide eyes, adjusting the various arms as she peered through one lens after another.

Iver smiled as he watched Natalia pour over the gift. "It allows one to see the unseen . . . invisible clues left behind by, for instance, faerie magic. It's the perfect tool for a promising detective such as yourself." Natalia spun around the room a few times, flipping through the lenses, with a smile as wide as a Cheshire cat's.

"Now, for Master Eisenstein," he continued, turning to Harley. The largest of the Griffins grinned as he ripped open the packaging of his tiny box, only to reveal a smooth stone with a hole bored right through the center.

"It's a Faerie Ward!" Natalia gasped. "Whoever holds one is immune to faerie magic. It only works if the hole in the rock was formed naturally, of course. But there aren't very many known to exist. They're super-valuable — like a force field or something."

"Cool," Harley said. Then he unlaced off a shoestring and threaded it through the Faerie Ward before tying it around his neck. "So I'm invulnerable now?"

"They only protect you from magic, not from being squished by a troll."

"Now I have one more gift . . . ," Iver said, excusing himself before slipping out the door. It wasn't long before he returned with an old cherrywood box, scuffed from long years of use. About the size of a cigar box, it had a golden clasp and hinges, though it was otherwise unadorned. "Here you are, Master Sumner," Iver offered, handing the container over to Max. "Go ahead and open it," Iver urged with a smile. "It won't bite. . . ."

Clicking it open, Max found two neatly stacked decks of Round Table cards nestled into felt compartments. Their color was faded and corners frayed from use.

"These cards," continued Iver, "come from the decks that your grandfather and I played with when we were just about your age," he explained. "William wanted you to have them."

Max smiled as he shuffled through the decks to reveal cards he never knew existed. There were Dragon Riders, Griffin Squadrons, Light Elves, Fire Giants, and even a Doppelgänger — whatever that was. "Wow . . . thanks."

"You are most welcome," Iver replied with a slight bow of his head, but just as Max was about to slip the gift into his backpack, Iver interrupted. "Perhaps you'd like to test that new deck of yours today?"

One of the most exciting they'd ever played, the game went back and forth for hours. Iver and the Griffins gobbled down dozens of cookies chased by frosty glasses of milk. Round Table was usually fought as a multiplayer game, with each player out for himself. Lately, though, Iver had been teaching them the value of teamwork. He emphasized, time and again, how important working together truly was — especially if they hoped to survive another attack from the Black Wolves. Iver would often reference the actual battles they'd faced with the Kobolds or werewolves, instructing the Griffins through card play on what they could have done better.

The basic rules of Round Table were fairly easy to follow. It was played with trading cards that each combatant collected in order to build the perfect battle deck. Then each player would set about concocting strategies to defeat the other combatants. The Griffins each had a particular style of play, and the cards they placed in their decks reflected their own tastes. Harley, for example, had a propensity toward brute strength, overwhelming his enemies with bruising monsters. Fighting Harley head-on was never a good idea, and for that reason, Natalia preferred to collect copious amounts of tiny pixies that were as impossible to hit as mosquitoes and twice as annoying. They didn't inflict much damage, but they drove Harley crazy. He could never get his hands on her stupid cards.

While Max could have used his family fortune to build the deck of his wildest dreams, the game had built-in equalizers to prevent just such an occurrence. Knucklebones. They were special dice that introduced an element of chance into the game, so that maybe, just maybe, a pixie might be able to defeat a dragon (possibly by flying up its nose and causing a disastrous chain of sneezes). Each player had a favorite set of knucklebones, from ghostly pale to sparkly pink. Yet however they appeared, casting knucklebones was both the single greatest and most horribly gut-wrenching aspect of the game — frequently allowing the element of chance to snatch victory from the jaws of defeat.

Yet no matter how well the Grey Griffins worked together, they were never able to defeat Iver. Even today. With only a single Grease Gremlin left in his hand, Iver managed to outmaneuver the team of Griffins. He took them down one at a time until his card was the last left, and the three friends were left brooding, elbows on the table.

"Excellent!" Iver beamed proudly as he gathered up the cards and cleared the table. "You're certainly becoming a formidable team. Soon you'll be ready for the next level."

Natalia raised her eyebrows. "What do you mean? The rule book doesn't mention any other level."

"Not *your* rule book, naturally," Iver replied with a twinkle in his eye. "But that's all for today. I'm afraid it's getting late, and I must finish packing. I will miss you all — each one of you," he said as he reached into a pocket and pulled forth one last gift. "If Ernie should wake before my return, please give this to him, won't you?"

Taking his leave, Iver disappeared into the adjacent apartment. Natalia and Harley soon left as well, but not until Max told them to go on without him. He'd noticed a small envelope sitting on a shelf just in reach, and he wanted to check it out. The name of an airline was written on the outside, so that meant it was probably Iver's ticket. Max didn't want to be a snoop, but the temptation was too much. . . . He peeked inside the envelope.

MALTA.

Max paused, cycling through his geography lessons. Malta was in the middle of the Mediterranean Sea, a tiny island of rock. So this was where the Grand Council would be held. But why didn't Iver have a round-trip ticket?

Max stepped into the night, shutting the front door to the Shoppe of Antiquities behind him. As he did, an overwhelming loneliness crept over him; he was worried that he'd never see Iver again. Shaking his head to clear his thoughts, Max took in the rich aroma of gourmet cuisine. Just a couple blocks down the street, Grandma Caliburn, his mom, and his baby sister, Hannah, were waiting at Café Boa. Max was supposed to be with them right now, laughing and pretending to be part of a real family.

Though it was a short jaunt away, Max wasn't supposed to be outside alone at night — especially after the incident at Thistlehaven Wood. Nevertheless, he sighed, zipped up his coat, put on his gloves, and headed toward the restaurant. The Guardian of the *Codex* kept to the shadows, trying to remain invisible. The Spider's Web was already closed, as was the bakery and Changing Hands, the little bookstore across from the beauty salon. Max hurried along, only a block away from his destination now, but from the corner of his eye, he caught sight of movement. A shadow swept across the street only to disappear into one of the alleys. Max's heart began to race, but he tried to stay calm, telling himself it was just his wild imagination. He picked up the pace anyway, even contemplating pulling out the *Codex* from his backpack.

That's when a second shadow darted out of the alley and into the night, landing on a street sign right in his path. It was a raven. The bird regarded him with soulless eyes, but it made no sound.

"Just a stupid crow," Max murmured, trying not to notice the hair on his neck rising.

Then a second raven appeared, flying down to roost next to the first. Though on the verge of being horrified, Max was rooted by curiosity as countless more flew in, landing on the eaves, electrical wires, rooftops, and street. Like a pestilence, there was hardly a patch of Main Street that wasn't covered by the strange birds. But the most disconcerting part was that none of them made a sound.

Max's skin began to crawl.

Suddenly, there was the sound of footsteps just behind him. Max spun around, eyes wide, but all he saw was a patch of fog drifting over the snowy street. "Who's there?" Max called, but no answer came. Then Max heard the faintest sound of mocking laughter. Max spun around again, trying to find where the sound was coming from. The laughter grew louder, and suddenly the street was filled with the ravens' mocking song.

Max had had just about enough. He put his head down and raced through a flock of the birds, sending them bursting into the air like shadowy fireworks. The Guardian didn't stop until he reached the Café Boa, where he plunged inside without looking back.

At the same time, the silhouetted figure of a man materialized amid the swirl of ravens, watching Max's retreating figure with hungry eyes.

When Dreams Come True

"You're telling me you'll bark at Dennis Stonebrow, but you're scared of a few crows?" Harley teased as they sat in a booth the next evening at Leonardo's Pizza Parlor. It was known across the county for a giant display window where patrons could watch the employees toss pizza dough high into the air.

"I told you that there were at least a thousand of them," Max tried to explain. "And they weren't alone." He was growing frustrated, but maybe Harley was right. Max had to admit that he sounded paranoid. Even the howling rainstorm outside seemed out to get him.

"Really? Who was there?" Natalia pressed, pouring herself another glass of soda.

Max shrugged, starting to wonder if he'd seen anything at all. "I didn't actually see anyone. It was more like a feeling, but I heard laughing."

"It was probably just a bunch of teenagers goofing around in the alleys," Harley said as the rain outside shifted direction and slammed against the windowpane. "But if you were so freaked out, why didn't you just pull out the *Codex*?"

"I dunno," Max said, shrugging. "I'm going to check on the pizza." As he made his way through a red-and-white-striped hallway, Max passed by a table ringed with children singing "Happy Birthday" to a little kid who'd just turned six. They looked happy, like they didn't have a care in the world. Max thought back to when he was six and wished he could go back in time, long before he found the *Codex*.

As Max neared the front of the restaurant, he paused to look out the window, where he could see the Shoppe of Antiquities right across the rain-drenched street. It was depressing. The doors were locked, the lights were off, and a CLOSED sign hung in the window. Iver had only been gone for a few days, but it might as well have been a hundred years.

Suddenly, the front door burst open and Logan stepped through a curtain of rain. Without saying a word, the Scotsman's presence rolled across the restaurant. Everyone grew silent as his eyes scanned the interior of the restaurant. In half a second, he located Max. In another instant, he had the Guardian of the *Codex* by the collar and was pulling him back out the door. "We're leaving. Now!" Logan commanded.

"What about Harley and Natalia?" Max argued as Logan ushered him into the rainstorm outside.

"No time," Max's bodyguard replied. Logan opened the door of an armored Mercedes sedan and pushed Max inside. The door slammed and Max's heart began to race as he spied Athena sitting in the driver's seat. No longer dressed as a doctor, she made the engine roar under her impatient foot. There was a wall of privacy glass separating the front from the back, and she wasn't answering the intercom. Max knew bad news was on the way. He gulped. A moment later, Logan slid in beside him, wiping a raindrop from his sunglasses before signaling Athena. The car rocketed into the falling night.

"What's going on?" Max asked, his agitation thinly veiled as they raced along the icy streets of Avalon. Outside, the storm was raging, but Logan remained calm. Without a word, he turned on a television. As the monitor flared to life, Logan's eyes met his, and Max could feel a sense of dread wash over him.

"Watch," Logan commanded.

As his gray eyes adjusted to the monitor, Max could see that some news channel was broadcasting an emergency report about an explosion. A swarm of helicopters hovered over a towering pillar of smoke that snaked its way into the atmosphere. Max's jaw dropped. "What happened? What am I looking at?"

Max watched the words scroll across the screen: *LIVE — TERRORISTS STRIKE MALTA!*

Malta? That's where the Grand Council was meeting. Where Iver had gone . . .

As the camera zoomed in, Max could see smoking wreckage strewn over the hills as emergency vehicles raced along dusty roads toward the scene. Miles of land had been scorched black, trees were blown flat like matchsticks, and if there had been a town in its path, nothing recognizable remained.

Logan growled through gritted teeth. "There's only one power that could do this."

Max's mouth fell open as he watched the flickering screen in front of him. "The Spear of Ragnarok," he breathed. "But Iver . . ."

Logan shook his head and put his sunglasses back on, his voice suddenly growing cold and distant. "I'm sorry, Max. He didn't make it."

Chill wind swept across the cemetery as a thin drizzle fell. Iver's funeral had been absolutely dreadful. Quite a few people had come to pay their respects — many of them Max had never seen before that dark day. Most were about Iver's age, though some were even older. They were an eccentric lot, so Max figured they were probably part of the Templar old guard — friends of Iver's, and probably of Max's grandfather's, too. Like relics from a time long past, they wore strange clothes: waistcoats, cloaks, spats, and bowler derbies. It looked as though they'd all stepped out of a Charles Dickens novel.

Cain Lundgren was there as well, speaking in hushed tones with several of the other mysterious strangers. Max had no idea Iver and he knew each other, yet in a town as small as Avalon, he figured it wasn't that big of a surprise.

"It's not fair," Natalia mourned, a bouquet of flowers dangling from her soaked mittens. Tears were streaming down her face and even her lungs hurt. The three Griffins remained at Iver's grave long after the others had left. "He didn't deserve this!"

Max's shoulders slumped. "I guess that's it, then. Iver said our only chance to defeat the Black Wolves was to stop them before they could use the Spear. Now . . . well . . . I guess we're all goners. The only question is who's next . . . My grandma? Mom? Sister? One of us?"

"Don't talk like that," Natalia admonished, wiping away a tear. Harley was the only one not crying. Instead, he stood stone silent, running his fingers over the Faerie Ward Iver had given him.

"It's true and we all know it," Max said in frustration. "It's like we're wearing giant targets on our backs, and now that my dad has Ray to work the Spear of Ragnarok, he doesn't need me anymore. I'm just a loose end. We all are."

"We don't know anything for sure." Natalia sniffed. "But what I *do* know is that Iver would never have given up hope." Max said nothing. "I'll miss you, Iver." Natalia's voice wavered as she placed the flowers next to his grave. "And I'll think about you every day. . . ." With that, she turned and ran back to the car where Athena waited with arms open wide.

After a moment, Harley pulled out a favorite pair of knuckle-bones and placed them next to the flowers. "Thanks," was all he could manage to say before he walked away.

Alone, Max stood next to the gray tombstone in the drizzle. "I'm sorry," he mouthed. It wasn't what he wanted to say, but he was sure Iver understood. He always did.

Alone in the half-light of the world's most amazing tree house, Max thumbed absently through a comic book. Doubling as the secret headquarters of the Grey Griffins, the structure spanned three trees, each tower connected by suspension bridges. There were even spiraling slides, a moat, and zip lines. Outside, the sky was hidden behind a curtain of mist, and twenty feet below, the forest floor was spongy from the relentless drizzle. Max was too distracted to care about the weather, though. He'd tried throwing himself into his kung fu training with Logan so he'd be too exhausted to think about everything that had happened. But nothing could dispel the realization that this whole thing had been Max's fault. Since he had handed over the Spear to his father, the Black Wolves had grown unstoppable. First, the Templar outposts fell. Next, their leadership was wiped out at Malta. Now, there didn't seem to be a single day that Max didn't hear of yet another Templar fortress being burned to the ground. The knights were on the run, and with no leadership to turn to, the outlook was bleak. The pit in Max's stomach was growing.

Without warning, a bolt of light ripped through the room. Max jumped as a portal formed, hanging in the air like a window into the unknown. And something was coming though. Something he never expected. . . .

Slowly, a catlike creature limped through the portal, and it snapped shut behind her. The creature's eyes were luminous and her lashes long. The faerie's tail twitched nervously as she looked about. This was the spriggan, the shape-shifting creature that had saved Max's life. He thought she was dead.

"Sprig!" Max shouted, still wondering if he wasn't looking at her ghost. "You're really alive?"

"Yes, Max Sumner. We are alive," the spriggan answered.

Max couldn't believe it. He wanted to pick her up in a giant bear hug, but something was wrong. Instead of elation at their reunion, she looked depressed, wringing her hands as nervous eyes darted about.

"I . . . I thought you were . . . ," Max breathed, still in awe.

"No. We are not dead," the spriggan replied. "But we have not the time to explain . . . not now, anyway."

"What's wrong?"

"Your friend . . . the funny boy with the spectacles. He's going to die. Tonight."

8 Back from the Dead

LIGHT FLASHED. The air near Ernie's bed began to ripple like water. An instant later, Max and the Spriggan stepped out of the portal and into the hospital. Ernie's bare room lay wrapped in sterile shadow, and the door was magically sealed by Sprig to keep out prying eyes. Max approached Ernie's still form, cringing at the oxygen mask and freakish tubes. "What do we need to do?"

"Take out the *Codex* and turn to the black pages," the spriggan instructed, purring nervously before licking at her injured paw. It was the same wound she had suffered when she saved Max's life.

As Max brought out the book, the room shimmered in golden light. He'd read the *Codex* a thousand times and had never come across any black pages before, but Max was learning to expect the unexpected. Sure enough, there they were, just as she said. That section of the book was filled with magical rings, lightning hammers, bottomless wells of wisdom, and other mysterious items. The last time Max had used the *Codex* at Sprig's urging, things had gone horribly wrong. Needless to say, if it wasn't for the fact that he knew Ernie really was dying, he wouldn't risk it again. Besides, the Griffins had made a pact never to release anything without all of them agreeing on it.

"There," Sprig said with wonder in her voice. She limped closer, though not too close, before pointing at an object that looked like a Viking horn. It was etched with runes and wrapped in bronze and silver fittings.

"What is it?"

"A miracle," Sprig replied with a clicking sound, her eyes igniting with fire. "I warn you, though, give him one drop only. No more, lest he be destroyed."

Max's skin began to crawl with fear. "Destroyed?"

"No time to hesitate, Max Sumner," Sprig urged, drawing closer. "Your friend is dying. Soon it will be too late!"

Max swallowed hard. "*Antalexi untalmo*," he said, reciting the strange words that were inscribed on the page. Immediately, they unlocked the contents within. The temperature dropped as frost swept across the room and crept up the bed, sheathing Ernie's oxygen mask in ice crystals. The Guardian glanced around, hoping Sprig hadn't actually tricked him into releasing a leprechaun, or something even more sinister. Then he caught sight of a horn, just like the one in the picture. It was lying near Ernie's feet. Cautiously, Max reached for it, and as he did, his fingers went numb. The horn was freezing cold.

"Remember . . . only one drop," Sprig cautioned, backing away. Max nodded as he uncapped the horn, which felt deceptively heavy in his hands. With gentle care, he tipped the device to Ernie's mouth and watched as a single crimson drop fell. The alien liquid beaded on Ernie's lips like water on a newly waxed car, but nothing else seemed to happen.

"What is that stuff?" Max asked, looking back at Sprig.

"Faerie blood . . ."

At the same moment, the droplet started to shimmer, then burst apart into hundreds of smaller drops. Those, too, split. It happened again, and again, until Ernie's entire face was covered in the strange faerie blood. Then, as one, the drops sprouted legs like a sea of tiny spiders, racing over Ernie's body only to quickly burrow beneath his skin.

Max gasped as the heart monitor screamed. Then, just as quickly, everything fell silent.

"Wha . . . what happened?" came Ernie's feeble voice.

"Ernie!" Max shouted. "You're alive!!!"

"I think so," Ernie answered, trying to pull off his oxygen mask. At the same time Max watched as a long scar on Ernie's forehead disappeared right before his eyes. Within moments, there was no visible sign of Ernie's injuries.

"How do you feel?" Max inquired carefully.

Ernie paused, his brown eyes squinting under the hospital light. He looked around, taking in his surroundings. He seemed about to say something, then looked down at his body covered under a mountain of sterile sheets. His feet wiggled, and his stomach growled. Then Ernie patted his belly and turned to Max, grinning.

"Hungry."

"I'm seeing it, but I still don't believe it," Max proclaimed, shaking his head as he watched Ernie down his tenth bottle of Plumples in less than an hour. Not a week out of the hospital, Ernie sat stuffing his face in the Grey Griffins Secret Head-quarters. He'd already devoured three bags of corn chips, two candy bars, an apple, six peanut-buttered celery stalks, and a half-dozen oatmeal cookies. If food wasn't locked up or nailed down, it was as good as gone. No one was complaining, though. Ernie was alive, and that was all that mattered.

When Max had told the rest of the Griffins about Sprig showing up and insisting that he use the *Codex* to save Ernie, there was a smattering of mixed emotions. Sure, the *Codex* had healed Ernie. But at what price? At the moment, however, the only side effect seemed to be a heretofore uncharted level of hunger.

Of course, Ernie's appetite wasn't the only oddity surfacing since the hospital. Whatever had saved his life was *still* healing him. Scrapes on the knee disappeared in seconds. No more sore throats, allergies, or asthma. In fact, just the other day, Ernie had nearly cut off his finger and watched it repair itself right then and there.

"You're just a worrywart," Ernie said, discarding Natalia's incessant worrying like yesterday's news. "Besides, what if I turn into a superhero? I mean, faerie blood's not gamma radiation, but it's gotta be close!" Max smiled reluctantly. The old Ernie wouldn't have been quite so enthusiastic when it came to playing the role of a guinea pig in a half-baked science project.

With a loud belch, Ernie patted himself on the belly and reached for the remaining package of powdered donuts, offering a piece to Winifred, his pet ferret. She was a cute bundle of silver fur stretched across a long, acrobatic body. The ferret's eyes were black, as was the fur around them. It made Winifred look as if she were wearing a burglar's mask.

Just before they left for Scotland, Ernie's parents had given her to him as a Christmas present, and at first the two of them had been inseparable. That was, until Ernie's accident. Since then, or more particularly since Ernie's miraculous resurrection, Winifred wanted nothing to do with him. Even now, despite the offered treat, she only growled.

"Do you still have Ernie's present from Iver?" Max asked. At mention of his name, the joy was sucked right out of the room and into the frosty air outside. Natalia had spent most of her days imprisoned between the joy of Ernie's return and despair over Iver's loss. It didn't take much for her to snap at the boys, her family, and even her teachers, which left them speechless. No one dared to challenge her, either. Even the Triplets had given up.

After an awkward silence, Natalia finally offered a deep sigh, as if mentally pushing away a dark cloud. She reached into her satchel and pulled out a small box, handing it to Ernie. "Here."

Ernie looked down and slowly peeled back the tape. There was a small box with T.H.O.R. written in strange letters above a hammer insignia. Cracking open the lid, Ernie discovered a small circular object about the size of a pocket watch. It had the same hammer etched across the top side.

Like Natalia's magnifying glass, the object was tarnished. When Ernie spied two tiny hinges on the backside, his fingers raced and quickly found a lever. Pushing it, the lid swung open, revealing a mysterious interior. It resembled the face of a compass, but there were lots of arms made from a myriad of different metals, each set with jewels.

"It's a compass," Natalia said, reading a note she'd found in the box. "Instead of pointing you north, though, it'll guide you to wherever you need to go."

"Cool," Ernie said, spinning the compass around to test it. "So if I lose my homework, it'll find it?"

"As if you actually *do* your homework." Natalia sniffed.

Then a knock came from the trapdoor. As one, the Griffins held their breath. Visitors weren't common at their secret hideout, which was the entire point of keeping it a secret. Certainly, they couldn't be too careful nowadays — not with all the weird things happening around town: disappearing pets, inexplicably soured milk, and trees picking up and moving themselves at night.

"Hope I'm not interrupting?" they heard as Logan's head popped into view, his signature sunglasses glinting. He was holding a white envelope and signaling toward Max.

"What's up?" Max inquired, rising from where he was sitting and walking over.

"You've got a date tonight," his bodyguard replied with a wry smile. Even when Logan tried to say something humorous, it always seemed to come out as ominous.

"A date?" Natalia asked with eyebrows raised. "With whom?"

Embarrassed, Max took the envelope from Logan. Holding it up to the light, the Guardian squinted as he tried to get a peek at the contents.

"You can read it on our way back to the house," Logan stated impatiently. "The rest of you need to get your things together. You're going home."

9

How Max Survived the Inquisition

As it turned out, Max hadn't received an invitation. It was an order. Max had been summoned to appear before the Templar High Command — or at least what remained of it after Malta.

"I want you to be strong tonight," Logan instructed as they drove through the city streets. Logan had been shuttling Max around in a veritable tank disguised as a sleek sedan. The windows were bulletproof and two inches thick. The tires were run-flat. Both gas tanks were practically missile proof, and there was a foldout console on the dash that displayed a collection of dangerous-looking buttons that Max didn't even want to know about.

"So where's this meeting taking place?" Max pressed, trying to look through the windows. Pushing a button near his arm, the passenger-window tint faded and the landscape shimmered into crystal-clear view. Outside, he could see they were winding their way along Lakeview Terrace Boulevard, not far from his house. The view didn't last long. Logan hit a button, and the tint returned. "I need to keep you safe, so let me do my job and don't touch anything, okay?"

"I'm going to find out where we're going sooner or later," Max pointed out.

"Sooner than you think," Logan replied, turning back to the road.

With a defeated shrug, Max pulled out his grandfather's deck of Round Table cards from his pocket and shuffled through them absently. He knew each one backwards and forwards by now — every decent player had to — which was why he knew something was out of place right away. Max counted through the deck, and then again. A card was missing. He paused and scratched at his head, unable to remember lending this deck to anyone.

Max shuffled through a final time, trying to recall which card was missing. The Stone Troll was there, and so was the Dwarf Sapper. There were the Kobolds, Gallow Goblins, and the Frost Giant. Then he knew. The Doppelgänger! Which was kind of weird. He hadn't even played with it yet. It was a hard card to work into his deck. All he knew for sure was that Doppelgängers were murderous shape-shifters. Losing one of his grandfather's cards was bad news — and worse yet, it was the last thing Iver had given him before he'd left for Malta. At that moment, Max realized for the first time that Round Table was finished. The game was over. Iver was dead. . . .

The armored Mercedes rolled to a stop on a wet drive of intricate brickwork. Max stepped out of the car and into the evening drizzle, expecting to have arrived at some underground secret lair. Instead, he saw familiar gargoyles flanking by the same rough-hewn stairs he used to play on as a kid. That was, before his father forbade him to play there ever again. It was the home of Dr. Cain Lundgren, Brooke's father.

A parade of vehicles lined the drive: elegant sedans, angry-looking motorcycles, and blacked-out trucks. Many of them had chauffeurs standing near at hand, but roads were not the only means of arrival. Out back, on the waters of Lake Avalon, a pier brimmed with a collection of mysterious boats.

Rain pelted their umbrella as Max and Logan ascended the stairs to the front entrance. Max didn't know what to say, or expect, when the door opened. Would Brooke be there waiting? If she was, what would he say? Once the best of friends, Brooke and her house had been off-limits to Max for years. If Cain was as bitter about the argument as Lord Sumner, Max was in even bigger trouble than he thought.

Logan grasped a knocker and let it fall heavily three times, followed by a pause, and finally a fourth knock. That was the same covert knock the Grey Griffins used to access their secret tree fort, Max marvelled.

On cue, the door swung open, revealing a well-dressed man with razor-sharp cheekbones and mottled skin that was stretched across his frame so tautly that it seemed as if it might crack at any moment. His eyes flickered eerily in the torchlight, but his smile was kind and inviting, despite the fact that Max was sure he could see fangs. White gloves covered long, careful fingers, and well-polished shoes adorned his feet. Max had never seen him before, but something about this man was eerily familiar.

"Evenin', Throckmorton," Logan greeted after clearing his throat.

The dark man bowed slightly. *"Guten Abend*, Herr Logan. *Wieviel?"*

"Just the two of us tonight, *natürlich*," Logan replied, handing the invitation to the servant and nodding toward Max. Max looked over at his bodyguard, thinking of all the strange places Logan had been. Languages came easily to him, but so did danger. With the Scotsman, they often went hand in hand.

Throckmorton's flickering eyes fell upon Max. *"Sprechen Sie Deutsch*, young master?"

Max shook his head. He'd barely managed to survive Latin last semester, despite the private tutor. German wasn't even a thought — at least not yet.

"That won't be a problem," Throckmorton replied in flawless English, smiling in assurance. "The gentlemen you will meet this evening are conversant in many languages." He then turned back to Logan. "The baron is in the parlor awaiting you."

"Baron?" asked Max.

Logan ignored the inquiry, stepped over a threshold etched with arcane symbols, and handed the damp umbrella to Throckmorton. He quickly shook it and placed it next to at least a dozen others that were resting nearby.

As the door shut behind them, Max looked around in wonder. It had been so long since he'd been there that he'd forgotten just how large the Lundgren house was. Somehow, it seemed even bigger on the inside than on the outside. In their early years, he and Brooke had adventured all through the house, finding undiscovered rooms and mysterious staircases that led to new floors and wings with each expedition. The house seemed to go on and on, as if it were continuously building itself.

Throckmorton motioned for Logan and Max to follow as he set off down a hallway lined with paneled wood, eventually passing a staircase that curved up to dizzying heights. Perhaps he'd been too young to notice before, but Max now descried Templar motifs lurking almost everywhere, with symbols etched atop every door and stained-glass window. The entire house was a bit of a puzzle box. Hallways zigzagged into the darkness, windows skewed in all direction, and flickering lamps burned with no oil or wick. It was as if Max had stepped into a haunted mansion. Creepy. Yet at the same time it felt like the safest place in the world.

They finally came to a pair of doors. Max could see a firelit parlor on the other side, filled with the soft murmur of voices.

"Now," Logan began as he knelt down and locked eyes with Max. "I want you to be on your best behavior. There're powerful men inside, and they're bloody well used to wielding that power. They're gonna test you, so remember to control that temper of yours. Don't give them a reason not to trust you. Just smile, be polite, and answer their questions. Then we'll go home and get a bite to eat. Understand?"

"They are ready for you," Throckmorton stated, before turning to leave. As Max's eyes followed, he gasped. Just as the butler disappeared around the corner, Max could have sworn he saw a tail swish out from beneath the servant's jacket.

"He's a . . . ," Max exclaimed, unable to finish.

"He's not your concern right now," Logan replied sternly, turning Max back toward the parlor. "You need to stay sharp. Speak clearly and breathe. Project your presence like we've talked about. You ready?"

"You're coming with me, right?"

Logan smiled reassuringly. "You bet your breeks."

Apart from the warm glow of a fire crackling in a hearth, the parlor was swept under a thick blanket of shadow. From what he could see, it was drenched in rich leathers, warm carpets, and the elaborate tapestries that covered the walls. Although it may have looked comfortable, it definitely didn't *feel* that way — especially once Max caught sight of the grim men who were there.

"Gentlemen, it appears the son of Lord Sumner has chosen to accept our invitation," Cain Lundgren said in a flowing baritone voice. Max studied him closely. Cain wore a red cape over his dark suit, and as his eyes fell upon Max, the Griffin shivered. Ever since Max had discovered the *Codex*, he could detect the telltale signs of power. This skill was what helped him track down goblins and trolls to put them back into the *Codex*, but as Max looked at Cain, his senses went into overload. Here was a man whose power was beyond Max's comprehension. Why had he never seen it before?

"Please, step toward the light," Cain entreated. The firelight seemed to blaze brighter as Max obeyed. "There are some gentlemen I think you'll be interested in meeting." On either side of Max were at least a dozen men dressed like kings, who were seated on leather couches and leopard-print chairs. Behind them stood a row of knights, stone silent in the darkness. Max could feel all their eyes boring into him, as though he were about to be dissected.

"I want to begin this meeting by telling you how sorry I am for your loss," Brooke's father offered, his own eyes filled with sorrow. "Your mentor and trainer, Olaf Iverson, was a valued friend and an esteemed member of the Templar. We all grieve with you."

Max said nothing.

"In the cataclysm of violence, we have lost many who were dear to us. More important, the Templar have lost their leaders in a single blow. Fortresses are falling as our armies are overrun by the growing shadow of the Black Wolves. We are fighting to prevent our extinction." Cain's voice fell upon Max like a suffocating cloud. "Yet, despite how far we have fallen, there is still hope. That is why we have gathered here today and *that* is why we have summoned you, Guardian." Dr. Lundgren's eyes narrowed as he studied Max; then he gestured to a figure reclining near the firelight. "I would like to introduce you to the Templar Grand Inquisitor. He has come to ask you a few questions. I advise you to answer honestly, for your own sake as well as ours."

Max swallowed uncomfortably, then nodded. Was he about to be interrogated?

"Thank you, Baron Lundgren," came the thin but potent voice of the Grand Inquisitor. Max paused — there was the word again! *Baron* Lundgren. Max tried to piece the puzzle together. His own father was a *lord*. Now, Cain was a *baron*. He'd never really thought about it before, but it seemed royalty had surrounded Max all his life, and he hadn't known it.

"Your name," the Inquisitor pressed Max. "Full name, if you please."

"Grayson Maximillian Sumner the Third," Max replied slowly.

"And your mother?"

"Annika Caliburn Sumner."

"Your father?"

"I don't have a father," Max replied coldly, his own eyes narrowing.

Slowly, the shadows gave way as the speaker leaned forward in his seat, revealing oily hair pulled severely back across his expansive forehead. His eyes were ravenously intelligent, and his nose, which dominated an ashen face, cast a long shadow over a disapproving mouth. "You have your father's eyes, you know." The Inquisitor's thin lips dryly parted, revealing a set of perfectly white teeth. Whatever his intention, it looked more like he was snarling than smiling. "My name is Ulysses of the House of Belisarius. I serve as the Grand Seneschal — the chief advisor to the Grandmaster — though, thanks to you and the gift you supplied to the man you seem reluctant to claim as your father, our leader, the Grandmaster, is now dead, as are many of my brothers of the Order."

Silence fell over the room as Max looked to Logan for support, but the Scotsman remained silent.

"I didn't mean to give him the Spear of Ragnarok, if that's . . . ," Max began.

"Of course you didn't," the Inquisitor snapped in sarcasm. "Yet, child, if you had no intention of handing that weapon to the enemy, then why retrieve it in the first place? Isn't it true that your Templar mentor counseled against it? Didn't he tell you what would happen if it fell into the wrong hands?"

Max bowed his head in shame.

"Nothing to say in your defense?" Ulysses inquired with a penetrating gaze. "I'd imagine not, since your actions, from the beginning, have already spoken volumes. You aren't wholly to blame, I think. After all, you *are* but a child. Perhaps the mistake stemmed from the misguided trust we placed in Iverson. This isn't the first time he's failed."

"Don't talk that way about him!" Max shouted. His fists were clenched, as were his teeth.

"And if I do . . . ?" Ulysses replied with the smile of a cunning snake. "Will you tell your father on me? Oh yes, he'd make me pay, wouldn't he? He has the Spear of Ragnarok, after all. . . ."

Max seethed, but said nothing. Inside him, he could feel his fire starting to boil, just as it had with the Tundra Troll. Ulysses seemed unimpressed, however.

"You see," Ulysses continued, "how can the Templar trust you? You are young, impressionable, and entirely ruled by your emotions. Your lack of judgment has likely led to the single greatest disaster in Templar history — and you aren't even twelve years old yet. My boy, you are a catastrophe in the making. A murderer. An offspring of a villain. And I will go on record as saying that if you haven't betrayed us voluntarily, it is only a matter of time."

Silence filled the room as all eyes turned to Max.

Max's eyes, however, were locked on the Grand Inquisitor. With each venomous insult, the fire inside Max grew more intense. Even now, flames burst from the tips of his fingers. He hated this man.

Ulysses smirked as he shook his head. "As I foretold, it didn't take long for the boy to show his true colors. Baron, put a leash on your dog!"

Immediately, Baron Lundgren raised his own hands and Max's fire smoldered, spat, then fizzled into nothing as the flames retreated to the farthest corners of his mind. Like the setting of a lock, Max next heard an audible *click* in his head. The fire was gone. Max's anger turned to wonder, and that wonder turned to panic. What just happened?

Cain Lundgren walked over to Max, leaning on his cane as he placed his hand on the boy's shoulder. "Come with me," he said flatly. It was not a request. As they passed through the exit, Cain shut the doors and turned to him, studying the Griffin intently. "That was exceedingly foolish," he began. "The Grand Inquisitor was testing you. You knew that, yet you allowed your emotions to cloud your judgment. You've lost Iver already. If you burn this bridge, you'll truly be alone. Do you understand?"

"What did you do to me?" Max asked, though hesitantly. "I mean, the fire. You made it go away?" His voice betrayed both shame at having nearly lost control, and the fear of possibly never experiencing the thrill of that fire again.

Brooke's father offered a reassuring smile. "Nothing permanent, I assure you. Take some time to clear your head, and you'll be back to full strength in no time. I'll send for you shortly."

Cain disappeared back into the parlor, his cane clicking on the floor before he closed the doors behind him, leaving Max alone in the hallway to contemplate just how badly he'd screwed up. Logan had warned him to stay in control, but Max had buckled under the pressure in a matter of minutes. Logan would never let him live this down. . . .

The Guardian of the *Codex* sighed as he sulked down the hallway, unexpectedly discovering a deck of Round Table cards that were lying on a side table. Outside of the Griffins (and Iver), he hadn't known anyone else to play the game. Furrowing his brows, Max walked over to get a better look. As he picked up the deck and began to look through it, his eyes grew. Max hadn't seen any of these cards before.

Suddenly, a flash of light appeared behind the deck in his hands and out darted a small pixie. A trail of glitter fell away like the tail of a comet as the gossamer-winged faerie shot over Max's head. Spinning to see where she'd gone, Max nearly stumbled in shock when he found her. Arms folded disapprovingly, she was hovering over the shoulder of Brooke Lundgren.

10

The Tale of Bounders

"BROOKE!" LIKE a thief caught with his hands in a safe, Max dropped the stack of cards as the pixie buzzed around him like a mad hornet. "What are you doing here?"

Brooke smiled in amusement, her eyes the color of warm chocolate as she entered the light. "I live here, remember?"

A long silence fell over the hall as Max regarded Brooke and her flying faerie in astonishment, wondering what this could all mean. Unable to find the words, instead he bent down to pick up the cards. "I understand," she admitted casually, looking at Max as he fumbled with the mess. "You didn't know about my secret. Kind of hard to explain, but I guess you know all about that...."

Max stood up too quickly, catching the top of his head on the corner of the end table, earning another mocking laugh from the faerie. Quickly, he handed the cards to Brooke. "Thank you," she offered, taking the cards. "I really shouldn't have left them lying around like that."

"Where'd you get 'em, anyway?" he asked, eying the pixie warily as it whispered something in Brooke's ear. She smiled at the faerie and whispered something back. Then the pixie spun to face Max, its tiny eyes narrowed and lips pursed indignantly, before disappearing down the hallway in a huff.

"Never mind her," explained Brooke. "Honeysuckle doesn't trust boys. Not many pixies do. No offense."

"No bid deal," Max managed as casually as he could.

"I have a lot of Round Table decks, but this one's my favorite," she said, shuffling through the cards. "They were my dad's."

"Really? You're a Templar, too?"

Brooke shook her head. "No. Not really," she explained, carelessly running her bare foot along the corner of a rug. Her toenails were painted and decorated with glittering flowers.

"I don't understand," protested Max. "I thought only Templar used Round Table cards. . . ."

"It's kinda complicated, but my dad can probably explain what he does for the Templar better than I can. In the meantime, you can just think of him as a kind of consultant, I guess. The Templar come to him for advice from time to time." Then she paused, brightening with an idea. "Hey, wanna go for a walk?"

Max hesitated. "I should probably stay here just in case they send for me. Besides, I don't think Logan wants me wandering around alone."

"You won't be alone, because you'll be with me," she said, laughing. "Besides, we'll be back before you know it — I know a shortcut." With that, she led Max around the corner and into a vast hall, each wall lined with shining coats of armor holding menacing weapons.

"These are part of my father's alarm system. The suits of armor are . . . well . . . I guess you could call them enchanted, though I'm not sure that's the right term. Anyway, you don't want to know what would happen to a burglar if he tripped the alarm."

"You mean the knights come to life?"

"Something like that," Brooke said as she looked from left to right to make sure they were alone. Convinced they were, she hurried over and opened a visor on one of the helms, before pushing a series of buttons. When Brooke finished, a section of paneling that lined the wall opened to reveal a slide. "You coming?" asked Brooke as she closed the visor and paused a moment before disappearing.

As they slid through the darkness, the wind whistled through their ears. Unlike normal slides, Max could swear this one didn't just go down. It felt like they were zipping up, straight, and every which way. Eventually, they burst into the backyard on a soft patch of sand. Ahead lay Lake Avalon, where a stone pier was lined with the mysterious boats Max had seen when they pulled into the drive.

They weren't the standard crafts that locals used for water skiing or fishing. One looked like a Viking longboat, and there was a weird submarine made entirely of polished copper. Max thought it resembled something taken from Captain Nemo's private fleet. Each craft was somehow stranger than the last, and where they'd come from, Max couldn't begin to guess — that was until, in the distance, he saw the shimmering light of a massive portal open up. Brooke and Max watched as a ghostly ship passed through the ethereal gateway, sliding through the lake toward the pier.

A half-dozen broad-shouldered men filed onto the pier to greet the boat with the words *Kon-Tiki* written across the bow. They were dressed in glittering armor with long flowing capes of crimson. "Who are *they*?" Max wondered as they marched past.

"The Templar Honor Guard. They're here to escort the surviving dignitaries," Brooke answered solemnly. "There aren't many left now. Most were at Malta when . . ." Her voice trailed off cautiously as she saw Max's jaws clench.

The two friends remained silent as the new arrivals quietly disembarked, striding past the two of them without so much as a glance. Rich robes flowed from the shoulders of gray-bearded men and radiant women. Even their servants looked regal.

"They're the leaders of the Templar Great Houses," Brooke said, as though reading his mind. "There're thirteen houses in all, including the House of Caliburn. They're all gathering here to prepare for the End," she explained, pulling Max back down the pier.

"What?"

"Yeah. When the Spear was re-formed, that started it." Max's jaw dropped. "You didn't know that?"

"I do *now*."

"Haven't you been watching the news?" she asked. "The signs are everywhere."

Max shook his head. He hadn't been watching much

television. Logan kept Max on a need-to-know basis ever since Malta had been struck. "But I thought Ragnarok could still be stopped?"

Brooke nodded. "It can, but we still need to be ready, just in case. Haven't you heard about those holes opening up in corn fields?" Max shook his head. "Lakes drying up in the middle of the night?" Still nothing. "What about all the herds of cattle disappearing?" Max was dumbstruck. "There's more stuff, too," she continued. "Things that would really freak you out."

"Like what?" he ventured cautiously.

Brooke paused. "I overheard my dad talking to a stranger the other day. He runs the cemetery a few towns over, and he said it was emptied out overnight."

Max shrank back. "Grave robbers?"

"No," Brooke said, shaking her head before looking over her shoulder anxiously. "That's what the police thought until they found skeleton footprints leading from the graves into a nearby field. It's like the dead got up and walked out on their own."

Max could feel the hair on his arms rise. Things were creepier than he could have imagined. Goblins were one thing, but zombies? Max rubbed his arms to warm up, but nearly jumped out of his shoes when he spied something out of the corner of his eye. A dark blur sped across the lawn, quickly disappearing into the shadows. "Did you see that?" he murmured.

"See what?"

"Over there," answered Max, switching to a cautious whisper as he pointed toward the park across the night-cloaked road. Then his heart skipped a beat as he heard a terrible cry. Looking up, he could just make out silhouettes of ravens circling in the night sky. "Great," he muttered under his breath, realizing his fears had been confirmed. Those birds were following him. "They were probably listening to everything we were saying. . . ."

Instantaneously, as though she'd been reading their minds, Honeysuckle appeared at Brooke's side. They exchanged a look, and then the pixie shot toward the birds. The ravens shrieked before flapping away in a storm of angry wings. Honeysuckle didn't return, though. Instead, she patrolled the sky, ensuring there were no other surprises.

After a few moments, Max and Brooke relaxed. "I've been meaning to ask you how you got a pixie," he began. "Is she a pet or something?"

"She's my Bounder," Brooke said as if that particular term explained everything.

"Your what?"

"Are you serious?"

"I . . . ," Max began. "I mean, I've seen lots of pixies, but I just haven't heard of a Bounder before."

"Bounders are faeries that are *bound* to people, Max. Have you been sleeping through your lessons?" Max tried to look like he'd simply forgotten, but it wasn't working. Instead he stared at the ground. "They serve and protect one particular human their entire lives. I thought everyone knew that. . . ." She paused, looking over at Max's confused expression, then smiled reassuringly. "I'm sorry. I guess I just thought that because you were the Guardian, you'd know everything already."

Max said nothing, wondering the same question. Then finally he looked back up. "How do people get a Bounder?"

"Sometimes it's because the person saved the faerie's life, but there are lots of other reasons. It's pretty amazing, really. There's a whole rule book on it in my dad's library. I can show you later if you want."

"So, how'd you get one? Did you save her life?"

Brooke shook her head. "She's been with me ever since I can remember. My parents said she showed up at the hospital when I was born. . . . I don't know the reason. Anyway, my dad has a Bounder, too. Maybe you met him already? Throckmorton . . . he's a gargoyle."

"I saw his tail," admitted Max.

Brooke nodded. "It's kinda hard to hide. But . . ."

"What?"

"Well, it's just kind of weird that you're asking me about Bounders, because . . . well . . . you have one, too."

Max paused as he tried to sort out Brooke's statement. Then it came to him. Sprig! So that's how it worked. "How'd you know I have a Bounder?"

"I've known ever since you tried to hide her from me in your locker last fall." Brooke smiled. "Anyway, every Bounder marks a territory so other faeries know to beware. You were marked. Simple as that."

"Where?" Max took a step back and examined himself suspiciously.

Brooke began to laugh. "No, silly. It's invisible to most people. You'd never see it. Only faeries."

"Then how can you?" Max replied, but Brooke only shrugged.

"It's just a gift, I guess. Dad says everyone has a gift."

Just then a great horn sounded, startling the kids. The portal above the lake shimmered to life again as the prow of a great vessel broke through, sending angry waves into the night as it headed toward the Lundgren pier.

The ship had three masts with enormous sails billowing in the icy wind. A single flag snapped over one mast, green with a black dragon. Its bow was carved to resemble a leaping dragon, complete with spectral eyes glowing in the darkness. There was a team of strong men working the rigging and mooring ropes, and there, standing on a platform overseeing it all, was the one man Max hadn't expected to see again.

Vlad Dracula.

The Doomsday Deadline

THERE WAS a murmur as Dracula strode through Baron Lundgren's study, his heavy boots echoing on the stone. Two menacing knights from the vaunted Order of the Dragon flanked the warlord. Heavily armed, they looked ready for battle. So did Dracula.

Head held high, Vlad's black hair flowed over a green cloak draped upon his shoulders. There was something about the Dark Prince that sent shivers down the spines of everyone who met him. Maybe it was his intense emerald eyes, or perhaps the way the air around him seemed to grow chill. Certainly, rumors of his past crimes — none of which could be substantiated outside of children's stories — left everyone with the feeling that crossing Vlad Dracula would be the last mistake one would ever make.

As the Dark Prince entered, all eyes turned to him. Some voices shouted with support. Some cried out in anger. The room was spilling with intrigue and heated arguments. Max was contemplating sneaking away, as he noted that the only person who didn't seem shocked to see the Walachian prince was Baron Lundgren. Brooke's father rose easily from his chair, as though merely greeting an old friend. "Dracula. Thank you for accepting my invitation," he offered. The room hushed.

"Upon whose authority did you invite this warmonger?" Ulysses demanded, standing with indignation.

"My own," Baron Lundgren proclaimed. "This is, after all, *my* house and none may enter without my leave."

"This is Templar business," the Grand Seneschal argued, pointing at Vlad. "Not a circus of freaks."

Dracula remained silent, but his eyes seemed to flicker in response to the insult.

"The End concerns us all," countered Cain. "Too much is at stake to act otherwise. So, if you please, we shall get down to business."

"Indeed," Vlad's voice broke over the crowd, creeping into their minds and chilling their blood. "And let the business be brief. I do not have time to waste with cowardly deliberation. The facts are apparent. The Black Wolves have the Spear. They will use it to bring Ragnarok down upon our heads. We must stop them. Now."

"What you may call cowardice, others may well consider prudence," Baron Lundgren offered deftly, showing he wasn't necessarily in Dracula's camp.

"And we have not been idle," argued one knight clad in crimson. The parlor was now filled with the newcomers Max had seen arrive earlier. "Already our intelligence . . ."

"I have my own intelligence," interrupted Dracula, waving away the comment. "Every morsel of information you hold, I know of . . . and more. I have urged the Templar to action three times in as many months, yet you do nothing." The last statement was directed at Ulysses. "You did the same with the Black Witch. Do you not remember? Were it not for me, she'd have destroyed you all by now. I alone overcame her, destroyed her fortress, and she now rots in my dungeons. You all owe me your lives *and* your allegiance."

The entire room erupted in chaos as Vlad stood there, unmoved by the shouts of anger. Yet some agreed with the warlord and didn't mind voicing as much.

"So, you urge us to march under *your* flag into battle?" interjected Ulysses as the voices faded. "And after your defeat of the Black Wolves, I suppose the payment for your services will be the Spear itself! Is that it?"

Vlad's eyes flickered once again.

Ulysses continued, "You can relieve yourself of any such pretensions, Lord Dracula. The Spear will never be yours. That is, unless we elect to trade one tyrant for another."

Vlad strode across the hall with great purpose. Reaching Ulysses, he snarled, "Know that the only reason I let you live is for the single hope that the others will finally see you for what you truly are."

"And what am I?" Ulysses sneered in return.

"A tool of the enemy," Dracula spat.

Ulysses' hand reached for his sword, though he was not foolish enough to draw. "Are you calling me a traitor, sir?"

Dracula paused for a moment. Max wasn't sure if Vlad was taking the challenge seriously or not. "While I admire the lack of regard you hold for your life," Dracula began smiling coldly, "I find myself wondering why you're not so courageous in your dealing with the enemy."

There were snickers in the crowd.

"Because Sumner holds the Spear," Ulysses snapped, his hand

still on the hilt of his sword. "Confronting you is one thing. There, at least, I'd only be risking my own life. However, I'd be risking the lives of countless others if I were to challenge the power of the Spear. You may be prepared to make this sacrifice, but I am not."

Vlad said nothing. Again the room fell into heated deliberation, as Ulysses sat back down upon his leather chair. "You see, we are simply outmatched, great Prince. My counsel is that we wait until we know more. At any rate, how could we possibly take the offensive at this moment? Our leadership has been wiped off the planet. Even with your troops added to our own, we're grossly outnumbered."

"I did not invite you all here," the Baron interrupted, "to discuss battle plans. That time has long since passed. We are hopelessly outnumbered . . . and outmatched. Neither Vlad's power nor my talents could stand against the Spear. It's a fact beyond debate. Yet wars are not always won on the battlefield. I have asked you all here to discuss an alternate means of victory. I wish to discuss the Eye of Odin!"

An audible hush fell over the room.

"What's the Eye of Odin?" Max asked, feeling naïve, even as he spoke.

"Legend tells of an amulet called the Eye of Odin that was forged by the dwarf lord, Regin. If the stories are true, the Eye is one of the most powerful objects ever created. No kingdom, no king, and no creature could stand against its subtle enchantment. Thankfully, before it could be used against humanity, the amulet disappeared. Some claim it has slipped into the sea;

others say it was melted in the heart of a living volcano. None know for certain, though, and so the legend grows."

"Even if this trinket of yours exists, it surely isn't a match for the Spear," spoke Ulysses, sarcasm lacing his every word.

Cain shook his head. "The Eye is not an offensive weapon, like a sword or spear. Its power is more basic. That is, anyone who wears the amulet can steal the essence from *anything* they touch, be it rock, tree, magician, or faerie."

"That is what you offer?" the Grand Seneschal snorted.

"Believe me, Ulysses, that's quite enough," Cain replied. "When the essence is drawn forth, the wearer of the amulet has the choice to do whatever he wants with the power. Imagine, if you will, that the wearer were to keep the power he stole for his own purposes? The owner of the Eye would essentially become an unstoppable parasite, jumping from one victim to the next until he was omnipotent and entirely beyond the challenge of anyone in this room. Including the power of our esteemed guest Lord Dracula."

Silence filled the room.

"Why would you seek such a powerful object?" Ulysses argued. "Better to keep it hidden, lest it fall into the wrong hands. . . ."

"Because with the Eye," Cain answered, "we could significantly change the balance of power without shedding a drop of blood."

Vlad rose. "So where is this Eye of Odin that can siphon off the power of the Spear?"

Cain signaled for Logan to approach the table. The Scotsman had been hiding in the shadows, and as the assembled knights cleared a path, Max could see that Logan was carrying an old box about the size of a briefcase. Logan set it on the desk next to Baron Lundgren and slowly opened the lid. With careful hands, Logan pulled out a book bound in cracked leather with a thick strand of string wrapped tightly around its cover.

"This book is the final diary of Lord Saxon," Cain proclaimed as the Scotsman handed him the diary. "In it, the author tells of a journey into the Underworld. It was a treacherous journey, yet he escaped, chronicling his entire expedition."

"Did he find the weapon?" inquired Dracula.

"He did, though it nearly cost Lord Saxon his life. Indeed, it may well cost us our own in the end." He paused, looking out over the audience as if measuring the strength of their hearts. "The Eye of Odin is our only hope of defeating Lord Sumner, and thanks to Saxon's diary, we know where to find it. Even so, time is against us. Lord Sumner has the Spear. All that remains is for him to locate the World Tree, into which, we all know, the Spear must be driven." Max looked up anxiously. He'd never heard of the World Tree before, but Cain didn't seem interested in explaining. "This is no small task," Cain continued. "But it is not beyond Lord Sumner, I think. Within a month, perhaps a bit longer, he'll have solved this last riddle. Then heaven help us all."

"So you propose to set out immediately on this quest of yours?" Vlad inquired.

Cain shook his head. "Not yet. I'm afraid there are things we must first do to prepare. One cannot simply walk into the Underworld and snatch the Eye of Odin from its resting place as easily as pulling an apple from a barrel."

Dracula raised a threatening finger toward Cain. "Then take your month to prepare. But no longer. If you have not secured the amulet by then, I will take matters into my own hands. And I cannot promise you will approve of my methods."

Early the next morning . . .

"I thought this was supposed to be official Grey Griffin business," Natalia commented, looking directly at Max as she joined Brooke and the other Griffins under the looming trees of Mystic Bay Park. In Natalia's mind, Brooke Lundgren represented everything she hated, a pampered princess who didn't deserve half the attention she got.

The Griffins were once again bundled in winter gear. The weather had taken another turn for the worse. Dark clouds sat motionless overhead, choking out the sun, and a creeping mist hung over the streets, slithering here and there, making it impossible to see so much as six inches in front of your nose. It was dark, damp, and dismal, and none of the Griffins wanted to be there. Were it not for Max's urgent message, they'd still have been in bed, warm and considerably less soggy.

"I'm sorry," Brooke apologized to Natalia. "Maybe I should go. . . ." She rose and turned in the direction of her house.

"Hold on!" Max pulled Brooke back, then faced his friends. "A lot of stuff has happened that I have to tell you guys. And I need Brooke here to back me up."

"Is that so?" Natalia placed her hands on her hips and arched a disapproving eyebrow in Max's direction. "Well, this had better be good, Grayson Sumner. Logan told you not to go out wandering alone, and here you are, inviting us to a secret meeting in a foggy park."

"At least there's a dragon slide," Ernie commented.

"It's not nice today," Natalia replied. "And we're taking a risk just being here. I don't care if it's across from Brooke's house. It was a stupid idea."

"I know. But it was the only place my dad would let me go," Brooke said. She was truly apologetic. "He probably has Throckmorton spying on me."

Harley had enough. "Stop gripin', Natalia. We're here already, so let's just listen to what Max has to say."

With Brooke filling in the gaps, Max spun his tale about the meeting, Vlad's appearance, the crows, and his suspicion of a supernatural stalker following him around. The Griffins looked at one another uncomfortably. They were fairly certain that one way or another, they'd end up looking for the Eye of Odin down in the Underworld. That's the way these things always seemed to work.

"Hey! There they are again!" Max exclaimed, pointing to a few nearby ravens that had perched on the snout of the dragon slide, which looked eerily alive in the half-light and fog. "Those are the same stupid birds I keep telling you about."

At that same moment, the temperature dropped.

"See what I mean," Max complained.

Suddenly, the entire park was flooded with an endless sea of ravens. Then the laughter came. Like a haunting melody, it rolled over the children, chilling them to the core. The fog was too thick, though. They couldn't see a thing.

"I told you we shouldn't have come here," Natalia reminded them.

"Yeah, maybe we should make like a banana, and split," added Ernie, as he backed away from a raven that had landed a little too close.

"I'm with you," Brooke agreed.

Then the birds attacked. It started with one, but soon the entire flock of hundreds was diving at the Griffins — pulling at Harley's jacket, tugging Natalia's braids, and swarming over Max's backpack. The angry ravens snapped at his fingers whenever Max got close to the latch where the *Codex* rested.

"Forget the *Codex*," Harley yelled, waving his fists at the black tempest of feathers and claws. "Use that fire!"

Max tried, but no fire came. His mind seemed to fog over, as there, standing amidst the flurry of wings, Max could see sharp fangs. There was no body, though, only a menacing smile shrouded in the mist. It drew closer, until Max realized there were invisible fingers around his throat, slowly tightening. He began to choke as the other Griffins fought for their lives under the barrage of furious ravens.

Just then, the headlights of a black sedan flooded the park, and a car skidded to a halt. The doors burst open, and Logan and Søren raced out. The ravens retreated into the murky sky, just as those invisible fingers relaxed from around Max's throat.

Because Practice
Makes Perfect

A Week Later . . .

"You find anything yet?" Max asked Natalia as the Griffins stood looking out over the glistening waters of Lake Avalon. Throckmorton, the Lundgrens' gargoyle servant, had herded them onto the pier behind Brooke's house. They had no idea where they were going, but Harley was hoping it was a fishing trip. For the first time in days, the sun had broken through the thick vale of clouds, and he hadn't been fishing in weeks. Nothing was biting.

"Unfortunately not," complained Natalia, shaking her head. She'd hardly been sleeping since Max told her about the Eye of Odin. With unequaled tenacity, she'd been throwing herself into research, trying to find any nugget of information about the relic. The school library certainly didn't mention it, nor did the town library for that matter. She eventually contacted the Templar Librarian that they'd met during their winter holiday. Much to her pleasure, the Librarian had issued Natalia a remote-viewing library card. It just hadn't arrived yet.

The Templar Library wasn't like other libraries, of course. There was simply no peer to its selection of books, not to mention that it was located in the bottom of a volcano. But the best part of all was that you didn't have to actually go to the Library to check out a book. Remote viewing allowed you to access the library from anywhere in the world. Natalia had no idea how it worked, but for those watching from inside the Library, when someone remotely viewed a book, it looked like the manuscript was floating in midair, the pages turning without aid.

"Come, children. It is time," the gargoyle spoke, leading them toward a long, narrow ship at the end of the pier. In single file, they boarded the boat, watching as Throckmorton pushed off. Soon, the craft was silently plying through the icy waters of Lake Avalon.

Though the meeting had been dreadful, Max learned that the Templar High Command had agreed to assign Baron Lundgren as his new mentor. In fact, Cain would be training *all* the Griffins. He wasted no time. All four of them had been thrown under an avalanche of lessons, despite their homework from King's Elementary. Every day after the final school bell rang, they made their reluctant way over to the Lundgren house, where they were handed another mountain of dusty old books.

The idea of training through games of Round Table had been all but forgotten. So had the *Codex Spiritus*. That was, until today. *Today* they would face the SIM Chamber, an advanced Templar training room. Inside its walls, anything was possible. Dream and reality were woven together so intricately that no one, not even the creator of the simulation, could tell the difference. Max had been told it was a little like walking into the middle of a video game, though not nearly as safe. . . .

"Um, how are we moving?" asked Ernie, looking nervously

back at their wake. "I don't see an engine, and nobody's rowing." Throckmorton said nothing.

Lake Avalon was the perfect getaway during the summer, but at the moment, it was miserable. Rotten ice crept about the shoreline, and the beach houses were abandoned. Theirs was the only boat in sight as they headed toward Lake Avalon's darkest mystery — the nameless island that sat ominously in the heart of its waters. Covered in menacing pines and riddled with caves, the island was the one place every mother begged her child not to go. There were stories of fishermen who had disappeared without a trace, leaving nothing but strange footprints found upon the shore, and, despite its being uninhabited, spectral lights could be seen flickering in the night. The townspeople had no name for it. They simply called it cursed and vowed never to set foot on its shores.

"Welcome," extended Baron Lundgren, as Throckmorton tied the boat to a rotting dock that jutted from the island's shore. "Please watch your step as you disembark. I wouldn't want you to fall in."

"Too cold?" asked Natalia.

"No. The serpents," the Baron replied casually.

"My mom said I wasn't supposed to come out here," Ernie said, looking into the shadows of the trees. Cain ignored Ernie and ordered the Griffins to follow him. For almost a mile, they trekked along a little-used path, but soon Ernie lagged behind, struggling with his jacket.

"You brought that stupid weasel of yours, didn't you?" Natalia complained.

"Whaddayou mean?" Ernie stuttered, as he readjusted his strangely lumpy sleeve.

"Ernest!" Natalia narrowed her eyes. "You know very well what I'm talking about. I can smell that stupid ferret from a mile away." Ernie was about to object to his ferret being called stupid when Winifred poked her head out of his collar and hissed at Natalia. The animal then turned and hissed at Ernie for good measure, biting his ear before disappearing back into the warmth.

"I don't recall permitting pets in our training sessions," Cain Lundgren spoke as he looked disapprovingly down at Ernie, who, in turn, fell to the back of the line, avoiding eye contact with the baron.

Max wandered in Cain's wake, thinking about Iver. The old man had shepherded the Griffins with a gentle hand and a kind smile. He was wise, his heart was warm, and he was never critical. Cain was altogether different. Stern and aloof, the Griffins couldn't remember the last time he'd offered a word of encouragement. Nothing seemed good enough.

"Did you guys see that?" Ernie gasped after trudging another mile or so, pointing into the thickest part of the woods. "Something's watching us from under that tree."

"Would you stop being so paranoid?" complained Natalia, putting her hands on her hips. "Everyone knows those stories about monsters on this island were made up to scare off tourists."

"Are you willing to bet your life on that fact?" Baron Lundgren inquired.

Natalia didn't answer, though her eyes narrowed. She didn't like being questioned about her facts. Facts were her specialty.

Cain held her gaze for a few moments, then stroked his goatee thoughtfully. "Those *stories*, as you call them, are circulated for a reason: your protection. This island is anything but safe. In fact, that creature over there, the one Ernie somehow managed to spot? It's called a Snatcher. I'm certain you've come across them during Round Table, no?" The Grey Griffins nodded silently. "Then you know that they're always hungry and aren't particularly picky about what they eat." None of them said a word. "You are currently under my protection, which is why you haven't been picked off and dragged into the woods by now. Remember that and stay close." With that, Baron Lundgren led the Griffins deeper into the woods, but they were doubly vigilant as they watched for Snatchers. Soon, their leafy path led them to a surprise. In the middle of an overgrown clearing were the crumbling remains of a massive structure.

"I didn't know anyone had ever lived on the island," ventured Natalia in a whisper. None of the Griffins felt comfortable replying, as if to break the silence would be to invite a curse. There was something about this place that felt like a freshly dug grave.

Baron Lundgren paused before walking under an arch layered with dormant vines. He looked thoughtful for a moment as he leaned on his cane, surveying the ruins. "It's a place of regrettable mistakes and great possibilities." He motioned at the skeletal remains of the building. "It may look like a forgotten wreck, but deep below the frost, its heart still beats. Come and see. . . ."

The Griffins followed Cain over hillocks of half-swallowed chairs and tables and down a dark staircase strewn with shattered brick. At the bottom lay a rusted door of iron. Their eyes moved quickly over its intricate scrollwork, obscured beneath layers of grime. There wasn't a knob, a handle, or even a hinge.

"Beyond lies the SIM Chamber," Baron Lundgren explained, motioning toward the door. "Everything you have learned in Round Table with your previous mentor must now be employed within these walls. Think about what Iverson taught you, and recall that those were not simply games. If you listened, you should do well. If you did not"— Cain paused as his gaze lingered on Ernie — "you will have to use your wits. Once inside, I cannot help you."

"We're toast," grumbled Ernie, the worst of the Round Table players, as he absently petted Winifred, who'd appeared to take a look for herself. Finding the entire scene rather droll, she hissed at Ernie and disappeared back inside his jacket.

"The Chamber is safe, to a degree," the Baron continued. "But I must warn you not to take that safety for granted. And leave the ferret here, if you please," Cain added. Reluctantly, Ernie set his pet in a nest of leaves under the stairs.

The door of the SIM Chamber suddenly swung open, and as one, the Grey Griffins stepped into darkness.

Beware the Iron Maidens

AN OMINOUS shadow sailed across the evening sky, casting darkness over the burning landscape. It was a world of fire, and in its roaring midst laid the smoking ruins of a city. Explosions filled the air and projectiles screamed overhead. The Griffins had stepped into the middle of a war zone.

"Over here!" shouted Harley, scrambling over a pile of rubble to find shelter. The others followed, ducking beneath girders and skirting the shells of charred automobiles until they came to the remains of an abandoned restaurant. Across the way, the Griffins could see a team of figures race off into the shadows. Not all of them had escaped, though. One was left behind, lying motionless just a few paces away.

"Oh no," Natalia breathed. "He's . . ."

"He's still breathing. At least I think he is," Harley interrupted.

Natalia shook her head. "No, I mean . . ."

"He's a Black Wolf," Max said, completing her sentence. Indeed, the figure was wearing the familiar leather and runes of the Black Wolf Society. The fire illuminated a ghastly face that was stuck in the transition between human and wolf.

"Why does it always have to be werewolves?" Ernie complained, inching away.

A stream of headlights suddenly flooded the street and the Griffins ran for cover as a convoy of Jeeps shot past, dodging the carcasses of tanks and supply trucks. The men inside were grim and wore berets upon their shaved heads.

"More werewolves!" cried Ernie.

"No," Harley disagreed. "Look at the markings on that truck. They're British." Harley was about to run out and flag them down when Max pulled him back. He pointed up at the sky, and all eyes turned in that direction.

The Griffins gasped as they watched ten thousand rays of light shoot out from the belly of the shadow above. They raced toward the British convoy, trails of fire sputtering in their wake. "Fireball Pixies," Ernie exclaimed, as the creatures shot past at impossible speeds.

In their last encounter with the temperamental faeries, small as they were, it only took one of them to nearly blow an entire forest sky high. But ten thousand in one place? That British convoy was in trouble. Yet even as the Fireball Pixies took the sky, the air filled with the sound of countless engines roaring to life.

Squadrons of British fighter planes now zigzagged through a barrage of exploding fireballs high above. Under attack, the pixies turned to engage the fighters. Soon, another squadron of warplanes appeared, evading the explosive faeries and setting their sights on the hovering shadow above, now illuminated by the beams of a hundred searchlights.

"It's a zeppelin!" Harley confirmed as the fighter planes

opened fire on the aircraft. Vaguely resembling a modern-day blimp, this zeppelin would have dwarfed an aircraft carrier. It was a floating fortress bristling with armaments, and as the fighters approached, those weapons came to life.

"We've got to get out of here!" shouted Max, signaling for the Griffins to follow him through the back of the restaurant and toward a line of trees on the horizon.

"I don't remember reading about Black Wolves or Fireball Pixies in any of my history books," Natalia noted as she ran alongside Max. "Is this make-believe?"

"It sure feels real to me," Ernie complained, racing ahead of the others in a blur. He passed under the leafy eaves and waited for the others. Together they trekked deeper into the woods, deciding to take cover in the rotting belly of a fallen tree.

"We should be safe here," Max said, breathing heavily.

"So how'd you become so fast?" Natalia's brows furrowed as she examined Ernie. "More faerie magic from that blood Max dumped into you?"

"I was always fast," Ernie proclaimed.

"No way. Not like that, anyway," Natalia pressed. "You were goin' at least fifty miles an hour."

"I was?"

"Don't play stupid. You eat more than a hippopotamus, you can't get sick, and now you have super-speed? What the heck's going on?"

Ernie grinned. "Well, I was going to wait to tell you, but . . ."

Suddenly, the Griffins realized they weren't alone in their

secret hiding place. At the entrance of the hollowed log, several small figures with green tunics and red caps stood staring at them. "Gnomes!" Natalia smiled.

"Are you sure?" asked Harley. "I thought gnomes . . ."

"Don't argue with me," Natalia interrupted. "I know that *Round Table Creature Compendium* backwards and forwards. These are definitely gnomes." As she finished, the small figures began to approach warily. They had long beards, but their faces were still wrapped in shadow. "Gnomes are perfectly safe. They're probably just looking to hide somewhere — like us."

"You're sure that all gnomes are harmless?" Harley pressed. "Iver said there was no such thing as a safe . . ."

"Of course," Natalia interrupted again, waving at the nearest gnome. She paused thoughtfully. "Well, all except one strain of gnome called Creepers."

"Creepers?" Max asked.

"They worship trees," Natalia explained as her face slowly paled. "Creepers sneak up and trap you with a sleeping spell. Then they drag your body to their sacred tree and bury you alive under its roots, which wouldn't be so bad if you just died. Unfortunately, you stay alive until the roots of the tree have completely devoured you. It can take years. Sometimes hundreds of years." A shiver ran down her spine. "At least that's what the book says. It could be wrong, though."

At that moment, a flash of light reflected off of Ernie's compass, illuminating wicked faces. The Griffins could finally see the yellow eyes and jagged teeth. Creepers!

"Get the *Codex*!" Harley shouted, but Max was already reaching for his backpack. He didn't have enough time, though. Already, the Creepers had begun their sleeping spell. It floated toward the Griffins like a shimmering green cloud, ready to turn them into plant food.

The spell struck Harley first, but when it did, the Faerie Ward around his neck flashed. He hadn't taken it off since Iver had given it to him. Immediately, the sleeping enchantment dissipated into nothingness, unable to strike at the rest of the Griffins. Amazed at his luck, Max unleashed the power of the *Codex*, launching five fiery orbs of blue energy that raced out of the pages of the book. They quickly engulfed the Creepers. With a snarl and hiss, they were pulled back into the *Codex*, where they disappeared onto the pages, alongside the hundreds of other creatures Max had captured over the last few months.

"Wow!" smiled Harley, cracking his knuckles. "That was awesome! This thing really works."

"Don't get cocky," Natalia warned. "Remember, it only works on spells."

Proud of themselves, the Griffins sat there waiting for Cain to release them from the training session. After all, they'd captured their target. Their smiles quickly faded, though, as the ground started to shake violently. The temperature dropped, and that's when the Griffins spied frost creeping up the throat of the fallen tree. "Shhh!" Natalia warned, just as Ernie opened his mouth to comment. "If we play dead, whatever's out there might pass by."

That's when the world seemed to turn upside down. Dirt and

decay poured over their heads, and the Griffins slid down the throat of the rotting tree. Like dice poured from the hand of a giant, the Grey Griffins tumbled to the forest floor, landing in a tangled pile of arms and legs. As they looked up, their blood chilled. Towering over them stood a beast from their worst nightmares.

Tall as a bull elephant and just as thick, the monster's face was lost behind a mask of iron, clasped shut with a single lock. Beady eyes regarded the Griffins with hunger through the rough slits that had been forged in the mask. Its skin was bumpy, lumpy, and the color of coal, and it had long, matted hair that hung greasily from its shoulders. Natalia gasped when she caught the worst sight of all — a string of threaded skulls that was hanging from the monster's neck.

"It's an Iron Maiden," she stammered. According to the *Round Table Creature Compendium*, these lumbering monsters were all that remained of the souls of women who had betrayed their own children. They were forever cursed to walk in the world of shadow, hated and feared by all living things.

The Iron Maiden let out a roar and snatched up Max, his *Codex* falling uselessly to the ground. With its other hand, the beast grabbed hold of Harley's leg.

"That could have gone better," Baron Lundgren noted as the forest evaporated and the metal dome of the SIM Chamber returned into focus. Cain stood with a disapproving look as he handed the *Codex Spiritus* back to Max, who accepted it sheepishly.

"What you just experienced was one of your grandfather's missions during the war, when he was pitted against the Black Wolves for the first time. In fact, if he and Olaf Iverson hadn't succeeded in their mission, the Allies may well have lost the entire war. I find it an intriguing parallel to what is happening today, for once again the Black Wolves threaten the world and our only chance of victory may lie in the hands of a faithful few."

Max nodded, wondering if Cain would tell the Griffins a bit more about the Eye of Odin and who would be going after it. But if the Baron felt any inclination to explain, he quickly changed his mind and continued his deconstruction of their training session.

"You'll note that your grandfather wasn't eaten by an Iron Maiden, of course," Baron Lundgren continued. "In fact, he didn't go running off into the woods at all. He stayed and fought. Though, since this was your first lesson in the SIM Chamber, I'm willing to extend a bit of grace, hesitant as I am to do so."

"What'd we do wrong?" Harley asked.

"Why don't you give me *your* assessment?" Cain replied.

"Well," Natalia began, "I think it went pretty well until the Iron Maiden."

"Did it?" Cain interrupted. "If it wasn't for Harley's Faerie Ward, you'd have been stopped by the Creepers."

"We still stopped it, though," she pressed.

"You should never have been in the forest in the first place," countered Cain, his eyebrow raised by Natalia's pluck. "The mission was to take down the zeppelin."

"But you never told us," complained Ernie.

"You need to be able to deduce tactics on the fly," the Baron explained.

"Fine," Natalia admitted. "We blew it. But I have to tell you, that *Codex* really stinks. I mean, it takes forever to pull it out, and it's huge, too. If Max hadn't dropped it — not that I'm blaming you, of course —" she said, turning to Max, "he could have at least captured the Iron Maiden so we'd had another shot at the zeppelin."

"Precisely," Cain agreed, much to her surprise. "William Caliburn had a distinct advantage over Max when it came to the *Codex*. If you'll allow me . . ." With that, Baron Lundgren passed his hand over the cover of the book as it rested in Max's hands. The *Codex* shimmered, then it appeared to melt away. With wonderstruck eyes, the Griffins watched as the air rippled around Max's hand. Then, in a flash, a shining armored glove covered his hand, wrapping halfway up his forearm. On the top of the palm, there was an embossed hammer insignia — just like the T.H.O.R. patches.

"Now that's cool!" Harley exclaimed. "A gauntlet!"

"This," the Baron explained, pointing to the hammer insignia, "will act as your early warning system, illuminating whenever there are faerie creatures nearby." As Max raised the gauntlet to show his friends, the Griffins noticed the insignia growing brighter whenever it neared Ernie. Max quickly dropped his arm and hoped the Baron hadn't seen anything. The healing was still a secret. He didn't know how people would take it, especially Cain Lundgren.

"This is the *truest* form of the *Codex*," Cain continued, motioning toward the gauntlet. "Under my tutelage, you'll be able to capture faeries as before, though without the encumbrance of an awkward book. Additionally, this gauntlet will help you control your Skyfire as well."

Skyfire. At last Max had a name for the blue flame that burned inside of him.

"It's a gift given only to the Guardians, and can be both dangerous and unpredictable. You've discovered that quality already, no doubt. But with this tool, the fire will one day obey your every thought — with practice of course."

The four Griffins looked at one another in wonder, a million questions in their heads. Harley wanted to know about the insignia, and if it meant Max was also a member of T.H.O.R. Ernie wanted to know if there was any Werewolf-Be-Gone spray in the fingertips of the glove, and Max wanted to know why he hadn't been told about this earlier. All they could manage was a dumbstruck expression, though.

"There's still a problem," Natalia pointed out, after a few moments of careful consideration.

"Yes, Ms. Romanov?"

"Well, if he thought carrying around a big, fat book was a pain, now Max has some kind of medieval robotic arm snapped to his body. How's he supposed to hide that at school?"

Baron Lundgren smiled. "Let's see if we can't remedy that." Brooke's father reached over and touched a hidden switch near Max's wrist. With a shimmer, the gauntlet faded from view, leaving a simple silver ring in its place. Max grinned from ear to ear.

"Just what are you thinking, Grayson Sumner?" Natalia asked, her eyes narrowing suspiciously.

Max twisted the ring just as he had seen Baron Lundgren do moments before. Holding the gauntlet high, he smiled mischievously. "I think it's time for another shot at that zeppelin."

The Grey Griffins had been invited to a party at Brooke's house Saturday morning. No reason was given, but the invitation clearly stated that Round Table cards would be required. After reading the note, Natalia quickly tossed it over her shoulder and sighed dramatically. The last thing she needed was some snoopy girl spoiling their Saturday mornings — mornings that the Grey Griffins had always reserved to play Round Table *alone* with Iver. She sighed again and pulled on her jacket. "Well, I can't very well let them go alone," she mumbled to herself as she grabbed her *Book of Clues.* "This Brooke business is getting mighty suspicious. It looks like her father is some sort of wizard. She just happens to own a deck of Round Table cards. And she has a pet pixie named Honeysuckle, of all things?" Natalia scoffed as she closed the front door behind her and stepped out into the morning fog. "What sort of name is that, anyway? Honeysuckle?"

Natalia grabbed her bicycle from the garage, stewing with every step. She checked the tires, the bell, and the unicorn flag. Everything was ready. She just needed to make a side trip first. Her Round Table cards were still at the secret tree fort in the Old Woods. It wouldn't take long, and she'd take Ernie with her. After all, he lived only a few houses away. Besides, she wanted to ask him some questions about that faerie blood, anyway. It just wasn't natural, and she was convinced there'd be a price to pay — sooner or later.

"You know, your new powers have me worried," Natalia said, walking her bike down the road, the precious Round Table cards now resting safely in her satchel. She couldn't wait to trounce Brooke Lundgren. Natalia had been strategizing late into the night, and she'd devised the perfect deck. "You *do* realize that having faerie blood running through your veins can't be good for you," she said, turning her thoughts from Brooke to Ernie. "Something terrible will happen, mark my words."

"You're just a worrywart," Ernie dismissed. After a few moments of walking, however, a sneaky smile crept across his face. "You know, I have a new superpower that I haven't told anyone about."

Natalia stopped and put her hands on her hips. She studied Ernie closely, looking for wings or pointed ears, but nothing seemed out of order. "All right, so what's this big secret of yours?"

Ernie cracked his knuckles. "Watch this!" In an instant, he had raced back up the hill in a blur of motion. A second later, he was back and smiling at Natalia without so much as breaking a sweat. "Super-speed! It started a couple days ago." Natalia struggled to remain unimpressed, but her jaw continued to dangle. "Pretty cool, huh?"

Natalia snapped her mouth shut and pointed a warning finger at Ernie. "You just be careful. It may be super-speed today, but it may be a lizard tongue tomorrow."

"Gross!" Ernie complained, examining his own tongue to make sure it hadn't already happened. Satisfied, he shrugged at Natalia. "Anyway, at this point, I think it's obvious what I am."

"And what's that?"

"A superhero," Ernie explained, folding his arms and puffing out his chest. "I just need a costume."

"Aren't you the least bit worried about what will happen to you next?"

"I have to admit that I *am* hungrier than usual. I'm taller, too. I betchya I'm even taller than you."

"Not yet," Natalia argued, straightening her posture. From the corner of her eye, she noticed another toadstool ring. Hundreds had been popping up all over the place. She wasn't sure if it was another sign that the world was coming to an end, but toadstool rings were never good omens. One wrong step inside and you could disappear forever.

"Wow, who's that?" Ernie exclaimed, as he pointed down

the hill toward a figure that had broken free from the tree line and was slowly crossing the road.

"That's strange. I've never seen anybody hiking in this part of the woods before. Especially not in weather like this." Natalia then held out her hand to feel the patter of rain.

"I think it's an old woman," Ernie posited. Beyond the super-speed and accelerated healing, he seemed to have enhanced vision, too. "She's probably lost. I've heard before about old people wandering away from nursing homes. Do you think we should go help her?"

The two Griffins hopped back on their bikes and slowly coasted down the gravel road, veering around mud holes and rolling over washboards. As they neared, the Griffins could see that the woman was wrapped in a shawl that clung loosely to her fragile frame. She was walking hunched over with a cane in her unsteady hand, looking positively miserable. Yet she turned her face away from them, as though she was hiding something. Chills started racing up Natalia's spine. Something was very wrong. She raised her finger to her lips and motioned for Ernie to follow. Together, they coasted by before pedaling up the hill.

"Man, she gave me the creeps," Ernie whispered when they were a safe distance away.

"Me, too," agreed Natalia, looking over her shoulder. She wished she hadn't. The old woman had turned toward them, and something about the way the crone stood there gave Natalia the feeling that she was being sized up for a meal. The woman dropped her cane. Her shawl fell next. Then she rose up to full height, threw back her head, and howled.

"Werewolf!" Ernie shouted as the blood rushed from his face. "I'm outta here!" Although he was sure his new powers would safely take him out of harm's way, his super-speed kicked in at the wrong time, and Ernie's bike chain was thrown loose. Instead of rocketing away, he was laying face first on the gravel.

"Ernie . . . get up!" Natalia shouted.

"But my bike!" Ernie looked at the wreck in a panic, knowing he'd have to abandon it.

"Forget your bike!" she yelled, waving for him to get onto hers. Even as he ran over, the werewolf wasn't more than a few meters away. "You drive!" she shouted, hopping onto the handlebars. "Just *don't* throw the chain. It's our only ticket out of here!" Ernie nodded, taking over the pedals.

Their ravenous pursuer was now within striking distance. Natalia could hear its ragged breathing.

Ernie tried to ease his way into the super-speed, but it wasn't happening fast enough. The wolf was already in the air, and as Natalia screamed, Ernie crossed his fingers and gave the pedals everything he had. A rush of wind hit Natalia's face as they lunged ahead. Holding on for dear life, Natalia watched the landscape speed by in a blur.

14

Just like Hansel and Gretel

"I'M VERY serious," insisted Natalia. "It was a werewolf, teeth and all. I don't know what it was doing sneaking around the woods, but I don't plan on going back to that tree house of yours anytime soon. And that's a fact."

"So you saved the day, huh?" Harley said, patting Ernie on the back.

Ernie grinned, puffing up his chest. "All in a day's work for a superhero."

The Griffins finally found themselves marching behind Brooke as she led them through a rough patch of thicket at the back of her house. "It's not much farther now," she said, smiling as she led the Grey Griffins down an overgrown path that was enclosed on either side by bramble and thorn bushes. By the look on her face, one might have thought that she was skipping through a field of wildflowers, instead of trudging through a network of neglected gardens that was smothered in shadow. Yet despite the gloom, Brooke was as cheerful as could be, wrapped in a soft yellow jacket with matching boots.

Natalia, on the other hand, was dressed head to foot in black, accented by a particularly sour expression. As far as she was concerned, spending time with Brooke was about as agreeable as chewing a bag of glass.

Max watched silently as Honeysuckle bobbed along next to Brooke, illuminating the air as she flew. The pixie seemed the perfect complement to Brooke in every way. Then he caught movement in the underbrush, where Sprig was peering up at him nervously. Though his Bounder could be secretive and shy, the spriggan always seemed to come through when it counted most.

"Where are we, anyway, Sleepy Hollow?" Natalia grumbled to no one in particular as she shielded herself from the constant barrage of branches that were whipping into her face. It was suspicious that Brooke wasn't suffering. "For goodness' sake, the next thing you know, the Headless Horseman will be trampling over us."

"Ever think you read too much?" taunted Harley, ducking below a stray branch that had caught one of Natalia's long braids.

"Have *you* ever thought about wearing deodorant?" Natalia quipped, before turning to glare at Ernie, who had just let a sharp branch slap her in the face. As usual, Ernie's nose was stuck deep into one of his comic books. Ernie never seemed to take a misstep. Instead, he'd just blur right through the hazards. She considered offering another sensible warning about the dangers of his new powers when Natalia heard a suspicious noise near her feet. She stopped and looked around. Somehow, those yellow clumps of grass near her feet had moved.

"Are you coming?" asked Brooke, noticing Natalia had lagged behind.

"Oh, don't you worry about me." Natalia sniffed. Reaching

into her satchel, she pulled out the strange magnifying glass that Iver had given her. As she passed the lens over the grass, it revealed a nest of tiny faeries hunched over, looking up at her with bashful eyes. Not much bigger than a hedgehog, each one had a long, curious nose and twitching whiskers. They blended perfectly with the grass, and indeed their own backs were covered in the same bristling blades as the flora around them.

"They're called Quivering Quillbacks," Brooke explained, walking over to Natalia. "Humans can't see them with the naked eye unless you know exactly what you're looking for. Otherwise, you'd need a special instrument like yours. Aren't they cute?"

Natalia remained silent as she pulled out her *Book of Clues*. She immediately sketched a picture of the nearest Quillback and jotted some notes, intent on cataloging her new discovery.

"It's kind of like they have a cloaking device," Harley said with admiration, peering through Natalia's magnifying glass.

"I guess you could say that," agreed Brooke, reaching down as one crawled into her hand. She stroked its neck and cooed as the Quillback relaxed under her soft touch. "They really are sweet, and they're amazingly helpful at keeping the bugs away . . . especially the mosquitoes."

"Do they always walk on all fours like that?" Ernie asked without bothering to look through the glass. Brooke, who hadn't been told about Ernie's emerging powers, gazed at him curiously.

"It's strange that you can see them," she commented. "I've never met anyone who could. At least not the first time."

"I don't get it," Natalia interrupted, tucking her pink note-pad back into her satchel. "I mean, faeries are dangerous, right? Iver told Max at least a hundred times that he was supposed to capture them before they hurt anybody."

"Not all faeries are bad, but I suppose they all *could* be dangerous," Brooke said, smiling down at the Quillback, who had fallen asleep. "Max told you about his grandma's greenhouse, right? Well, it's kind of the same thing here," Brooke said, waving in a circle around them. "You can think of this as a sort of wildlife refuge for faeries. My father created it to give these creatures a place where they don't have to worry about being run over by cars, sprayed with pesticide, or tortured by some mean kid. Anyway, we can talk more about all that later. Right now, I want to show you something that I know you'll like."

Natalia gasped as she broke through the final tangle of bushes. There, in a sumptuous clearing, sat a tiny cottage bathed in sunlight. It was warm, cheery, and seemed to glow with a life of its own.

"Oh my," Natalia murmured, half expecting to see the White Rabbit come skittering by with his pocket watch in hand.

"You have no idea," Brooke said, smiling as she walked lightly down the path.

Everything was perfect. Almost too perfect, actually. The sun above was shining brilliantly in a cloudless sky. There was a rich carpet of grass beneath their feet, a cheery brick path leading to the doorstep, swaying violets in the window boxes, and even a smoking chimney that peeked through a thatched roof. Speechless, the Griffins followed Brooke inside. Harley, the tallest of the five by some margin, was just able to duck beneath the doorframe without hitting his head. "That's odd," he said as he turned to study the door. Either he'd somehow shrunk, or the door had just grown. He wasn't sure which.

The interior of the cottage was just as extraordinary. It was as if the Griffins had walked into a vibrant storybook, saturated in pastels and floral print. More importantly (at least to Ernie), just beyond the staircase was a kitchen where the scent of freshly baked cookies and fruit pies, as well as brownies and chocolate cake, wafted with inviting delight. Somehow, the individual scents were magnified so that Ernie was sure he could smell at least seven different colors of sugar sprinkles. Along the counters were pitchers of milk — chocolate, white, and strawberry — and there were three others filled with frothy lemonade.

"Isn't it amazing," Brooke began, handing a glass of lemonade to Natalia, who eyed it suspiciously, looking for signs of poison or perhaps faeries swimming among the ice cubes. At the same time, Ernie was racing from pastry to pastry, leaving a trail of crumbs swirling in his wake.

"Who made all this food?" asked Harley, filling his plate with brownies.

"The house did," she explained casually. Natalia looked at her as though Brooke had gone completely mad. "I know it sounds strange, but that's the way it works."

"It's a bit far-fetched, don't you think?" Natalia asked, setting aside her drink without so much as taking a sip. Nothing could be this perfect. Not even in fairy tales. It had to be a sham. A game. Yes. That was it! It was just a creepy game. In fact, Natalia was starting to come to the conclusion that unless the Griffins evacuated immediately, they'd soon end up sharing the witch's oven with Hansel and Gretel. So with a condescending sniff, she excused herself. Natalia decided she needed time alone, which she would put to good use exploring the house for any traps. She figured that's what Sherlock Holmes would do.

The remaining Griffins didn't appear to share Natalia's concerns. The boys simply accepted what they saw as fact, and that's all there was to it. Perhaps that's what frustrated Natalia the most. That, and the fact that even after she had been sulking for twenty minutes in the parlor flipping through the photo albums of one *W. Rabbit*, they hadn't come to see if she'd been abducted by the Mad Hatter. With a sigh, she set aside the book just as someone knocked at the door with a fist made of stone.

"Hey, Throckmorton!" Brooke greeted. The gargoyle stood dressed in butler attire, and perched on his fingertips was a silver tray that held a rather curious box.

Throckmorton bowed, his tail lowering deferentially as well. "*Guten Tag, meine Damen und Herren.* I am pleased to make your acquaintance."

"He's a . . . he's a . . . ," gasped Ernie in horror, having nearly being eaten by one of Throckmorton's less cultured cousins a few months before. "Gargoyle!"

"Naturally," agreed Brooke. "And he's a Grand Master, too. That's the highest Round Table ranking in the world."

"Oh, of course," Natalia replied with a careless sigh, thinking the stories Brooke was telling were getting harder to believe.

Throckmorton regarded Natalia for a moment, then nodded. "The rankings are quite like chess, you see. The main difference is that both individuals and teams can be rated at the Grand Master level. Further, in chess, the Grand Master title, once gained, is always kept. But, as there are a number of players with considerably long life spans in the world of Round Table, the title must be defended, just as in prizefighting."

"Why didn't Iver ever tell us about all this stuff?" Max wondered, scratching his head.

"I'm certain his reasoning for the omission was sound. Olaf Iverson was a man of impeccable character. He will be greatly missed." Quietly, Throckmorton handed Max an old picture from the mantel. It was a black-and-white photo of students posing with medals proudly pinned to their chests. "This photograph was taken after their school won the Teutonic Tournament," explained the gargoyle. "And that's young Olaf and William in the back row."

"Their school had a Round Table team?" Ernie asked.

"Highland Academy at Crusader Castle," Throckmorton

clarified. "Of the thirteen schools of the Great Houses, it's still one of the best."

"So you're telling us that there are actually schools with official Round Table teams?" pressed Natalia, scribbling furiously in her *Book of Clues*.

Throckmorton raised a hand, waving away the question. "When you are ready, your mentor will explain."

Natalia rolled her eyes and sighed in disgust.

"Anyway," Brooke interrupted. "We don't really have time for an official tournament today, but I thought we could still have some fun. There're six of us, so we'll divide into three pairs and go head-to-head, like they do in the regional qualifiers. We just need to draw names to see who plays who."

"If this is really a tournament, don't we need a prize or something?" Ernie pointed out.

"If you don't mind, I believe I can solve the predicament," offered Throckmorton, pulling out of the box a pair of magnificent knucklebones made of transparent crystal that held a flickering green flame. "These are the Dice of Damascus, said to have been created by a desert genie over a thousand years ago. I won them in a tournament when I was traveling the old Silk Road. I'd be happy to offer them as a prize."

Ernie's eyes peeled back and his jowl dangled as he devoured the sight of the knucklebones. He'd never seen anything he wanted more.

Natalia wasn't so sure. "What do they do?" she asked skeptically. "They could be cursed."

"If you're wondering what magical powers they possess, I cannot tell you," the servant replied. "Perhaps none . . . or perhaps they haven't found the right owner."

"I think I forgot something at home," Ernie exclaimed after drawing Throckmorton's name as his opponent. He still didn't trust gargoyles. Not after what had happened a few months back outside the church in downtown Avalon. "Don't worry. I'll just see myself out."

Harley caught him by the back of the collar before Ernie could bolt away. "Just relax. Maybe you'll win."

Sweat formed on Ernie's brow as he looked over at Throckmorton. "Not all gargoyles eat kids, right? Because I had a bad experience once. . . ." A long, uncomfortable pause followed as Throckmorton arched a heavy brow but said nothing. Ernie gulped.

"You're funny," Brooke answered, laughing as Throckmorton handed her the box. All the combatants took their seats at a long table just off the kitchen. As everyone prepared his or her cards, Brooke went over the tournament rules. "Okay. We'll have to set a time limit, of course. I think an hour should do."

Everyone nodded in agreement. "Now, to win, your enemy has to be completely defeated. Ties are handled with a sudden-death match."

"This is gonna be good," Harley said, rubbing his hands together in anticipation.

"Can we refer to any outside material for reference?" Natalia asked. "The *Round Table Creature Compendium* would come in handy, you know."

"This isn't an open-book test," Harley complained.

"Unfortunately," Brooke explained, "you aren't allowed to use anything other than your deck and knucklebones. I'm pretty sure you all know the rest of the rules, so I think we can start. Is everyone ready?"

"Let's do it," Max declared, reaching into his backpack to pull out his grandfather's Round Table game box. As his hand ran carefully over the weathered cover, he imagined that his Grandpa Caliburn was smiling down at him. As he shuffled through the cards, he paused, though.

"What's the matter?" asked Brooke.

"I already lost one of my grandfather's cards. I guess I'm just kinda mad about it."

"What card is missing?" inquired Throckmorton, eying Max curiously.

"The Doppelgänger," Max confessed with a regretful sigh. "I don't know much about it, so maybe it wasn't that good of a card, anyway. It's just that it was my grandpa's."

Throckmorton's eyes flashed momentarily — as if the news alarmed him — but any reaction was quickly subdued behind his stony brows. "I wouldn't think about it too much. I'm sure it will turn up. . . ."

"I brought *my* Round Table box as well," Natalia said proudly. "It may not be as old as Max's, but I've put a lot of thought into it." Natalia's box looked more like a hastily painted pink tackle box with stickers of prancing unicorns and flowers stamped around the outer edge than it did an heirloom. She flipped open the latches and carefully selected a pair of knucklebones from one of the trays.

"So this is real, right? Winner gets the magic knucklebones?" Ernie turned his eyes to the grand prize resting nearby and smiled broadly.

"Are you suggesting gargoyles are liars, young man?" Throckmorton replied, eying Ernie coolly.

"Time to begin," Brooke exclaimed, picking up a nearby hourglass. "Get ready. Set. Go." With that, she placed the timer on the table and the cards began to fly.

Ernie managed to draw first blood from Throckmorton's cards. Unfortunately for the hapless Griffin, it got fairly ugly after that. In two consecutive turns, Ernie lost both his Dwarf Sappers and a Viking Berserker in terrible fumbles. From there, his entire game plan fell apart. Ernie spent the rest of the match avoiding eye contact with the gargoyle, who was watching him intently from the other side of the table.

Max started off rather poorly, surprised by Natalia's unusually aggressive play. Her high rolls coupled with a barrage of snide comments kept him off balance, but then, in a stroke of luck, Max rolled a perfect 100, wiping Natalia's Frost Dragon off the map.

"That was ridiculous," Natalia exclaimed, stuffing her knucklebones back into her box with a sniff. "I had you. You know it, and so do I."

Harley was a formidable player, and clearly he hadn't

expected Brooke to be such a challenge. With shrewd tactics, she had him on the ropes right away. Soon his army of Tanker Trolls ended up tangled in the webs of a Gossamer Trap. Harley bit his lip, as one monster after another was tied up by the most ridiculous cards he'd ever heard of: Moonglow, Buttermilk Skies, and Faerie Glam. The frustration was killing him.

Even Natalia had to admit that she'd never seen anyone play the way Brooke did. Brooke seemed entirely satisfied with letting Harley wear himself out, and the strategy worked brilliantly.

"Time's up," Natalia said, looking at the hourglass as the last grain of sand emptied from the top chamber. Harley ran a hand through his mop of hair and let out a ragged sigh.

"You're good," he proclaimed to Brooke, sifting through his remaining cards and shaking his head in wonder.

Brooke laughed and shook his hand. "You nearly had me with the Frost Giant. They're really tough. Anyway," she continued, "since we're missing enough players to fill the semifinal bracket, I have to forfeit."

"Why?" Max asked. "You're better than all of us. It's your house, after all. You should play."

"If it's my house, that means I make the rules. Besides, Throckmorton and I play all the time. I think he'd enjoy play-ing *you*." She pointed a finger toward Max.

"As you wish," the gargoyle said with a deferential nod.

Though Max was the undisputed champion among the Grey Griffins, he'd never been able to beat Iver. Iver, at least as far as

Max knew (which was admittedly very little, it seemed), wasn't a Round Table Grand Master like Throckmorton, either. The Guardian of the *Codex* began piecing together a new battle deck, mixing some of his familiar cards with a few of the cards from Grandpa Caliburn's stash, hoping they'd bring him good luck.

Throckmorton, on the other hand, left his deck as it was. The game began in a blaze of action that Max would remember the rest of his life. There were armies of skeletal warriors, Rings of Fire, and even the newly discovered Traps of Terror that opened up underneath his characters in the blink of an eye, swallowing them whole. Max played valiantly, pulling from every lesson or trick he'd ever learned. Yet even with knucklebone casts that would have been the envy of any player, Max couldn't seem to get an edge. Every move he made seemed as useless as trying to sink a battleship with a fistful of rocks. Soon the last drop of sand fell in the hourglass, and Max had to admit defeat.

"I can see why you're a Grand Master," Max admitted. "You're awesome."

"On the contrary, Master Sumner," began the gargoyle. "It is *you* who have shown your qualities today. *Gratulieren!* To stand your ground against a Grand Master, especially during your first competition at this level, is a remarkable achievement. Your grandfather would be proud."

15

A Peek into the Past

THE CHAPEL of Mist stood upon the shores of Lake Avalon like the ghostly remains of some vanished world. Gray stone, moldered but unbroken, formed its skeleton, and stained-glass windows filled its heavy sockets. Built before the first settlers arrived in Avalon, the architects were a source of mystery. The Vikings? Templar? Aliens? Nobody really knew.

"So why do you come all the way out here?" asked Natalia as she accepted half of the sandwich that Athena offered. Despite the difference in age, the two had become close. They'd spend hours talking about school, world travel, and just about everything Natalia found interesting (which was, admittedly, almost everything). The only topic off-limits was Athena's past. Whenever Natalia got anywhere close to the subject, the female Templar would promptly change the topic.

"I guess I just like it here," Athena answered, pulling out a juice box and handing it to Natalia. "It's so peaceful."

"So's the morgue," Natalia quipped, admiring her own wit for a moment. "Why here?"

"I'll be in a morgue soon enough. Why rush it?" Athena replied with a smile. "Besides, morgues don't decorate like this, do they?"

Natalia looked around admiringly at the frescoes on the walls, then took a bite of a bagel neatly slathered with raspberry jam.

"You know," Athena began, looking up at the ceiling. "This reminds me of home . . . a little."

Natalia's ears perked up, wondering if Athena was finally going to allow a peek behind the curtain of her past. "Really?"

Athena sighed, continuing to look up as her ponytail dangled behind the pew where she sat. "I grew up in eastern Europe. Romania, actually. There're lots of old churches and chapels there. This has the same sort of feel."

"But you don't have an accent," Natalia pointed out.

"I lived in the States until I was about your age," Athena answered. "My parents were missionaries."

"You have parents?" Natalia asked. It was a poor attempt at humor, and she knew it. So Natalia frowned in embarrassment and apologized. "I mean, I know you have a family and all. I just hadn't heard you mention them before."

Athena's eyes dropped from the ceiling, as she straightened in the pew. She seemed to consider saying something, then promptly reached into her bag for the smoked salmon. As she cut off a piece for Natalia, Athena shook her head. "Not anymore."

Natalia's mouth fell open. "What happened? Don't you get along?"

Athena smiled briefly. "They're dead."

Natalia sat stunned for a long while before clearing her throat. "What happened?"

"The world's not a nice place," Athena replied coolly, turning back to her lunch. "My dad made the wrong enemies. The next thing you know, someone broke into our house and everyone was killed . . . . well, everyone except me."

"Oh my . . . ," breathed Natalia.

"I had a little sister," Athena recalled as she looked into the distance. "I miss them a lot." Then she turned to Natalia, her face deadly serious. "I haven't told anyone about this. I'm trusting you to keep it a secret."

Natalia nodded vehemently. "Cross my heart."

Athena absently smoothed her jeans. "Anyway, that's all in the past. The Templar adopted me some years later. Now I'm here eating lunch with you," she said, offering a forced smile.

"I'm really sorry," Natalia spoke gingerly. "Especially about your sister."

Athena looked over at Natalia, who had begun to sip her juice box self-consciously. "Maybe that's what brought us together," Athena offered. "You know, you kind of remind me of her."

"Right." Natalia laughed uncomfortably. "Your family were probably all beautiful. Look at me. . . ." She pulled at her red braids. "Carrots." She shrugged. Then she pointed at her freckled nose and stuck her tongue out in disgust. "The only person I remind anyone of is Pippi Longstocking."

"Do kids tease you?" Athena probed, her eyes narrowed in concern.

"All the time," Natalia admitted, sliding down in her seat.

"If I didn't have the Grey Griffins, my life would be a perfect tragedy. I'd be an outcast. A social pariah! And just because of my red hair . . . well, mostly, I guess. I don't know . . . but I *do* know they hate me."

Athena's brows furrowed protectively. "Who does this to you?"

"The girls at my school." Then Natalia paused as a related topic slammed into the front seat of her mind. "What do you think about Brooke Lundgren?"

"Brooke teases you about your hair?" Athena seemed notably surprised.

Natalia shook her head. "No. At least not that I know of. But she *has* been hanging out with Max quite a bit lately."

Athena nodded. It was her job to notice. Everything. "How do you feel about that?"

Natalia bit her lip as she thought about it. "I think she's up to something. . . . How long have you known her?"

"A long time," Athena answered. "In fact, I've known her father for years, though I haven't spent as much time with Brooke. She seems nice enough, though."

"That's the problem," Natalia confessed, throwing the remainder of her bagel into the paper bag. "She's always so nice. No one can be that nice, can they?"

Athena measured Natalia with her eyes, then nodded. "So, what are you going to do about it?"

"I haven't made up my mind yet," Natalia replied thoughtfully. "What do you think?"

Athena sat forward. "Let's go over the facts, Ms. Detective." Natalia straightened up and took out her *Book of Clues*. She loved facts. Facts were sensible, and so was Natalia.

"Brooke is popular," Athena began.

"Check," replied Natalia with a roll of her eyes. These weren't the sort of facts she had hoped to review.

"She's also rich."

"Check." Natalia bit the inside of her cheek, wondering where this was leading.

"Pretty," Athena continued.

Natalia offered a dramatic pause, followed by a reluctant: "Check."

"She's also nice and has never been mean to you."

Another pause. Natalia squirmed. "You aren't playing fair...."

"Are you?" Athena replied. For a long, uncomfortable moment, neither said anything. "I think you should know something about me. When I joined the Templar I was pretty young, and young people can do stupid things."

"What do you mean?" Natalia asked.

"There was a girl," Athena began slowly, then laughed despite herself. "You know, I really hated her guts."

Natalia laughed as well. "What was she like? Anyone I know?"

Athena nodded, smiling. "Oh, I used to call her 'Little Miss Perfect.' She was the daughter of a lord from one of the Great Houses. She went to Cambridge, was swimming in money, and had one of those sickly sweet smiles I just wanted to punch.

Compared with my life, hers was a fairy tale, and it made me mad."

"So what happened?"

"Eventually we were both assigned to the same mission," Athena continued. "It was a glorified recon mission, and I got bored, so I spent most of the time making catty remarks under my breath. I hated everything about her, and I wanted her to know it."

Natalia nodded appreciatively.

"Anyway, things went south pretty quick. We were set up, and I was lazy and got captured."

"Oh my . . ."

"Yeah. I'd be dead if she hadn't come back for me."

"Really? What happened?"

Athena shrugged. "She died saving my life."

Natalia's face fell. "Wow . . . I thought you'd have a happy ending."

"I wish it was," Athena said, her voice trailing off in reflection. "I just don't want you to make the same mistake."

One week later...

THE SPIDER'S Web was Avalon's one and only comics shop.
Crowded floor to ceiling with every conceivable collection that
a superhero fanatic could conjure up, the aisles were walled
in by looming towers of overstuffed boxes so constricting that
even Ernie, one of the skinniest kids in school, had to walk
sideways to find what he was looking for. It could never take the
place of Iver's shop, which now sat looking forlorn, boards
nailed over the windows and door. But at least it gave them
something to do on Saturdays.

Of course the decision to go there wasn't entirely random.
All the Griffins read comic books — even Natalia, though only
when she thought no one else was looking. Ernie, on the other
hand, was a professional. He had started collecting comics
long before he could read them. In fact, he'd proudly been
planning his own series, using some of the hundreds of colorful
characters he'd created from scratch. He knew their birth
names, bases of operations, where they were born, how tall
they were, the color of their eyes, and, of course, what superpowers were lurking beneath the convincing camouflage of
their secret identities. So when he wasn't hanging out with
the Griffins, Ernie spent most of his free time lurking about

the Spider's Web. It certainly didn't hurt matters that he and Monti, the owner of the shop, were two peas in a pod.

"So . . . ," began Ernie, leaning over the counter toward Monti, almost in a whisper. "Let's say super-speed was possible."

"It's not," Monti countered, looking defiant as he stood there with spiky brown hair, baggy jeans, and a vintage corduroy jacket. "There are laws of physics."

"Yeah, I know," Ernie replied impatiently. "But let's say it was. Let's say you suddenly had super-speed and you wanted a costume. What would you need?"

Monti paused from bagging a back issue and stared up at the lights in thought. "Hmm . . . I guess you'd need glasses or something. You know, to keep the bugs out of your eyes."

Ernie copied it down onto his yellow notepad. "Yeah, I wonder how Superman deals with bugs. Wouldn't they get in his teeth when he's flying so fast?"

"Then again, glasses can fall off," Monti reconsidered. "Maybe goggles."

Ernie erased his last line and scribbled some more. "And?"

"Well, you'd need really good shoes."

"Tell me about it," Ernie sighed, looking down at his shredded sneakers, which hadn't fared so well at high speed. When he looked back up, he found Monti gazing at him curiously. "I mean, I've always wondered how the Flash's boots don't get all messed up when he runs."

"Special material," Monti replied casually. "The Flash is also a scientist, so he created his boots and costume in his laboratory."

"I don't have a laboratory," Ernie noted glumly, but smiled innocently as Monti caught his eye.

"What's this all about?" Monti inquired suspiciously. "Halloween was five months ago."

"Just curious," Ernie replied. "Do you think tire tread would work? . . . You know, if you glued it to the bottom of your shoes?"

Monti scratched his chin in thought. "Depends on how fast you go. I'd get the best shoes available, then throw on the tire tread last. It couldn't hurt."

Ernie nodded. "Check."

"And a helmet," Monti added quickly. "In case you run into anything at high speed. Better be a good one." .

"Check!"

Ernie and Monti droned on in meticulous detail as Brooke and Natalia meandered through the dark recesses of the shop. Natalia, taking Athena's advice, tried to make polite conversation with Brooke. It was a hollow sort of dialogue that left Natalia feeling fake. Her heart just wasn't in it. She watched Brooke closely, though, just in case her hunch had been right. Nothing. Brooke appeared to be as sweet as she seemed. Confounded, Natalia sat down at a table and pulled out an old romance comic from a nearby rack. She hadn't even realized what she had in her hand and sheepishly replaced it when she found Brooke watching her curiously. Natalia sighed and be-gan to look as engrossed in her *Book of Clues* as she possibly could.

"What's that book you're always writing in?" Brooke asked, coming to look over Natalia's shoulder. Natalia, in turn, quickly flipped the notebook shut and bit her lip. "Is it a diary?" Brooke pressed, though not rudely.

Natalia shook her head.

"Then what?"

"It's kind of a secret," Natalia alluded.

"It's really pretty. Where'd you get all the unicorn stickers?"

Not expecting a compliment, Natalia bit her lip even more. She tried not to swell with pride but found it difficult. So instead, she shuffled her feet rapidly until the feeling went away. "Yes, well, I've spent a lot of time on it. Anything worth doing is worth doing well."

"So what is it?" Brooke smiled innocently.

Natalia sighed and put it back in her bag. "I'm a detective," she replied, thinking that that was all the explanation required.

"So it's your clue book?"

"My *Book of Clues*," Natalia corrected quickly.

"Like Sherlock Holmes?"

Natalia smiled in self-satisfaction. "I'm going to be bigger than Sherlock Holmes. I'm going to be the greatest detective this world has ever known."

"You know what? I believe you," Brooke commented appreciatively. "Everyone in school talks about how smart you are."

Natalia's smile faded as her thoughts returned to the kids at King's Elementary harassing her on the playground, calling her, among other things, the Dictionary Dork. "Sure they do," Natalia answered sharply with a roll of her eyes. "I'm *so* popular." The sarcasm was not lost on Brooke, who fell quiet. Still, she didn't leave. Instead, she took down the romance comic Natalia had been thumbing through and sat beside the red-headed Griffin. Neither said a word.

Natalia felt so uncomfortable that she wanted to crawl under the table and die. She would have written that down in her *Book of Clues* if Brooke wasn't sitting so close. Instead, she bit her nails.

At that moment, there was a crash out in the back alley, as if a trash can had been knocked over. Natalia's brows furrowed as she rose to her feet and looked in the direction of the back door.

"That's strange," she commented. "No one's ever in that back alley."

"Maybe a dog got loose?" offered Brooke.

Another crash! This one louder than before, as it shook the back door. Then they heard a terrible moaning sound. Natalia took a step back in alarm just as the other Griffins rushed up next to her.

Something screamed, followed by the sound of an avalanche of *bangs* and *booms.*

"Somebody's in trouble," Harley noted as he warily approached the back door, which was shaking as if it were sitting on a washing machine. He looked at Max. "We have to do something."

"We could call the police," Ernie suggested, too busy sketching out some ideas for the speedster costume. He glanced over his shoulder toward Monti, hoping he'd make the call, but the shop owner had thrown on some earphones and was oblivious as he listened to music.

Max shook his head. "No. Whatever's out there is pulsing

with faerie magic. I can feel it." He walked up to the door and placed his hand on the knob. Then Max paused, just for a moment. "Maybe you should stay, though," he said, looking at Brooke.

"Thanks, but I think I'll come along just the same," she said, buttoning up her jacket. "I'm always up for an adventure." Max rolled his eyes, wondering what Baron Lundgren would do to him if anything happened to Brooke. Then he took a deep breath, twisted the knob, and quietly led his friends out into the darkness.

To no one's surprise, the alley was smelly and the pavement was damp. With the days still dreary under the unrelenting grasp of winter, dismal shadows made the alley even creepier than usual. The Griffins quickly stepped around icy puddles and over broken bottles, heading in the direction of the terrible sounds. The screaming had stopped, but a low humming sound had taken its place, broken every now and then by a long, suffering moan that made the Griffins' stomachs churn.

"Is it getting colder, or is it just me?" asked Ernie, vapor rising from his lips as they moved deeper into the alley.

"No. You're right. It's freezing, which means we're probably heading straight into another preposterous trap," warned Natalia. "Maybe we should get Logan ... or even Brooke's dad. If we called him, I bet he'd send Throckmorton to help us."

"We don't have time," Max countered as he stepped over a broken crate. "We have to help whoever is out there. What if it was your sister or something?"

"Fine, but don't say I didn't warn you," she huffed, watching the ground as a creeping frost approached.

The Griffins turned around a corner of moldering brick and found themselves peering into a dead end. It wasn't empty, though. "Look!" Brooke called, spotting a body lying in the middle of a pile of garbage. "It's Dennis."

Above Dennis Stonebrow's prostrate form, a swarm of small, but disgusting, creatures buzzed like wasps streaming from a hive.

"Hold on," Harley urged, holding her back. They hadn't been spotted yet, and Harley didn't want to take an unnecessary risk — especially for Dennis. Why the most notorious bully in the history of King's Elementary School had been there in the first place was anyone's guess, but the oaf looked like he was about to be the entrée for a swarm of hungry faeries.

Not much larger than a spriggan, these little beasties were a bizarre fusion of icy blue skin, bony wings, rows of silvery teeth, and beady little eyes. Max hated flying faeries. They were hard to hit with the Captivity Orbs from his *Codex*.

"They're Ice Imps," Natalia noted. "Kind of like sprites, but twice as vicious. They're a bit like piranhas, I guess. I read somewhere that a swarm of them once stripped a Bull Dragon to the bone in thirty seconds."

"Great!" Ernie complained, looking down the alley for a quick escape route.

"We have to do something before they kill him, Max," Brooke pressed.

"I'm on it." Max's *Codex* was already in its shimmering

gauntlet form — the T.H.O.R. insignia glowing intensely. This was going to be the first time he'd used his new weapon outside of the SIM Chamber, and he hoped it would work. Normally, he'd just try to capture the Ice Imps, but he'd never tried to capture this many faeries at once. Controlling half a dozen Captivity Orbs was one thing, but trying to manipulate a whole horde of them while chasing after flying imps was different.

Max concentrated. Sure enough, cobalt flame flickered in his palm, and the fire grew until it illuminated the alleyway. Raising his arm like a cannon, Max steadied his wrist with his free hand. Instantly, a stream of fire shot out of the *Codex* gauntlet, tearing into the Ice Imps. Max's aim was terrible, but there were so many of the winged faeries that it didn't seem to matter. Wherever the fire landed, the monsters would burst into a shimmering cloud of ice flakes. If Logan was right, they weren't dead. They would have to go back to the Shadowlands to get fitted with a new body, though, and that was good enough for now.

Harley and Ernie cheered as the Ice Imps shot into the air. Max could hardly contain a smile. Things would be different now. With the *Codex* on his fist, and the Skyfire at his beck and call, anything seemed possible. Unfortunately, the imps didn't see it that way. Enraged, they doubled their attack on the children, though they'd learned to stay clear of the boy with the blue fire.

Natalia wasn't going to sit on the sidelines. In one fluid motion she reached into her satchel and let a spray of nails fly. The Ice Imps shrieked as the Faerie Bane tore through their wings, sending them plummeting to the ground just as Max's Skyfire burst upon them.

"I'm going in," Harley said, turning to Ernie. "Can you cover me?"

"You're gonna save Dennis?"

"I don't like it any better than you, but we can't just leave him here like a stranded water buffalo."

"What the heck am I supposed to do?" Ernie asked. "Shoot 'em with my inhaler?"

"I dunno." Harley shrugged. "You'll think of something."

Ernie shrugged, took a deep breath, and then blurred into super-speed. In an instant, he reached Dennis's fallen form and started pulling the tails of Ice Imps. They swatted at him with claws and hissed their icy breath in his face, but he was moving too fast to be caught. He circled once, twice, three times, working the imps into a frenzy. Then, with a yelp, Ernie tore off down the alley with a swarm of Ice Imps on his heels.

"Ernie's super-speed is a secret," Natalia noted to Brooke with a warning glance. "So don't tell anyone."

"Your secret's safe with me," Brooke agreed, smiling as she watched Ernie blaze away.

Unfortunately, that was about the time Max found a chink in his armor. With so many Ice Imps swarming, he'd poured on the heat, unleashing the Skyfire like there was no tomorrow. The problem was that he didn't have an endless supply. The flame of his was beginning to sputter and fade.

At the same time, Ernie couldn't seem to shake the flying monsters. They weren't as fast as he was, but they didn't have to be. Ernie couldn't hit full speed in the alleyway, for fear of smashing into a wall. That meant he had to stop from time to time to get his bearings and figure out where to run next. No matter where he turned, though, the Ice Imps were there.

Cheers of triumph turned to an overwhelming sense of fear as Brooke and the Griffins realized they'd bitten off more than they could chew. "We're gonna die before I could make my costume!" Ernie complained.

"Oh, brother," Natalia breathed, rolling her eyes before she threw her last fistful of nails at the large swarm of Ice Imps just overhead. They nimbly moved to the side, and the projectiles passed through harmlessly.

His arm shaking, Max was spent. He felt like all his energy had been zapped and could hardly stand up any longer. Harley was swinging at any imp that got too close, but they were laughing at the boy, nimbly dancing out of range of his iron ring. Now that Ernie was cornered, and Natalia was out of ammunition, there was nothing left to do.

At that moment, when all hope was lost, something flashed in Brooke's pocket. In an explosion, Honeysuckle burst into the sky, lighting up the entire alley. Glittering faerie dust rolled in her wake as her eyes sparkled. Then, without fear, she flew into the heart of the swarming beasts. The air started to buzz so loudly that the kids had to cover their ears for fear of their brains falling out. "No!" Brooke screamed in sudden realization. "Honeysuckle! You can't do this!"

It was too late. An explosion of pink light tore through the alley, sending the imps careening in all directions. Countless disappeared in a detonation of snow and ice. The rest lay on the ground, stunned senseless.

Like a dying flame, Honeysuckle plummeted to the ground in a heap. She was fading before their eyes. Brooke raced over and fell to her knees in dismay. Gently, she picked up her pixie, repeating the word *no* over and over as she cried inconsolably. Honeysuckle had saved their lives.

"Is he dead?" Ernie asked, walking over to Dennis.

"No, he's still breathing," answered Harley. "But if we don't do something fast, he might be."

"I don't know," Max disagreed. "He looks pretty bad."

At that moment, Brooke walked over and placed Honeysuckle's still form in Natalia's hands. Then, with a heavy sigh, Brooke crouched next to Dennis. "I have a secret, too," she confessed. "I wasn't supposed to tell you . . . not yet, anyway."

"What are you talking about?" Max asked.

Brooke said nothing as she placed her delicate hand on Dennis's forehead. All at once a warm breeze rushed through the alley as the air began to shimmer. Even afterward, Max could never explain what happened. One minute, Dennis was on the brink of death. The next, he was standing next to them, looking confused. He didn't have a scratch.

"Don't worry," Brooke assured, turning to the Griffins. "He won't remember a thing."

17

MONDAY MORNING came far too quickly, as the Griffins piled in behind their desks after the first bell.

"Can you believe Brooke has power, too?" Harley whispered, taking a seat right behind Max. "Now you're not the only kid who can . . ."

"Hey," Ernie complained, plopping his books down. "What about me?" Then he pretended he was lining up at the starting block for a race.

"Whatever," Natalia said, rolling her eyes.

"I'm serious," argued Ernie as Mrs. Bone walked in. "I'm just about done with my superhero costume — speed-resistant boots and all!"

"Oh, *puh-leeze*," Natalia complained, waving his exuberance away. "I have no interest in seeing you in your long underwear *ever* again."

"Fear not, citizen," Ernie replied, trying to sound like a television announcer as he placed his fists on his hips. "Soon, your simple human ways will lead you into danger most foul. And despite your ungratefulness, *I* will rescue you." Ernie lowered his voice as Mrs. Bone gave him a curious look. "After all, that's what heroes do. We don't ask for much. Just the opportunity to serve and protect."

Natalia rolled her eyes, then promptly gave him a wicked pinch under the arm. Ernie shrieked like a baby pig, then he glared back at her, rubbing at the sore spot. "We'll see how smart you are when I save your life. *Again!*" He then put his arm around Max. "You see, me and Max are the same now. It's just too bad you guys don't have any superpowers. But we'll let you hang out with us, anyway. For now. Won't we, Max?"

Max tried not to laugh.

"But I *do* have a superpower," Harley replied, smiling roguishly.

Ernie's countenance brightened. "Really? What is it?"

"I call it the Atomic Wedgie!" Harley then leapt at Ernie, who quickly sat down, underpants safely out of reach.

Hidden under the guise of a simple silver ring, the *Codex* remained virtually unnoticed as Max passed through the halls of King's Elementary School. Just as Natalia had predicted, it was easier to hide a small piece of jewelry than a hulking book. Plus, the security of knowing that the power of his Skyfire was only a finger twist away was reassuring.

Despite the new weapon, Max's days were anything but peaceful. Even under the relentless eyes of the Templar, Max still couldn't escape the feeling that he was being followed by something sinister. It was as if a great evil was hovering just out of sight — waiting to catch Max alone. It left the skin on his neck in a perpetual state of tingle, no matter if he was by himself or surrounded by a throng of kids.

At the moment, Max and Ernie were picking up the last of the red rubber balls left strewn about the gym after a blistering game of dodgeball. Marked with a nasty burn on his shin from sliding across the polished wood floor, Max still managed to rise to the winner's circle. So did Ernie, which was something he'd never experienced. In the past, the clumsy Griffin had been a favorite target of everyone. But since the introduction of the faerie blood into his system, Ernie was untouchable. Fast as lightning, one moment he'd be in range and the next he'd disappear like a ghost, confounding every attempt to knock him out of the game. It was risky showing off like that. Yet, despite Max's warnings, Ernie was determined to get back at the same jerks who used to treat him like a walking piñata.

Dennis Stonebrow, in a strange twist of events, had switched roles with Ernie. Ever since the escapade with the Ice Imps, he'd become quiet and docile — despite not remembering a thing. Natalia had started calling him the Sedated Rhino. Ernie, on the other hand, took full advantage of Dennis's lethargy. With newfound glee in playing dodgeball, he pelted the lumbering giant with a rain of rubber balls for almost an hour. The entire gym class watched in bewilderment.

"That was fun, huh?" Ernie asked, smiling as he tossed the last ball into a netted bag before stuffing it beneath the gymnasium stage. "I didn't even work up a sweat. In fact, I'll be in the big leagues soon. I even have my superhero name — Agent Thunderbolt, the Cosmic Speedster! Whaddaya think?"

Max slid the bolts shut on the storage doors and sighed. "Just make sure you get hit once in a while, otherwise everyone's going to start asking questions. We can't afford that right now, okay?"

Ernie shrugged as they walked together down the stairs toward the locker room. "Who cares if they do? Besides, everyone else knows now — everyone that matters. Logan, your grandma, and even Brooke's dad." Max shook his head, recalling an uncomfortable conversation he'd had with Baron Lundgren a few days before. After hearing about the transfusion that had saved Ernie's life, Cain grew silent and contemplative, refusing to discuss the matter further. He hadn't returned Ernie's ferret, stating that Winifred's examinations weren't complete.

Ernie's spirits, on the other hand, weren't the slightest bit dampened. He was a superhero now, and even if a tail popped out of his pants, he couldn't have been more pleased with his present circumstance.

"Don't most superheroes have secret identities?" Max tried to reason, lowering his voice as they brushed past a nosy classmate. "I mean, they keep their powers secret to protect their families and stuff, right? Maybe you should do the same."

Ernie looked off wistfully, then smiled as they pushed their way through the locker room doors. "Okay. I'll keep it a secret" — suddenly, a rolling cloud of steam overtook them, and when it had cleared, Max found Ernie smiling mischievously at him — "for now."

Max's brow furrowed as he watched Ernie erupt into

another blur of speed, racing around the blue metal lockers like the superpowered speedster he envisioned himself to be. Unfortunately, just like a hundred times before, Max heard Ernie yelp in panic. The bespectacled Griffin had accidentally stepped into a puddle near the drinking fountain, and he quickly found himself sliding at high speed through the shower doors, sending his classmates tumbling like bowling pins.

Rolling his eyes, Max opened his locker and threw his sweaty gym shirt inside, just as the creepy feeling that he was being watched returned. Then he felt a cold chill sweep over him as something moved at the corner of his eye. When he spun around, no one was there, though. Max scratched his head.

Get a hold of yourself, Max, the Guardian of the *Codex* told himself as he shuffled over to a porcelain sink, turned the squeaky knob, and lowered his face into the stream of water.

Shortly after Iver's death, paranoia had started to set in. Ernie used to be the only one consumed by thoughts of monsters lurking in every shadow, but now Max seemed to have caught the virus. Just the other day, Max was checking out a book at the Avalon Public Library, talking with Mrs. Callahan about the erratic weather. Then a cold chill set in the room, and her eyes turned as black as pitch right in front of him. Max swore he could see fangs, too. When he ran into her at church that Sunday, Mrs. Callahan acted like they hadn't seen each other in months.

That wasn't the only time, either. It had happened with

Principal Hamm, and then a pimply-faced teenager who was working the drive-through window at Hasty Hamburgers. Even Rosa, the family housekeeper, had looked at him like she was sizing him up for a meal, and a few minutes later she was humming a tune, baking cookies like nothing was wrong. Max was starting to feel like one of the three little pigs in a town full of wolves. As Ernie liked to say, things were getting C-R-Double-E-P-Y.

Max was also becoming less resentful about all the T.H.O.R. agents Logan had assigned to "babysit" him. It wouldn't be easy for any Black Wolf to get past them, and that offered some level of comfort. The knights were keeping tabs on everyone who entered or exited the school, his house, the bus, and even the bathroom at the Spider's Web. There wasn't a single hair on anyone's head unaccounted for in all of Avalon.

Turning off the water, Max reached for a towel. Then he gasped as he caught sight of the mirror. Written in a desperate hand . . .

I'm watching you, Sumner!
Your pal,
Ray.

Ray Fisher? He was supposed to be somewhere in hiding with Max's dad and the rest of the Black Wolf Society. How'd he write that message?

Max turned to see Ernie hopping out of the showers, his

shirt dripping and his underwear pulled up near his shoulders. He'd been wedgied. As he limped over to Max, his face flustered and red, his eyes slowly rose toward the mirror where Ray's message was still dripping.

"Holy . . ."

"We've gotta get out of here," Max's voice fell as he looked nervously over his shoulder.

Max and Ernie, who had tamed his underwear malfunction, took their place in the growing lunch line. Each grabbed a tray. At the same time, they watched Harley scare off a flock of chattering fourth-grade girls who were moving in on the Griffins' favorite table. Natalia soon joined Harley, and without a word, she opened up her unicorn lunch box, folded her napkin across her lap, placed her food neatly upon the table, and began sipping daintily from her thermos cup.

The lunchroom was full of hungry students, laminated tables, and ketchup-stained ceilings — the latter being a relic of a massive food fight that happened long before Max or the Grey Griffins ever stepped foot in King's Elementary School.

"You know, the more I think about it, Ray couldn't have written that stuff on the mirror," Ernie argued, wringing out his shirt with his spare hand. "Somebody's just playing a joke."

"Who?"

"Dennis," Ernie stated flatly. "Then again," he considered, "Dennis never takes showers. Which, of course, explains why he smells like a skunk crawled under his shirt and died."

Max shook his head. "To get past the Templar, whoever it was probably wasn't even human."

Ernie paused with frightful eyes, nearly dropping the fork he'd just pulled out of a bin. "Do you think it's one of the dead people who jumped out of the graves? Brooke was really freakin' me out with that stuff."

"I don't know," Max replied in a lowered voice as a group of giggling girls passed by. "But we need to tell Logan. He'll know what to do."

Ernie set his tray aside. "I don't think I'm hungry anymore."

"That's a first," Max said, pulling Ernie back into line as he struggled to break free. "Look, you have to act like nothing's wrong, or whoever it is will know we're on to them."

"We *are* on to them," Ernie protested. "And I'm still not hungry."

"Have it your way then." Max sighed. "Just go tell Harley and Natalia. I'll be with you in a second. It's grilled cheese today, and I'm not letting a stupid monster wreck my lunch."

As Ernie left the lunch line with visible relief, Max grabbed his utensils and approached the counter where three lunch ladies wearing hairnets waited. He knew them well, since they'd been serving him the same food week after week since kindergarten. The first had red hair, though it wasn't a natural red like Natalia's. It was almost fluorescent and seemed to have a life of its own. She was the youngest of the bunch, but considering the two dinosaurs next to her, this was hardly a feat. In fact, the crone in the middle looked like a piece of gristle chewed on by the family dog, with a disgusting hairy mole near her pink-painted lips. The last of the lot was short, sour, and corpulently crammed into an ill-fitted white uniform. She reeked of cigarettes and never said much, relying more on her withering glare than her gravelly voice to let the students know that two meatballs were all they were getting. Luckily, meatballs weren't on the menu today.

Max set his tray on the rails and began to work his way down the line. He smiled at the first lunch lady, but he averted his eyes from the second and her hairy mole. His eyes remained downcast when he finally reached the smelly monster who controlled the bubbling pot of tomato soup. Hopefully, she'd just fill his bowl and let him go, but after a few uncomfortable seconds had passed, no ladle appeared.

"Sumner...." Her terrible voice grated, sending a shiver through Max. Hesitantly, he looked up at the old hag, but despite Max's weak attempt at a smile, still no soup appeared. Instead, the line was starting to pile up as the children looked at him suspiciously. In a few more seconds the complaining would begin.

"Sumner...," the voice repeated, this time darker. Was she asking him a question? Of course she knew who he was. It was the only school he'd ever attended.

"Uh...yeah, that's me," he confirmed slowly. As he did, an eerie light flashed in her blind eye. With a rush of speed, the lunch lady's hands gave way to clawed fingers as they shot over the rail and grabbed him by the collar, pulling Max across and into the kitchen. He could hear his classmates scream in horror, and he was only vaguely aware of their fleeing footsteps. His attention was quickly snapped back into focus, though, as his head crashed onto the tile floor. Vision filled with stars, Max could barely make out the grotesque monster that now pinned his *Codex* hand to the ground, rendering it useless. Her mouth was filled with needling teeth, and her eyes glowed. Somewhere, out of the corner of his eyes, Max could swear he saw a raven fly by.

"Dinnertime," the monster cackled.

The lunch lady never got a chance to finish Max off, as one knight, who was posing as a dishwasher, tackled the monster. Almost instantly, the kitchen was flooded with T.H.O.R. agents, helping to subdue the rogue lunch lady.

"The boy will die," the creature declared, though the voice was clearly a man's. "If not now, then next time. You can't stop the Black Wolves forever." Then the lunch lady's body evaporated into mist, as just outside the window, a flock of ravens flew into the sky.

Since the attack at the cafeteria, security had been increased around Max — something his mom had insisted on. Logan didn't argue. Instead, he took it to an almost impossible level. Nobody wanted another cafeteria debacle. Apparently, the result of that spectacle had been messy, and the Templar didn't like clean-up work. Any student or teacher who'd witnessed the event had to have their memories "tidied up," just in case. Max didn't exactly know what that meant, but he had his suspicions.

The Black Wolves and their assassin were growing stronger by the minute, just as Cain had foretold. Templar fortresses continued to fall, the survivors retreating to secret strongholds that the enemy had not yet discovered. Despite the urgency of their situation, though, Cain would not speak to Max about the Eye of Odin, or even Lord Saxon's diary. There'd been no further mention of the Underworld — or the World Tree, for that matter. If they were so important, then why wasn't he talking? Dracula's thirty-day deadline was almost up. If Cain didn't set out soon, Lord Sumner would arrive at the World Tree and destroy it, and the entire planet, with the Spear of Ragnarok.

Max was tired of waiting around to be plucked off by the assassin. Max wanted action. If Cain wasn't brave enough to face the Underworld, Max certainly was. All he needed was for Natalia to locate the Eye of Odin so he knew where to go. Max was meant to save the world. He could feel it.

Natalia pushed through the homeroom door and slumped into a seat next to Max. It looked as if she hadn't slept in days. "You can forget about the Eye of Odin," she sighed. "I finally got my remote viewing card. . . ."

"Cool," Max said. "Can I borrow it sometime?"

"Yeah. Fine. But I have some bad news. There're only three books on the subject in the entire library."

"That's better than none," Ernie commented, stating the obvious as he fumbled through a wad of paper, trying to find his homework. The page he finally pulled out was lined with a soda-ring stain from a can of Plumples, and had more than a few chocolate smudges traced along the top.

"Sure. If Brooke's dad hadn't checked them all out already," she complained, dropping her head onto the desk, pounding it once or twice on her folded arms for good measure. "I should have known. Even if he didn't need them, he'd check them out so nobody else could. It's ridiculous."

"I don't know," disagreed Harley. "Maybe he's just keeping it from Dracula. That's what I'd do."

"So why hasn't he said anything to Max?" Natalia pressed. "You'd think he'd tell the Guardian of the *Codex* what his plans were. Remember, the clock's ticking. Ragnarok is gonna wipe us all off the earth if we don't do something fast."

"Maybe they sent T.H.O.R. agents after the Eye of Odin already," Max countered.

"I doubt it. Not that they'd tell us, anyway. They just think we're a bunch of dumb kids," Natalia complained. "It's not like when Iver was around. He's the only one who's ever really trusted us."

"Then maybe we need to go get the Eye of Odin ourselves," Harley said with a shrug.

"I've thought about it," Max said, "but if Natalia hasn't been able to find anything, our only hope is to get our hands on Lord Saxon's diary. He's the one with the map to the Eye."

"I'm in," agreed Harley.

"It's not that easy," Max said, shaking his head. "The diary's locked away somewhere in Brooke's house, and she already told me about their alarm system. Ninjas couldn't break into that place."

"But *you* could," Natalia said, the light of an idea playing in her eyes as she perked up. Max didn't like the way she was looking at him. "I'm serious. Brooke would do anything for you. . . ."

Brooke agreed to meet Max in the basement of the library, the most secluded spot in school. Mrs. Aron, the librarian, had given them special permission to be there over the lunch break, thanks to some finagling by Natalia. She was Mrs. Aron's only student volunteer, and when Natalia told the librarian that Max was going to be joining her on Friday afternoons after school for the rest of the year, it sealed the deal.

The problem was that Max and Brooke really weren't alone. Søren, Logan's second-in-command, was standing watch at the door. Thanks to his custodial uniform, he'd already swept the entire library for anything out of the ordinary, all without riling the librarian.

"I don't know," Brooke admitted after hearing what Max had to say. "I mean, I want to help. I really do, but I wouldn't even know where to look."

"Where does he keep the important stuff?" Max asked.

Brooke shrugged. "You know my dad. Everything he has is important. He could put something in the kitchen drawer and it would be just as hidden as if he had dropped it into a safe guarded by a genie. If he doesn't want something found, you won't be able to find it."

Max chewed at his lip for a moment in thought. This would be difficult, but he felt sure it was their only chance. "You don't even have a guess?"

Brooke shrugged. "It might be in the Oubliette."

"Your dad has a dungeon?" Max asked. He'd heard of oubliette pits before: They were dark holes where prisoners were dropped and then left to be forgotten.

Brooke shook her head. "It's not really a dungeon, but the Oubliette is pretty deep underground. Dad doesn't talk much about what's down there, but some of the world's most notorious thieves have tried to break in. They've tunneled underground, used invisibility potions and time stoppers, and one even tried to drill in through the bottom of the lake. None of them have gotten very far, though."

"Really?"

"Yeah," she nodded. "Throckmorton told me they never send them to jail, either. I guess their punishment is lots worse."

Max's shoulders sank. He felt sure the Oubliette was exactly where he'd find Lord Saxon's diary, but if the best burglars in the world couldn't break in, he'd need a new tactic.

"You've been there before, haven't you?" Max began.

Brooke nodded slowly. She knew where Max was heading.

"Then you can help me get in. I mean, there's no way he'd let the security system hurt his own daughter, right?"

"I don't know, Max. . . ."

"Please?" he implored. "Look, I know it's my fault we're in this mess to begin with. I need to find that amulet so I can stop my dad from destroying the world. You're my only chance to make things right."

Brooke didn't say a thing.

"Look, I won't even take the diary with me. I just wanna read it, that's all. If Lord Saxon really has a map in there, I can find the Eye of Odin and stop my dad. Please, Brooke. I'd do anything. . . ."

Brooke offered a cautious smile. "You realize that you're asking me to disobey my father, right?"

It was Max's turn to sit in silence.

"If I do help you," she continued slowly, "you're going to owe me big time."

"I know."

"I'm serious," Brooke emphasized. "If I ask you a favor, no matter what it is, you have to do it. Deal?"

Max nodded, fearing a single word might change her mind.

"Okay," she finally said, standing up to brush herself off. "I'll do it. My dad isn't going to be home Friday night, and he's taking Throckmorton with him. If we're going to get the diary, it has to be then."

"Friday's good for me," Max said, trying to sound nonchalant. "What time?"

"I'll call you."

"Did someone order pizza?" Logan's stern voice issued from behind the couch where Ernie and Max were sitting, playing video games. "There's a guy at the front gate with a large pepperoni and extra cheese."

Max raised his hand as Ernie jumped up, tossing his controller aside as he licked his chops. Max was a little surprised the pizza had arrived so quickly. The day before, the sky had opened up and sent down a torrent of interminable rain, closing businesses and cancelling school. Max's school bus was found floating in its garage and would need a month to dry out. Thankfully, Leonardo's Pizza was still open, though how the delivery boy got there in twenty minutes was nothing short of a miracle.

Logan pointed a strict finger in Max's direction. "What did I say about things like this?"

"To ask you first . . . ," Max said, sheepishly.

"You know I don't like surprises," the Scotsman continued, growing hotter with each word. "I can't protect you if I can't count on you to protect yourself."

"From the mutant pepperoni monster?" Ernie said with a snort and a laugh. The act earned him a withering stare from Logan, who meant business. As far as he was concerned, Max's safety was no laughing matter.

Ernie cleared his throat self-consciously and quickly excused himself, just as Annika Sumner entered the room, carrying Hannah in one arm and a bag of cheese puffs in the other. "Did somebody order pizza?"

Tonight was family night, an old tradition in the Sumner household that they were trying to make new again. Originally, it was supposed to be just Max, Hannah, and his mom watching family movies starring his grandfather, but even though things were getting better, it still felt weird. So Max asked if Ernie could come over, too. That way there wouldn't be any awkward silences. His mom agreed, even though Max knew she was hoping for some time alone with her kids.

"Yeah. Your favorite," Max answered.

"Wonderful. I'll have Rosa get us some soda, and then we can meet down in the theater. Ernie, can you help me with the chips?"

Starving, Max raced after Logan, who was already halfway to the door.

"Has he been scanned?" Logan grunted into an earpiece as he strode through the hallway. Evidently, he received an affirmative from the other end, because he gave the go-ahead. But as Max reached for the doorknob, Logan stepped in front of him. "You know better than that," Logan warned in his Scottish brogue. "That's what I'm here for, eh? I am paid to be the one who gets skewered by the baddies. Now, stand clear."

As the massive front door swung open, it revealed a delivery boy with a piping-hot pizza box, flanked by two humorless T.H.O.R. agents in body armor. The delivery boy looked ridiculously small in comparison, but Max immediately recognized Johnny Russo. He was an olive-skinned high school kid with a flair for wild hairdos and ripped jeans.

As Logan regarded him, Johnny didn't return the Scotsman's gaze. Instead, he peered through the door, his eyes roving until they lit upon Max. Then he smiled.

"Just give the pizza to me, son," Logan said, stepping in front of Max.

Johnny continued to stare at Max, oblivious to the world around him.

Sensing danger, Logan nodded for the two knights to escort Johnny away, but it was too late. The delivery boy let out a shrieking howl as his body transformed into a hairy mass of teeth and claws. All at once, one of the most fearsome werewolves Max had ever seen was standing at his front door. Max watched in terror as the beast lashed out, its massive arms sending the T.H.O.R. agents hurtling through the air.

Cursing, Logan kicked the door shut with his boot and threw Max over his shoulder, turning toward the nearest escape route. Before he could get two steps, the door blew apart and the werewolf leapt after them with a roar. As the beast reached for Max, its hungry claws within inches of the Guardian's neck, he could see its eyes: the same eyes possessed by the feral lunch lady. The assassin was back.

Even as death seemed unavoidable, the monster was jerked up short and went crashing to the ground. Max looked down and saw that the werewolf's legs were wrapped up in a silver cord. Another cord bound its arms.

Standing with a heel on the werewolf's back, a young woman winked at Max, her silver forelock falling over one eye. "So . . . ," Athena began with a smirk. "Looks like I just earned a slice of that pizza."

Max began to smile, but his heart sank as once again the assassin melted into mist and disappeared.

He'd be back.

Friday arrived and along with it, Max's plan to sneak into Cain's Oubliette to get that map from Lord Saxon's diary. First, he needed a good alibi. Logan wasn't going to let him hop on a bike and ride over to Brooke's house, even if it was next door. No, he'd need something more cunning — something that the Scotsman would support.

"I have to go to Baron Lundgren's house and study," Max explained for the millionth time as the Land Rover pulled into the drive-through at Hasty Hamburgers. "Why do you keep asking?"

"Seems odd," Logan replied with a shrug, reaching through the window and bringing back two sodas, handing one of them to Max. "Cain never mentioned anything to me."

"Because I'm behind in my studies. I didn't want to tell him."

"So you waited 'til he was out to get caught up?"

"Well, this was the only night Brooke could help me," Max returned, taking his fries from Logan, then popping one into his mouth.

"What are you studying?" Logan pressed as he handed Max his double cheeseburger, special ordered with no tomatoes and extra pickles.

"The Siege of Acre," Max said, casually lying. He buried his discomfort in the straw of his soda.

Logan said nothing, but tightened his grip on the steering wheel as they turned in the direction of Brooke's house on Lake Avalon, a convoy of black vehicles following. Logan was clearly overdoing it, but Max liked that. Better safe than sorry.

Brooke's typical smile was replaced by a look of concern as Max told her about the werewolf attack. They were seated at a table in one of the windowless parlors, presumably studying for a fictitious test. Their privacy extended for about twenty feet to the door — Søren stood on the other side.

Max looked around, imagining there might be some kind of a secret passage through a grandfather clock, or maybe even a disappearing staircase leading directly to the Oubliette. If he were Cain, where would he hide his secret treasures? This new mentor of his was frighteningly clever, so it couldn't be that easy.

"Well, it's now or never," Brooke began. Opening a green velvet bag with gold strings, she reached in and produced an intricately designed brass doorknob. "You're sure you want to go through with this?"

Max nodded resolutely.

"Okay." Brooke sighed in resignation. She then rose and approached a large painting on the far wall. It depicted a dark tower upon a cliff that overlooked an angry sea. The painting was so real that Max could almost feel the ocean spray on his face. Suddenly, Brooke's arm reached right through the canvas, into the stinging rain, and plunged the knob into the surface of the tower door. Silently, the entrance swung open, and before Max knew what had happened, Brooke had grabbed his wrist and pulled him through.

Max had never seen anything like this before. The Oubliette lay deep beneath the earth, a vault, he was told, protected by sophisticated electronics, complex faerie enchantments, and even good old-fashioned head-chopper-offers that whistled across the neckline if you didn't know exactly when to duck.

They were now standing on a circular platform surrounded by a bottomless pit. Several bridges led off into the darkness, but Brooke ignored them all. Instead, she stepped off the ledge and into the air. Max leapt to catch her, only to find that instead of plummeting to her death, Brooke was walking briskly across an invisible bridge, waving for Max to catch up.

"This one's invisible," she explained, as they reached the other side. "The others are intangible."

"You mean if we'd have tried to walk on one, we'd be dead right now?"

"That pit is a lot deeper than you think," Brooke said. "We'd probably starve to death before we ever hit bottom." Max gulped as he tried to keep pace. Next, they entered a tiled chamber — each stone marked with a single rune. Brooke quickly traversed the floor, moving carefully from one tile to the next, sometimes zigzagging, other times hopping across several. Again, she moved without hesitation. Max followed, trying not to think about what would happen if he stepped on the wrong tile.

A short passage came next. "What's that?" Max asked, pointing to a tall glass at the far end of the hall.

"That's the Mirror of Mirander. If a thief actually makes it this far, his reflection is captured in the mirror. If the reflection isn't one of my family's, the thief's soul is sucked out."

"What about his body?"

Brooke shook her head. "Dad told me that I don't want to know the details, so I don't ask. I guess only three people have gotten this far."

"So how am I going to get to the Oubliette? I'm not in your family," asked Max, who was starting to get worried.

Brooke smiled. "Wait here." With that, she approached the Mirror of Mirander and made several strange signs in the air. Nothing happened. All Max saw was Brooke's reflection. So far, so good. A moment later, she waved for Max to step up. He approached cautiously, unable to stop thinking about what it would feel like to have his soul sucked out. Closing his eyes, Max stepped forward, but he wanted to scream. When he opened his eyes and realized everything was fine, the Guardian of the *Codex* let out a huge sigh of relief.

With a wink, Brooke stepped though the mirror and disappeared in a flash.

Max swallowed hard and stepped through.

"So what keeps the creatures with no reflections out?" Max wondered as he ducked under another swinging blade. Their adventure through the barrage of deadly traps seemed to be going on forever, making Max wonder who in their right mind, gold-hungry thief or not, would even attempt it. The wrong step, a sudden sneeze, or a curious glance could result in a horribly nasty death — or worse.

"You mean like faeries and vampires? The whole place is lined with iron," Brooke replied casually. She walked over what looked like a camera lens and looked inside. "And the air is humidified with holy water, too." A green strobe light scanned Brooke's eyes before an invisible door slid open to their right. "Biometric security," Brooke explained. She then placed a finger along the door panel, and Max could hear the clanging of chains. He could only imagine what trap had just been deactivated thanks to Brooke's fingerprint.

"Are we getting close?" Max asked.

"Very," Brooke replied as they avoided an inviting door and instead ascended an invisible ladder through the ceiling.

"How long have we been gone?" asked Max. "Do you think Logan will notice?"

"Time doesn't work down here the same way as it does in Avalon. We could probably spend weeks down here and no one would miss us."

The two friends soon found themselves staring at the final piece of the puzzle. They were in a circular room, a dead end, paved with rune-etched stones from floor to ceiling.

"There must be thousands of them," commented Max, staring up toward a towering ceiling obscured by darkness.

"In order to get through to the Oubliette, they need to be arranged in exactly the right order."

"You mean, they move like a combination lock?"

Brooke nodded as she walked up to the wall and slid a stone from right to left. Then another up and down.

"But it would take a million years to move all these stones even once!"

Brooke nodded again. "I know, but that's what you have to do."

"What if you were a wizard and used a magical spell or something?"

"It'd take the best sorcerer with the most powerful spells at least three hours to get the right combination."

"So it *can* be broken."

Brooke shook her head. "Once you enter this room, you have exactly seven minutes before you're dumped into a black hole."

Max paused, visualizing what it must be like to be atomized by a star-devouring black hole. Then he shuddered. "So if it can't be broken by a spell, how the heck do you get through in time?"

"A key, naturally," Brooke replied, smiling.

"Seems kind of easy to me." Max shook his head. "I mean, why all this protection if all you need is a stupid key. I bet even Harley could pick it."

"It's not just any lock and key." Brooke explained. She then brushed off her hands on her jeans and sat down upon the ground. Then she started pulling something away from her shoes. Max heard a couple of *pops*, like threads snapping, and a moment later, Brooke's shadow slipped away from her feet.

Brooke waved at her shadow and smiled warmly. The shadow waved back, blowing her a kiss. Max stared as the shadow pulled out a ghostly key from her invisible pocket, flew up into the ceiling, and disappeared. A moment later, the walls rumbled to life, each row beginning to spin and rotate, stopping now and again, then moving in the other direction, looking for the perfect alignment. Finally, everything stopped, and suddenly the stones began to rearrange themselves, parting and pulling away to form an entrance to the room beyond.

Brooke smiled as she reattached her shadow. "Next stop, the Oubliette!"

Agent Thunderbolt

MAX PASSED into the Oubliette as Brooke walked softly beside him. His eyes scanned the room cautiously, afraid that breathing too heavily might set off an alarm. Brooke was right. It was no dungeon. Not by a long shot.

In a way, Cain Lundgren's Oubliette reminded him a bit of Iver's Shoppe of Antiquities. Yet where Iver's store had been a clutter of curiosities, Cain's treasury was in strict order, with strange collections neatly labeled or under glass casing. The walls were lined by wood paneling, and kerosene lamps flickered, sending shadows dancing on recessed ceilings.

One of the walls was inset with giant panels of thick glass that held back a murky darkness. As they drew near, Max could see a kelp forest flowing back and forth in an invisible current, with a school of sunfish swimming happily by. Max walked up to the glass and smiled, but the sunfish scattered when a northern pike undulated into view, its toothy jaws snapping at the fleeing shadows. "Is that Lake Avalon?" Max asked in a whisper.

Even before Brooke could answer, a huge shadow rolled in, followed by a scaly head the size of a truck. In a frightening rush, a serpentine monster snapped up the pike in its jaws before disappearing in a cloud of murk.

"His name is Leviathan," Brooke explained casually.

"How'd he get in our lake?"

"Portals," Brooke explained, as though it should have been obvious. "How do you think the Loch Ness monster has been hiding for so long?"

"So why doesn't this one eat people when they go fishing or swimming in the lake?"

"Dad has a deal with him," she answered with a shrug. "Anyway, let's try and find that diary so we can get out of here before he comes back."

Max stepped away from the glass and looked around the room. There were books everywhere. Any one of them might have been Lord Saxon's diary. "Is it safe to walk around in here?"

Brooke nodded. "Yeah. But it's better if you stay close to me."

Together, the two walked along a line of exhibit cases that lined a far wall. Within it lay artifacts, including Egyptian scarabs, Arabian lamps, and something called the *Book of Armaments*, each more curious than the next. Max wouldn't have been surprised to find the Holy Grail in the Oubliette. So far, there was no sign of the diary, though.

As Max backed away from a cabinet of strange artifacts, he bumped against a pedestal, knocking off its contents. Max caught the plummeting object with his hands just before it hit the ground. With a sigh of relief, he brought it up to his eyes to take a closer look.

"Eden's Clay," Brooke read from the tag upon the pedestal.

"It feels like wet mud," Max observed as it slid around in his fingers. No bigger than a baseball, the object was elastic, but held together, and when he looked at his hands, they remained bone dry, despite the slick skin of the clay. "What's it do?"

Brooke shrugged. "I don't know. I think Throckmorton told me you can mold it into almost anything, and it'll look just like the original object that you're trying to copy."

"Don't you have to be an artist or something to make it work?"

"No," Brooke explained. "That's the point."

"Cool," he said, squeezing the clay in his hand as it squished through his fingers. Brooke went back to looking for the diary, but Max found it almost impossible to part with the clay. So, instead of putting it back on the pedestal, he decided to hold on to it a bit longer.

"How about those bookshelves?" Max pointed, walking over to a wall of shelves. Unfortunately, there were so many, the odds of finding Lord Saxon's diary was about the same as finding the proverbial needle in a haystack. Then Max took a double take. Had the books just moved? Max shut his eyes and spun around in a circle. When he opened them again, sure enough, the books had been rearranged once more.

"Wait a second," Max heard Brooke say. He turned to find her looking at the top of her father's desk, littered with maps, compasses, timepieces, and a thousand other oddments. Her eyes were locked on a crumbling book that was spread across the desk, though. It was open, with a magnifying glass lying on the moldy pages. When Max joined Brooke at the desk, his mouth fell open.

There, on two facing pages, was a detailed map drawn by a shaky hand in crimson ink. Yet what lay at the bottom is what caught Max's eye. It was an elaborate illustration of a necklace, though not just any necklace. It was an amulet. The Eye of Odin!

Brooke had found the diary of Lord Saxon.

Then Max sensed the presence of someone else in the room, as a tall shadow fell over the pages of the open book. Max turned to find two piercing eyes gazing back at him. Brooke screamed.

"I have to congratulate you," offered Baron Lundgren as he strode into view. His countenance was cold, his face emotionless. "I knew you'd likely try for the diary. I just hadn't expected you to use my own daughter against me."

Startled, Max was barely able to keep from dropping the Eden's Clay, so he hastily shoved it into his jacket pocket, hoping he wouldn't be accused of stealing.

Brooke stepped forward, shaking her head. "He just wanted a look, that's all. He wasn't going to take anything. . . ."

Cain raised his hand, cutting her off. Silence fell upon the room, and even if Max had *wanted* to speak, he couldn't seem to get his mouth to work. In the meantime, Max could feel Brooke's dad peeling away the layers of his mind, as if the Baron were searching for something.

"Why didn't you simply come to me with your questions?" Cain began, lowering his hand.

"You wouldn't have told me anything," Max countered.

"Perhaps not. But I would have known you were a gentle-man rather than a brigand. It's one thing to put yourself in danger, but when you place my own daughter in harm's way, I have to question your moral compass."

Brooke stepped protectively in front of Max. "He didn't think he was putting me in danger, Dad. I told him that the traps wouldn't hurt me. Anyway, it was my choice to bring him here. I'm the one who should be in trouble, not Max!"

Cain's eyebrow rose. "Does this boy really deserve your loyalty?"

"He deserves a chance!" Brooke shot back. "He made a mis-take with the Spear, and now he wants to fix it — even if it means sacrificing his life."

"And apparently the lives of anyone else foolish enough to follow him," Cain retorted, his heavy gaze returning to Max. For a long moment, no one said a word. Then, with a sigh, Cain sat down at his desk. "Let's begin with this...." His face softened as he regarded Max. "Why have you come here?"

"To look at Lord Saxon's diary. I needed a map to find the Eye of Odin, and I figured it'd be in there," Max replied.

"If you were able to locate the amulet, and somehow survive the creatures of the Underworld, what then?"

"Like you said to everyone at the meeting," Max replied. "I'd find a way to use it on the Spear and stop my dad from destroying the world."

"Your bravery is noted, Guardian. And I believe your heart

is in the right place. However, I wonder if you've considered all the variables."

"I just want everything to go back to the way it was," Max sighed. "I want it back to normal."

Cain paused, considering Max's statement with the faintest hint of a smile. "That all depends on what you consider normal. Certainly, if you manage to stop your father, life may return to the way it was — at least to the naïve," he said. "I'm afraid that life has never been normal in Avalon, Minnesota, though." A half smile crossed the Baron's face as he pulled out a nearby map and unfurled it on the desk. "Of course you can't read runes yet, but you will recognize several of these images. The sphere in the middle of this map surrounds . . ."

"Avalon," Max said quietly.

"Very good," the Baron replied with a nod. "By now you must understand that Avalon is not like the rest of the world. It's an ancient place . . . one of the last remnants of the Golden Age, though it's now entirely surrounded by the modern world. Think of it as a tidal pool, if you will. It remains, though the rest of the magical realm has been drawn back into the ocean of time and space."

Max raised his eyebrows. "You mean even before I found the *Codex*, Avalon was always like this?"

"Have you ever thought it was strange that we in Avalon can see the rest of the world, but few outside our borders mention us?" Baron Lundgren posed. "Few know of our existence and fewer still know where to find us. Even most of the residents of Avalon have no idea what sort of land they inhabit, blissfully going to their jobs and back again in convenient ignorance."

"Why not tell them?"

Cain shook his head. "Most would be happier not knowing, I assure you. Some have been relocated to Avalon for their own safety. Others wandered in by accident, and some by fate."

"But . . . "

Cain raised his hand. "At the moment, we must focus on why you came here in the first place. *The amulet.* What were you planning to do once you discovered its location?"

Max's eyes flickered. "The same thing you're supposed to do — go after it!"

"You're not concerned about what lies in the Underworld waiting for you?"

"I'm not afraid of anything."

Cain leaned forward, his eyes locked on Max. "You will be . . ." His voice left chills on Max's skin. It was though the hand of a corpse had brushed against him. "What lurks in the Underworld is a living nightmare that has driven braver heroes than you into madness. Even if you knew the way, were you to go there without my protection, you'd be lost forever . . . you *and* anyone foolish enough to follow you." His disapproving eyes flitted over to rest upon his daughter, then returned to Max.

"If it really is the end of the world," Max countered, undaunted, "then I'm as good as dead, anyway. The Eye of Odin is our only chance. You said so yourself."

Cain sat back, studying Max for a long while. "You know, I must admit that I wasn't quite honest with you. There is another possibility that your father may fail — but in a way that would seal all of our dooms. You see, there's a dragon that sleeps beneath the World Tree. It is this ancient monstrosity, not the Spear, that has been ordained to ignite Ragnarok."

"Then why does my dad need the Spear?"

"If the Great Dragon destroys the World Tree, as the legends say, then no one will escape annihilation, including your father. If, however, the Spear — in the hands of someone powerful enough — gets to the World Tree first, then that person may be able to control Ragnarok, and create the world that comes after. This, I fear, is your father's misguided plan; he must do all of this without waking the sleeping dragon — Malice Striker. Perhaps if he goes alone, in secret, he might have a chance. But if he brings his army with him, he'd be a fool. Once the Great Dragon is awakened, there will be no going back."

"Would my father be able to stop the dragon?" Max asked anxiously. "I mean, what if he uses the Spear of Ragnarok like he did with Malta?"

Cain shook his head. "Malice Striker is unstoppable, invulnerable, and impervious to almost every conceivable plot. To defeat the Great Dragon, it would take nothing short of a miracle — even with the full power of the Spear in his hands."

"But there's still a chance he could do it, right?" Max pressed.

Cain said nothing, but after a quiet thought, he conceded with a nod.

"Then we still have to get the Eye," Max replied, folding his arms defiantly.

"Not *we*," Cain corrected. "I'll grant you the quest for the Eye of Odin must be pursued. I had come to this conclusion long ago. But you will not be coming along," Cain confirmed, then turned a finger to his daughter. "Nor will you. It's far too dangerous."

Max's heart sank. "You can't keep me out of this! You have to let me get the Eye. It's my fault my dad has the Spear in the first place...."

"*Yes*. It is your fault," Cain answered, rising to his feet before leaning across his desk. Max sank backwards as the Baron's angry eyes seemed alight with fire. The mood passed, and within a moment, Cain sat back down and turned Lord Saxon's diary so Max had a better look. "What you see here is a map of the Underworld. Deep in the bowels of this nightmare, across forgotten roads of misery, beyond a thousand shocks and horrors, and through a maddening maze that is impossible to navigate — even beyond the Teeth of the Hel-Hound himself, there lies the Eye of Odin."

Max's eyes remained locked on Cain's. "I'm still not scared."

"And you're still not going."

"Meet the new Agent Thunderbolt!" Ernie proclaimed with a broad grin. After a parade of shopping at all the garage sales he could find, Ernie had finally finished his costume. He was wearing a blue T-shirt with a white lightning bolt that ran from his shoulder to his waist, but that was only the beginning. Somewhere he'd come across antique aviator goggles that sat atop a military helmet of the same vintage that was strapped around his chin. He was wearing a utility belt, where he'd somehow managed to secure the compass Iver had left him, on the buckle. The running shoes he'd selected had been reinforced with tire tread, and his hands were gloved to the wrist. "Chic, huh?"

"You don't even know what 'chic' means." Natalia rolled her eyes. The four Grey Griffins were aboard Baron Lundgren's boat on their way toward the island for another session in the SIM Chamber. "And that smelly old helmet is way too big. You look like a talking mushroom. Where'd you get it?"

"Some guy was cleaning out his closet. He said I could have it. Can you believe he was gonna throw it away?"

"One could hope," Natalia mused.

Ernie turned to look for a more receptive audience when he found Cain Lundgren staring down at him in disapproval. The Baron had not been amused after learning of Ernie's emerging powers. He hadn't asked for an explanation, instead chose to watch and study Ernie like the boy was a science experiment. Nor had Max volunteered any information to his new mentor, but the Griffins had a feeling that the Baron already knew more than they did.

A spray of lake water swept over the side of the boat,

hitting Natalia full in the face. She sputtered in annoyance and began to wring out her braids as Ernie handed her his blanket.

"What about you?" asked Natalia, looking at him suspiciously. "You aren't even wearing a coat."

"I don't get cold anymore," Ernie shrugged. "I never know what new power I'm going to get next. Tomorrow I might get superstrength."

"Or you could be dead," finished Cain Lundgren.

Ernie gulped.

As the Griffins approached the burned-out buildings that sat atop the SIM Chamber, Max could see that things were changing. Some of the forest had been cleared around the structures, though no footprints could be seen, nor any tire tracks for that matter. It was as if invisible hands had come in to clean up. Even though the Griffins had commented on this several times, all they could ever get out of the Baron was an acknowledgment that something was indeed going on. The man was impossible to read, and he seemed to like it that way.

"You never told us what this place was," Natalia pressed.

"A church or something?" guessed Harley.

Cain shook his head. "My daughter told you of the Templar schools, did she not?" The Griffins nodded. "This was once the site of such a school. In fact, this is the very school I attended with Max's father." With that, the Baron moved at a quickened pace down the path. "This way, please. Keep up and stay close. As you recall, this island is not entirely safe yet."

Max looked over at Natalia, who was looking back at him with the same question: Max's dad had attended a Templar school?

The Griffins stood just outside the SIM Chamber, looking in through the carpet of leaves that covered the floor at their feet.

"So what's the lesson today?" Max asked. Each session had focused on a particular discipline: teamwork, decision-making, and even a bit of history.

"Knowing your enemy," the Baron began. "It requires the understanding that things are not always as they seem. The foul may seem fair, and the fair foul. You must trust your instincts. Take nothing for granted. Now, are you ready?"

The Griffins nodded and passed through the entry — except for Agent Thunderbolt, that was. He just stood there with arms folded across his chest.

"What are you waiting for, Mr. Tweeny?" came the Baron's impatient voice.

Ernie shook his head as he wrinkled his nose. "Something doesn't smell right."

"Is that so?" Cain's eyebrow arched dubiously. "Ernest, you are my guest here, and only my guests have access to this SIM Chamber. I assure you that you're quite safe."

Ernie remained unconvinced. "Something's definitely wrong," he maintained.

"Ernie, I thought you were a superhero now?" Natalia called back from within the SIM Chamber. "Or is that costume of yours only for Halloween? Agent Thunderbolt? Seems more like Captain Chicken to me."

Ernie squirmed uncomfortably, then edged toward the door. "All right, but don't say I didn't warn you. I have a nose for danger — that's one superpower I've always had."

"Fine," Natalia huffed. "Just get in here."

Ernie tightened his chinstrap, defogged his goggles, and double-checked his tire-treaded shoes. Everything looked good. Taking a breath, he stepped inside and the door closed behind him.

It seemed as if Ernie's worries were completely unfounded. The training session went just as smoothly as the others before it. No one got hurt, and they even managed to pass the test without a scraped knee. Max had to admit they were starting to form a pretty good team.

This particular adventure had taken them to the arctic seas aboard a Black Wolf battleship, bristling with cannons. There had been a twenty-headed hydra that had nearly eaten their ship, as well as an aerial dogfight that had resulted in Agent Thunderbolt having to outrun a crashing plane, which he did without even breaking a sweat. His goggles had fogged up more than once though, causing some worry that he'd trip and fall over the side. Ernie's shoes were holding up, however. The tire tread was doing its thing.

When the program ended, the images faded and the door opened. Cain stepped in with a proud smile across his face.

"Well done, Griffins. You're improving nicely with every session — faster than I'd hoped, in fact. Especially you, Max. You made short work of that hydra."

Max smiled. The compliment was out of character — at least for Baron Lundgren — but it was a welcome surprise, nonetheless. Cain motioned toward the door, signaling the session was over and that it was time to return to the boat. As the Griffins passed through the door, Max felt a hand on his shoulder. "A moment, Max. I'd like a word with you, if you wouldn't mind?" Max nodded as the others exited.

As the door slammed shut, a chill suddenly crept up Max's spine. Then long, cold fingers wrapped around his neck. "What a tasty little morsel you are," a harsh voice whispered, as Max was yanked up off the ground. His legs dangling, Max's watering eyes met his assailant's.

It wasn't Baron Lundgren at all. Perhaps the program was still running, and this was another twist, or someone had broken through Cain's defenses, infiltrating the SIM Chamber. Either way, Max was in serious trouble.

Max watched in horror as Cain's face was slowly replaced by a werewolf's, with flickering yellow orbs in its eye sockets. "So you see, Sumner," it spoke, a haughty smile curling about its lips. "There's no place you can hide . . . no place that I cannot reach you."

"Who are you?" Max choked in desperation.

"Don't you recognize me, boy?" the creature mocked in a strangely familiar voice. "No? Think, O Great Guardian of the

Codex," it teased, but Max had no idea. "Oh, but I've waited a long time to be rid of you and your miserable pack of friends." Suddenly, the face of the werewolf morphed once again, revealing an all too familiar face.

"Dr. Blackstone?" Max whispered, his voice coarse from the pain. The vice principal had been the Black Wolf assassin all along!

"Oh yes, Sumner. You and I have a long history, don't we?" Max just looked at him with dread. "Do you know how many times I've stood over your bed at night while you were sleeping . . . wishing and hoping they'd finally release me to put an end to your miserable existence?"

Eyes smoking with hate, Diamonte Blackstone raised Max high overhead. "Time to die, Sumner."

Max felt his throat close in, but in the reflection of Blackstone's eyes, Max could see a figure of gray stone burst through the chamber door and soar with wings spread like a bat's. It was Throckmorton! He plowed into Blackstone like a runaway truck, hammering the Black Wolf into the wall. Beaten and broken, Blackstone lay sprawled across the floor beneath the threatening form of the gargoyle.

"You're dead, Sumner," Blackstone said through a fit of coughing. "I've waited so long . . . what's a few more hours?" With that, he burst into vapor and disappeared into the shadows, just as Baron Lundgren raced onto the scene.

THERE WAS no more debate. If Blackstone could find a way to penetrate Cain's defenses, Max wasn't safe *anywhere* in Avalon. Though it was the last thing Baron Lundgren had hoped for, he could no longer avoid it. Max would get his wish and join the expedition into the Underworld. It was too dangerous aboveground. Despite the atrocities that lurked below, Cain couldn't afford to leave Max unsupervised. The Guardian would be safer at his side, where he could keep a close eye on the boy. Regretfully, that meant the rest of the Griffins, and Brooke, would have to go as well, as the assassin would most likely target them next. Besides, if the world was about to be destroyed anyway, what was the difference? Better to die seeking victory than hiding in a closet until death finds you.

The fellowship would be led by Cain, with Logan, Athena, and Throckmorton to watch over the children. A select group of T.H.O.R. agents led by Søren would be waiting for them near the entrance to the Underworld. Stealth and speed were vital to success and help would not be coming from the armies of the Templar who, under the unstoppable on-slaught of the Black Wolves, were on the brink of collapse. The last Max had heard, the handful of remaining Templar fortresses were under siege and weren't expected to last much longer. It would be up to Cain and this crazy mission into the Underworld to save the day.

"You lot ready?" Logan asked, stepping into the armory. It was a narrow room constructed with walls of stone and lined with rows of laden shelves.

"I think so," Max said. He and the rest of the Griffins were seated with Brooke and Athena at a long table, stuffing their packs, under Throckmorton's supervision. He'd handed each a checklist that included items such as flashlights, rope, carabiners, flares, wool socks, dry goods, water bottles, and plenty more. By the time they were done, the packs weighed almost as much as the children did — except for Brooke's, that was. Throckmorton added most of her items to his bag.

"Good," the Scotsman said, inspecting their gear. "The baron asked me to give you a few gifts for our vacation. Here you go. . . ." With that, he threw each of the Griffins a hooded jacket. They were deep gray with griffin patches stitched on the shoulders.

"These are awesome," admired Harley, as he slipped his on.

"No kidding. It's like we're a real super-team," Ernie noted, strutting around the table. "And you guys have 'em, too." Sure enough, Logan and Athena were wearing the same jackets.

As Max searched the pockets of his old jacket to make sure he hadn't forgotten anything, his eyes opened wide when he came across a rather heavy lump — Eden's Clay. He'd been waiting for an opportunity to return it to Brooke's dad, but it was never the right time. So making the lame excuse that he had to go to the bathroom, Max disappeared so he could transfer the clay to his new coat without drawing suspicion.

By the time Max returned, Baron Lundgren had shown up. "So, how do you like the jacket?" he asked.

"It's awesome," answered Max, who had noticed that under the griffin insignia his jacket had one of the T.H.O.R. hammers as well.

"Excellent," Brooke's father said, rubbing his hands together. "These garments offer much more than protection from the cold. They're woven from a special substance imported from the Shadowlands themselves."

"Will it make me invisible?" asked Ernie hopefully, zipping his jacket all the way to his chin.

Baron Lundgren shook his head. "Nothing is invisible to the creatures of the Underworld, though the jackets *will* provide at least a modicum of protection from the things that go bump in the night. Just try not to put them to the test."

"What about our parents?" Natalia asked, checking her watch. She was starting to grow nervous. "I mean, I told them I'd only be gone a few hours."

Athena smiled, patting Natalia on the back reassuringly. "Don't worry. Where we're going, time doesn't exist. At least, not in the same way it does at your house. You'll be back before they miss you."

A few minutes later, packs zipped tight and strapped on tighter, the fellowship followed Throckmorton through a series of halls that seemed to offer an endless supply of choices.

Virtually every fork in the road allowed them to go left, right, or straight ahead — and they'd passed at least a dozen such intersections.

"I still can't believe the assassin was Dr. Blackstone all this time," Natalia said, turning to Athena. "I mean, what about the old lady in the woods who nearly ate us? That couldn't have been him, could it? And the lunch lady? A pizza delivery boy? There's no way. He'd have to be a Hollywood special-effects and makeup guru to have all those costumes perfected like he did. Besides, I didn't know werewolves could change shapes like that."

Baron Lundgren shook his head. "Blackstone is *not* a werewolf," he explained. "He's actually a Doppelgänger. . . ."

"A whatsit?" asked Ernie, who was loping between Brooke's father and Logan, figuring that was the safest place to be.

"Doppelgängers are shape-shifters of the most undesirable sort," the Baron continued. "These creatures have no bodies of their own, so they spend their lives stealing the shape of anyone they touch, be it the lunch lady, your fellow students, or even your own mother. When in the form of some victim, they are almost impossible to recognize, even by magic. Thus, Doppelgängers make the perfect assassin."

"Did you know it was Blackstone?" asked Harley, who was taking up the rear.

"I had my suspicions," Cain confirmed. "But I had no way to confirm them until now. Which reminds me," he said, turning a suspicious eye toward Ernie. "I believe it's time we discussed your new powers, Mr. Thunderbolt."

"Pretty cool, huh?" Ernie smiled, patting his helmet.

"You may not think so after you hear what I have to say." Cain's brow furrowed. "Your recent evolution is not by chance, and while you Griffins have been reluctant to explain what happened, I am not blind. You have found some way to infuse Ernie with faerie blood, but your reckless action has resulted in Ernie's becoming a Changeling."

"Ernie would be dead if it weren't for Max!" Natalia defended, glaring up at Cain.

"Would he?" Cain replied coldly. "At any rate, if Ernie had known the repercussions, he may well have preferred the alternative to his current situation."

"Whaddaya mean?" Ernie asked incredulously and looked down at his hands to make sure they were still there. "I feel fine! Is there something wrong with me?"

"You have become a Changeling," Baron Lundgren repeated.

"A what?" Ernie cried.

"A faerie creature that evolves from one species into another. Even as we speak, the faerie blood is mutating inside of you, changing you bit by bit into what you will become. Each time you use those new powers you've discovered, you take one step closer to becoming fully faerie, and there will be nothing left of you for your friends to recognize."

Ernie's mouth fell open.

"So that explains why he's taller and needs a haircut almost every week," Natalia gasped in realization while referring to her *Book of Clues*. She'd been tracking any strange occurrences involving Ernie since he'd returned from the hospital.

Max looked down at the ground, ashamed of himself for having done such a terrible thing to his friend. It seemed like no matter what he did, everything went haywire.

"If it helps, I would have made the same choice given the options," Cain said, seeing the glum look on Max's face. "Thankfully, the mutation appears to be slower with Ernie than other cases I've witnessed. Perhaps it will take a lifetime to complete. In the meantime, you must avoid using those powers, Ernie. If nothing else, that should inhibit the change." Cain took one more hard look at Ernie, as if he were mentally writing the warning into the boy's brain, then turned and headed down the hallway. "Come. The Underworld awaits!"

Afraid to move, Ernie had to be dragged along by his friends until his bundle of nerves untied themselves.

Soon Throckmorton led the group through a small door and into a dimly lit passage with low ceilings. The air was stale as they made their way steadily down into the bowels of the earth. It quickly became claustrophobic, even for fifth graders, and everyone was relieved when the end of the tunnel came into view. A round iron door, like a bank vault's, was fixed into the wall. It was dingy and rusted, and looked like it hadn't been touched in a thousand years.

Throckmorton didn't hesitate to turn the large wheel that

protruded from the door. It screeched as the gargoyle pulled hand over hand, until a loud clang echoed through the suffocating hall. A wall of rotten steam poured through the opening.

"You've got to be kidding me," Natalia complained, looking over at Brooke. "Why would you have something like this in your house?"

Brooke shrugged and wrinkled her nose. "I've never been here before. I didn't even know it existed."

Cain Lundgren was the first to pass through, carefully descending the steel grate stairs that led into the cloud of stench, the click of his cane echoing as he walked. Logan motioned for the Griffins to follow, which they did without a word. The heavy air seemed to drown any feeling of hope or adventure, leaving only the sinking sensation of entombment. It was only magnified when Max heard the gargoyle seal the vault behind them. There was no turning back now.

"Don't worry," Throckmorton offered in his German accent, catching the look of concern on everyone's faces. "We won't be in harm's way for at least another hour."

"Oh, that makes me feel a whole lot better," Agent Thunderbolt complained sardonically as drops of water pinged off of his helmet. With the slippery stairs and thick clouds of impenetrable putridity, a super-speed escape would be suicidal. What good were superpowers if he couldn't even use them to save his own life? The Cosmic Speedster muttered before glaring secretly at Throckmorton. For some reason, he just didn't trust the gargoyle.

"This way," Cain ordered as they reached the bottom of the stairwell. The Baron then led them along a brick path bathed in an eerie green light. All around, the sound of water trickled through the passage.

"This place looks and smells like a sewer," Natalia noted, plugging her nose as she looked about.

"Hey, Natalia?" asked Ernie with a mischievous smile, his eyes partially obscured by his fogged goggles. "Pull my finger!"

Harley snickered farther up the line, as Natalia glared at the bespectacled Griffin. "Boys are such barbarians."

"We're now entering the Roots of the Underworld," Cain explained, gesturing to an arched passageway. "Though your sensibilities may well trick you into considering this place little more than a sewer," he said, turning to Natalia, "I will remind you to take nothing for granted. Much like your expeditions on the island in Lake Avalon, I must ask that you stay close and be vigilant. If you wander off or become lost, I will not be able to save you. Remember, we are not welcome here."

At that moment, Max caught a glimpse of approaching shadows. A lump formed in his throat and his hand immediately reached for his ring.

"Who is it?" Harley pressed gruffly, his fists at the ready. He'd seen the intruders, too.

"I dunno . . . just a bunch of guys, I guess," replied Ernie, replacing his recently de-fogged goggles back on his face. His faerie-enhanced vision allowed him to see twice as far as his friends. "They look like knights, and they're carrying lots of weapons."

As the knights marched into view, Max spied at least a dozen T.H.O.R. agents, each more deadly looking than the next. Søren was at their head, and they were armed to the teeth, shielded by high-tech armor, and clothed in heavy boots and thick gloves. Some wore stocking caps, others ski masks, and some had greasepaint streaked across their faces. Though their armor didn't gleam like the knights' of old, it was ten times as strong, and probably worked just as well against modern weapons as it did against magic fireballs and dragon's claws.

The knights were stone silent as they marched up to Max and the others. Søren saluted briskly. Logan saluted back, and the agents of T.H.O.R. expertly took up positions around the company.

"With each moment, the Black Wolves draw closer to the tree," Athena spoke, her voice breaking the silence. "Is he coming or not?"

"Patience," the Baron advised. "He'll be here. We're a bit early."

"Is *who* coming?" Ernie asked, his voice barely above a whisper.

It was at just about that moment that a strange clicking sound echoed through the chamber. *Click. Click. Click.* It continued until Natalia gasped. Through the green glow of the sewer, she could just make out the silhouette of a freakish figure slinking through the fog. As it drew near, the Griffins could see an emaciated body suspended in the air by what must have been a dozen long, spidery legs projecting from its back, each as thin as the edge of a knife. Thrust out in all directions, they skittered along the walls of the tunnel, hauling the mysterious body closer and closer.

"Try to relax," Logan warned, walking over to the Griffins. "This guy is our ticket into the Underworld — and more important, back out."

"Who is he?" asked Harley.

"He's called the Custodian. I don't know if he has a real name, though he probably wouldn't remember even if he did. From what I hear, he's not..." Logan's voice trailed off ominously, as he seemed to be considering his words.

"Not what?" demanded Natalia.

"Not altogether sane," Logan answered after a moment's hesitation. "Keep your eyes open. He doesn't operate by the same rules as people aboveground." Logan looked into each of their eyes sternly, then nodded. "But if you do what I tell you, we should be fine."

Ernie reached for his asthma inhaler instinctively, even though he hadn't needed it for weeks. He kept the device nearby, however, just in case. It never hurt to be prepared.

The Custodian

As THE mysterious Custodian neared, his frightening features came into view. He was old and grizzled, much like a living corpse that had been dug up and chewed on by a junkyard dog. Wrapped in threadbare coveralls that likely hadn't been washed in a century, he smelled even worse than the slime that covered the sewer walls. In his hands was an old mop, and at his side jingled the largest ring of keys the Griffins had ever seen. Thick-lensed goggles were snapped over his carrotish nose, and his ears were pointy, with odd patches of hair crawling out from the inside.

When he smiled, the Griffins could see that his teeth were crooked and broken. In fact, they were so rotten that they almost glowed. Perhaps most disgusting was the inexplicable fog that rolled out of his lips, like stench billowing from a pile of month-old diapers. To top it off, the Custodian's eyes rolled around in their sockets like loose ball bearings and he bore a disconcerting grin shared only by grave robbers.

Ernie chewed at his nails nervously, wondering if he shouldn't risk losing more of himself and accelerating his faerie transformation by running for his life, when the Custodian slowly lowered himself to the ground and his wiry appendages folded into his back like a closing pocketknife. He looked at the children, one by one, with a gaze reminiscent of an overzealous puppy that hadn't played with anyone in weeks. Then he slapped his gloved hands together and started to laugh, though it quickly turned into a kind of chortle, then a terrible cough, and finally into several gross hacks that caused Natalia to reflexively step back to avoid being barfed on.

"Custodian," Cain began, after allowing the odd character to regain his composure. "I'm pleased that you've reconsidered my offer. After all, who knows the Roots of the Underworld better than you?"

"Ah yessss," a voice slithered out in a lisp. The Custodian sounded like a cross between a snake and the suctioning of shoe-sucking mud.

"I must say that your home grows more impressive every year," Cain continued. Max raised his eyebrows, wondering if Baron Lundgren had lost his marbles. The sewer was at best a slimy hole barely fit for the decaying remains of a bucket of catfish. Yet the Custodian seemed simply delighted by Cain's compliment, as he took in a deep, snotty breath before exhaling more disgusting fog from his gullet.

"Indeed, the Roots are particularly fine this evening," the odd little man said. "You couldn't have picked a better time to go on this little expedition. And lucky for you, I just got done feeding *most* of my pets. If we're particularly lucky, they'll be asleep when it comes time to pass by. If not, we'll just have to find something else to feed them." His eyes then fell menacingly on the children.

Then the Custodian broke into a slobbery smile as he turned to Athena. He seemed completely enraptured, his eyes roving wildly as he studied her like a lion eyeing a tasty gazelle. The strange man skittered across the slimy floor toward the female Templar, lifted her hand in his, and landed a messy kiss on her gloved knuckles. "Pleased to make your acquaintance," the Custodian offered, bowing low as his thin scrap of hair fell away from a balding pate. "I've been away from the surface for so long that I'd forgotten the exquisite nature of a woman's beauty. What is your name, my dear?" As he spoke, Natalia spied a worm crawl out his ear and disappear up into his nose hair. He didn't even sneeze.

"My name is Athena . . . ," she said, her voice flat and emotionless. If Athena was creeped out, Natalia couldn't tell. The female Templar was trained by the best and could probably eat a sack of spiders without so much as blinking.

"Ah!" The Custodian danced around in a clicking circle, laughing to himself. "Yes, I've heard of you, though who hasn't of course? What a delightful treat."

Max watched in revulsion as the Custodian clattered away on his spindly legs, key ring jingling as he went. But just as Max was about to look away, he noticed that the Custodian was now staring back at him. The hair on Max's neck rose and a chill swept over him. Something about this strange old man wasn't right. Max felt like he was being cataloged for the dinner menu.

The Custodian then pulled out a dingy pocket watch and

clicked the lid open. "Time to begin our little adventure, no?" he proclaimed, his white tongue wagging. Then those creepy legs unfolded from his back, lifting the small man off the ground. His eyes narrowed as he sniffed the air. "Oh yes, the weather is fine tonight! Excellent . . ."

Max's stomach crawled like a nest of worms.

"Shall we?" the Custodian asked. He stood above the assemblage, hovering in the air with the aid of his spidery appendages. Max noted how sharp each of them was, with edges like blades, and wondered if those legs weren't handy for more than walking.

"At your convenience," the Baron replied, before turning to the rest of his team. "I need you to spread out, and keep vigilant. Down here lurk your darkest nightmares. One mistake could cost all of us our lives. . . ."

"So true. Isn't it just scrumptious?" the Custodian concurred with glee.

Max felt a sudden compulsion to twist his ring and summon the gauntlet.

"Don't even think about it," the Scotsman warned, as he walked up next to Max. "Not down here — not unless there's no other choice."

Max looked up at Logan in confusion. "But —"

"No 'buts,'" Logan interrupted with a wave of his hand. "In the Underworld, everything is magical. Every breath of air. Every drop of water." He paused, looking over at Max. "What

I'm trying to say is that you're just a small fish down here. Your little fire will be a beacon to their legions, and we'll all be goners for sure. Understand?"

Max nodded, though he didn't like abandoning his security blanket like that. The Skyfire had given him confidence, and now Logan was trying to take it away from him.

"Too true," the Custodian agreed, poking his sharp nose into their business. "You mustn't use your powers. 'Tis a no-no, it is." Then the Custodian rose high above them. "I believe it's time for your first lesson. . . ."

"What's that supposed to mean?" complained Agent Thunderbolt, who was tightening up his gaiters and checking his shoelaces. Footwear was crucially important for a superhero — - especially a speedster like him.

The Custodian sidled up to the bespectacled Griffin. "Tell me, do you like roller coasters, my juicy little boy?"

Ernie nodded, stepping backward in revulsion.

"What do they tell you to do when you sit down on the ride?"

"To keep my hands and feet inside . . ."

"Exactly." The Custodian grinned. "Same thing here. Only instead of getting in trouble with your mommy if you disobey the rules, you'll get this. . . ." He then threw a large bone toward the nearby wall, and the kids watched in disbelief as the bone was caught in a swirl of teeth and fingers that lay just beyond the surface of the slimy wall. A moment later, after a terrible crunching sound, it was gone.

Ernie gulped.

"This guy's definitely a freak," noted Harley as Max nodded his agreement.

With that, the Custodian laughed and continued on, leading them into another murky passage. As the torches grew dim, Throckmorton handed out several Ever-Burning lamps. Max had seen these once before, when entering the Catacombs of the Chapel of Mist. Rumored to be a myth, these lamps could stay lit forever. As the lamps flared to life, they revealed crumbling walls of brick and mortar, stained with creeping patches of phosphorescent fungus. Sluggish water gurgled in the underground reservoir nearby, its surface black and mysterious. The entire place stank, and the air was heavy.

"It feels like a coffin down here," Natalia commented as she pulled out the magnifying lens that Iver had given her, before studying the ground at her feet. She quickly let out a shriek and dropped the instrument, rubbing at her eyes in pain.

"What's wrong?" asked Brooke as Athena helped Natalia along for a few steps until the pain subsided. "Oh . . . ," Brooke said, realizing what just happened. "Your magnifying glass amplifies magic, and this entire realm *is* magic. It was like you were looking directly into the sun with a telescope. You could have gone blind, you know."

"Now you tell me," Natalia complained, still rubbing at her eyes.

"You should have been more careful," Athena reprimanded.

"Yeah, Natalia," Ernie echoed, pointing to his goggled eyes. "You really should have been more careful."

"Thanks, Captain Obvious." Natalia glared back at him.

"That's Agent Thunderbolt!" Ernie complained indignantly. "What's so hard about remembering my name?"

"Because your name is Ernest," Natalia quipped, earning a heated glare from behind Agent Thunderbolt's goggles.

Minutes slowly drifted into hours. No monster had come out and devoured anyone yet, but Max started to notice something rather unexplainable. The size of the tunnel was shifting, depending on which gateway they'd enter. Sometimes it would be suffocatingly close, while other times it was cavernous, with fat drops of water plunging down on their heads from some invisible ceiling high above.

"This place is disgusting," Natalia groaned after another slimy drop plopped on her head. She looked absolutely miserable, with her hair matted and growing curlier with every reluctant step. "Where is this water coming from?"

"Maybe you should take out your magnifying glass and find out." Harley gave her a smile as he glanced back over his shoulder.

Natalia glared. "Maybe you should speak when you're spoken to." Harley chuckled. Natalia then looked over at Athena. Slimy rain was everywhere, oozing down in big drops, but somehow Athena was bone dry. Natalia shook her matted head and grumbled. She'd have to learn that trick. Maybe it was in the Templar rule book. She'd just have to find herself a copy.

The Custodian and Baron Lundgren continued to lead them. Despite his limp, Cain was able to maintain a challenging pace. Fatigue was starting to set in with Max, though. His boots felt a great deal heavier than they had at the start of the march. Worse, though, were the hungry stares from the Watchers in the walls. They were just waiting for one of the kids to slip up.

"Are you okay?" Brooke asked as Max stumbled, his mind growing numb. He could feel the dark creatures trying to pry open his mind like a can opener.

Throckmorton stopped, reached into his jacket, and extracted a glass jar. Inside was a mass of writhing, translucent bugs that looked like centipedes. The gargoyle unscrewed the lid, reached inside, and handed Max one of the insects.

"What the heck is he supposed to do with that?" asked Ernie, his ample nose wrinkled.

"Eat it," Throckmorton replied.

"Are you crazy?" Ernie exclaimed, earning a sharp look from the gargoyle.

Brooke walked up to Max and placed her hand on his shoulder. "It's safe," she encouraged with a smile. "I took one this morning. They're called Delirium Worms. They fight off hallucinations. Down here, you have to have them, or you'll go crazy."

Max paused. Even in his state, the idea of a bug crawling down his throat wasn't terribly inviting, but when he saw Natalia pop one into her mouth, he decided he needed to stop being a wimp. So Max raised the squirming bug to his lips. He hesitated, then closed his eyes and placed it in his mouth. The guts of the insect squished beneath his tongue and slopped against the inside of his teeth. It was warm and gushy, like hot pudding. If he had to admit it, the Delirium Worm was actually kind of tasty — for a bug. Remarkably, his head immediately cleared of the fog.

When it came time for Harley to eat his Delirium Worm, they discovered that he wasn't suffering from any of the hallucinations or side effects at all. His Faerie Ward was working perfectly. The rest of the party hadn't been so lucky. Though Ernie had to be practically force-fed, Throckmorton soon completed the task and replaced the glass jar into his jacket. "The effects last for six hours," the gargoyle explained. "If the hallucinations return, let me know."

Ernie spat, his face contorted in disgust as he chewed on his Delirium Worm. "This stuff is nasty," he declared. "Besides, it doesn't even work."

"What do you mean?" Throckmorton turned back to him with narrowed eyes.

Ernie pointed directly above them. "If I'm not supposed to be hallucinating anymore, how do you explain that thing with all the teeth and claws that's flying toward us?"

22

THERE WERE shouts as a swarm of leathery wings shot toward them. The nightmares were terrible to look upon, with gruesome faces dominated by milky white eyes and jaws full of sharklike teeth. Their howls were so piercing that Max fell to his knees, just as he caught sight of Natalia pulling her protective hood over her head. He feared he'd go deaf or, worse, that his brain was going to rattle out of his ears. Max instinctively reached for the *Codex* ring, ready to unleash his armored gauntlet and the Skyfire that screamed to be released, only to have Logan pull his arm back down.

"Easy," his bodyguard encouraged, pinning Max's arm so he couldn't reach the ring with his free hand. "Just let 'em go. No harm here. Remember what I told you."

Max shook his head, sweat beading on his brow. "I can't stop it! I can feel the Fire burning inside. It wants to get out."

Logan drew closer. "Max, listen to me! You have to control this. If you don't, you'll put all of us at risk."

Max nearly bit his tongue to keep the flame from escaping, but he could feel it creeping forward, trying to seep out of his nose, ears, and eyes. . . . Max felt as if he were a dam about to burst. There was something about this place — the Roots — that amplified the Fire, and it was nearly impossible to rein in. He shouted in pain as

Logan pulled him close. Max knew he couldn't hold it back much longer. Even his vision was starting to shift into the blue spectrum.

"You will control yourself, Guardian!" Cain commanded, his voice filling the passage like a wave crashing upon the rocks. Once again, Max could feel Cain's probing for the switch that controlled the raging fire. Like a trapped animal, Max felt himself trying to resist, but he couldn't, and with a *click*, the flames were snuffed out. He collapsed with a moan, just as the monsters disappeared into the shadows.

"Easy, Grasshopper," Logan said, checking his pulse.

"What happened?" the Guardian asked weakly. "I've never felt like that before."

"The Underworld is magnifying your Skyfire," explained Baron Lundgren, who looked gravely concerned. "I fear I will not be able to hold it back for long. It's imperative that you focus and keep those flames at bay. Do you understand?"

"Don't you think we should give him a break?" Natalia intervened. "He's doing the best he can."

"Oftentimes that is *not* good enough, Ms. Romanov," countered the Baron as Natalia bit her lip before she said something she'd regret. She was always taught to respect her elders, but this Baron Lundgren could be as mean as an old badger.

"What the heck were those things, anyway?" Harley asked, as Logan slowly helped Max back to his feet.

"Skreechers," Brooke explained. "They're usually harmless. We probably just frightened them, that's all."

"*We* frightened *them*?" asked Ernie. "Yeah, right. That's a good one. Did you see the size of their teeth?" He patted his helmet, then his chest to make sure he was still in one piece.

"Everyone accounted for?" Logan called out, doing a quick head count. Soon, the grim band was marching again, moving through the labyrinth of passages, turning first one way, then another. The place was a perfect rat's maze, and none of the Griffins had the slightest idea where they were heading, much less how to get back. Natalia was the first to point out that if the Custodian decided to double-cross them, they'd be lost forever. Max hoped Cain had a backup plan.

When they came to a narrow choke door, the Custodian quickly unlocked it with one of his thousands of keys. He allowed everyone to pass through before he joined, and as Max walked under the Custodian's gaze, he shivered. The Guardian of the *Codex* could feel the odd monster of a man leering at him through those ridiculous goggles. Max knew in his heart that the Custodian was a rotten apple.

"You sense anything strange?" Logan asked, breaking into Max's thoughts.

"What do you mean?" Max feigned. "Do you sense something?"

Logan whispered a single word.

"Ambush . . ."

"We'll make camp here tonight," Cain called out. No sooner had he finished the sentence than the T.H.O.R. agents broke ranks and prepared the camp with uncanny efficiency. Some set the fire; others pitched a small pavilion where Brooke, Natalia, and Athena would sleep.

"Who'll set watch?" Logan inquired.

"Throckmorton will be our eyes," the Baron responded.

"I'd feel more comfortable if Søren and a couple of the other blokes joined him."

Cain shook his head. "Throckmorton will suffice. As a gargoyle, he needs neither food nor sleep. His kind was created especially for this purpose. Your men, however, perform better when they've had adequate rest. There are more than enough challenges on this journey. Luckily, sleep won't be one of them."

Logan nodded coldly, then turned and relayed the order to his men. There were some confused looks at first, but no complaints. Besides, if Max knew Logan, he'd keep his eyes open all night anyway. The knights would likely follow suit. For now, things remained calm, and soon the fire was crackling as bedrolls were unfurled around the warm blaze.

"Nobody said anything about spending the night down here," Ernie protested. What Ernie meant to say was that he was starving. Back home it was meatloaf night, and now he was stuck with a fistful of salted nuts and a strip of shoe-leather jerky. There'd be no dessert, and all he could think about were the brownies and ice cream his parents were going to be eating without him.

"Nobody said we weren't, Agent Wonderbolt," countered Harley with a smile.

"Thunderbolt!" Ernie complained vehemently. "Now you're doing it on purpose!"

Harley laughed as he moved on. With plenty of excitement to burn, he decided to help the T.H.O.R. agents set up and secure the camp. Harley seemed to fit right in with the stoic knights, who were hardworking and only spoke when necessary.

"So we're following the map of some crazy dead guy, right?" asked Ernie.

Natalia nodded. "Lord Saxon. But why would you say he's crazy?"

"He'd have to be crazy to come down here," replied Ernie with a shrug. "Besides, I bet the longer you stay down here, the crazier you get. Just look at the Custodian!" Ernie noted, pointing in the direction of their guide.

"Hey, where's that creep going?" Natalia murmured as she watched the Custodian disappear into the darkness after talking in whispers with Baron Lundgren.

Harley shrugged. "Beats me. He lives down here, I guess. So maybe his house is nearby."

"Something's not right," she noted, and then set to chewing the inside of her cheek. "I just wish I could place what it is."

"That Custodian's crazy as a loon, that's what," Ernie offered, taking off his helmet, goggles, and gloves as he joined the Griffins around the fire. "He keeps eying me like he wants to eat me or something."

"Maybe it's all those sweets you keep stuffing into your mouth," Harley pointed out. "Did you ever consider using the name Captain Candypants?"

"Knock it off! I'm serious," complained Ernie. "Every time

somebody offers him food, he turns up his nose at it, then looks back at me and licks his lips. I bet he's a cannibal."

"Hmmm," Natalia considered. "I'll check it out."

"What?" Ernie exclaimed. "You're gonna follow him?"

"Logan said we needed to get to sleep," Max reminded her.

"Thanks, but I'm a big girl." With that, Natalia started toward the sewage canal, tiptoeing past the adults. She wished that magnifying lens Iver had given her would work down here, but she wasn't in any hurry to burn her eyes out of their sockets. Instead, she'd have to rely on good old-fashioned detective work. She made decent time and was just nearing the edge of the firelight when she sighed in frustration. A dark pool of stagnant water was blocking her path.

"And where do you think you're going?" a deep voice questioned. Natalia stopped dead in her tracks. It was Baron Lundgren.

Natalia slowly turned around, caught in an odd feeling of fright and frustration. "I was just going to look around for . . ."

"Yes?" Cain said as he approached, his brow raised.

"I don't know . . . Something isn't right. I can . . . well, I can just feel it."

"Is that so?" he asked. "And you thought it would be a wise course of action for a twelve-year-old girl to wander about the shadows where evil things lurk?" He nodded to the water nearby, where Natalia caught sight of two glowing eyes looking back at her. They quickly submerged. "You see," he explained. "One bit of bad judgment on your part, and I'll have to explain to your parents why all that remains of their little girl is a gnawed skeleton. Am I clear?"

Natalia's eyes narrowed. "Perfectly," she said sharply, before storming back to the fire. As she neared, Natalia saw Brooke sitting with Throckmorton, sipping a cup of hot cocoa. Natalia rolled her eyes and marched right on past. She didn't want anything to do with the Lundgren family. Cain had been nothing but mean to her since they'd first met. He was nothing, in her opinion, like Iver. One of these days, she was going to tell him so.

Natalia found a quiet spot away from the others and sat down next to a brick pillar. She was still within range of the firelight, but far enough away that it was obvious she wanted to be alone. Then Natalia pulled out her *Book of Clues* and started flipping through the pages, studying the various runes she'd drawn over the last few months. Languages were always a curiosity to her, and this archaic form of written communication was fascinating. Natalia had made up her mind to get Athena to teach her to read them.

"What're you doing?"

Natalia looked up from her studies to see Brooke's cheery face smiling down at her. "Reading," Natalia replied crisply.

Brooke's face fell at the sharpness of Natalia's tone. "Oh," she said, then handed Natalia a cup of cocoa. "I just thought you might like some, too."

Caught between anger and discomfort, Natalia didn't know what to say. So she stuck with, "Thanks." For a long while, neither said a thing, but Natalia was too angry to let it slide. "Can I ask you something?"

"Sure," Brooke replied.

"Why does your dad hate me?"

Brooke smiled and shook her head. "He's just like that sometimes. He doesn't mean to be, but . . . well, he's under a lot of pressure. I know he likes you, though."

"Yeah, right," Natalia huffed, rolling her eyes.

"Honest. He told me so. He said you're really smart and a great detective, too."

Natalia blushed at the compliment. An uncomfortable silence fell over the two girls as Natalia continued to sip at the cocoa, hoping Brooke might decide to go away. Every time she looked up, though, Brooke was still there, watching her thoughtfully.

"You know, I've wanted to talk to you about school for a long time," Brooke ventured. A pit grew in Natalia's stomach. "I know the other girls aren't very nice to you."

Natalia set her jaw and tried to appear casual, even though it hurt just to think about it. "I hadn't noticed," she lied. She scribbled in her notebook, avoiding eye contact.

"It bothers me, though," Brooke pressed on.

"Don't worry about it," Natalia urged, hoping the conversation was at an end. She was starting to get that same sick feeling that she felt whenever the mean girls would exclude her from their lunch tables or leave whenever Natalia showed up on the playground. She hated it, and at that moment she could feel herself prickling up like a porcupine.

"You know," Brooke continued, "they're just jealous of you."

"Oh yeah . . . right!" Natalia said, shaking her head. It was one of the most ridiculous things she'd ever heard. Those girls were all beautiful and outgoing, with limitless wardrobes and boys who would fall all over themselves just to get a whiff of their perfume. Their mothers even let them get their ears pierced and wear makeup by the fourth grade!

"No, seriously," Brooke maintained. "I hear them talking. You know . . . how Natalia is so smart and gets such good grades, and how hard they struggle to even pass."

"They don't care about their grades," Natalia stated plainly.

"Maybe not, but whether it's grades or who has the best wardrobe, they don't like being second. Whenever someone's better than they are, they start making fun of them. I guess it makes 'em feel better. Sad, huh?"

"Then why are you friends with them?" Natalia asked. She wanted to shout it, but instead she offered a careless smile and tossed her braids over her shoulder, trying to look completely indifferent.

Brooke sat down next to Natalia and set her cocoa mug to the side, glancing back toward the fire where Max was sitting next to Logan. "I wouldn't call us friends. I actually feel sorry for them. They're never happy about anything. In fact, they're miserable. I just try to be nice to everyone." Then Brooke paused, looking very concerned. "I'm nice to you, aren't I?"

"But when I see you with them, you're always laughing and having a good time," Natalia countered. "Iver always said that a person is judged by the company she keeps."

Brooke grew silent, obviously stung by Natalia's comment. She was trying to be nice, and Natalia immediately felt bad for saying it. When it came to social settings, she tended to say the wrong thing at the wrong time — especially when she felt vulnerable. Natalia just couldn't help it. "I'm sorry," she confessed, after a thoughtful moment. "It's just hard to imagine that you could ever understand someone like me ... someone almost everyone hates. Especially since everybody loves you."

"Those girls don't really like anyone. I've heard them say nasty things about me when they didn't think I could hear them."

"So why don't you say something?"

"What's the point?" Brooke shrugged.

"They might listen to you."

"No, they wouldn't," Brooke countered. "They'd just turn on me and I'd be the next . . ." Her voice faltered.

"What? Natalia Romanov?" finished Natalia smugly. "Well, just to let you know, it's not so bad on the other side. The quality of friends is better, for one thing."

Brooke looked uncomfortable for a moment, then stole another glance toward Max.

"You like him, don't you?" Natalia ventured, the scowl remaining.

"What do you mean?" Brooke asked, flustered.

"Max, of course," replied Natalia confidently as Brooke blushed. Then Natalia softened a bit. "It's okay, though. He likes you, too."

"I'm just worried about him, that's all."

"Join the club," Natalia answered as she offered the faintest hint of an understanding smile toward Brooke, who smiled back.

221

23

"MAX SAID there's gonna be a dragon once we get to the World Tree," Ernie pressed Athena as Max and Harley joined them for breakfast the next morning. "Do you think we'll have to fight it?"

"I hope not," she replied coolly.

"Is he big?" Harley ventured. He always loved dinosaurs, and dragons were their closest relatives. "Bigger than a T. rex?"

Athena arched a skeptical eyebrow at Harley. "One bite," she replied. "The T. rex would only be an appetizer. Anyway, it's not the size that you have to worry about."

The boys drew closer.

"They say dragons are the most ancient race in the faerie world, but that the Great Dragon is the oldest of them all. He's smart, too. Clever and cunning. That's the real trick. If given a choice, most people would choose to be eaten by a dragon than to be caught by their poisonous words."

"Oh right!" Ernie scoffed.

Athena turned toward him, her eyes narrowed. "Imagine standing there before this mighty serpent, caught by its hyp-notic eyes, unable to move as it scoured your brain, frying your memories one by one and turning you into an empty-headed zombie ready to do whatever it instructed. Then imagine it gave you the order to eat your own arm off."

"What? A dragon could do that?" Ernie was anxiously patting down his jacket as he searched for his inhaler.

"Just for the fun of it," Athena answered matter-of-factly. "Anyway, if we're lucky and are able to disable the Spear of Ragnarok before we even get to the World Tree, we won't have to worry about the Great Dragon."

"And if we don't?" Harley's voice grew quiet as chills rolled up and down the spines of the three boys.

"Lunchtime!" roared a terrible voice, nearly startling the boys out of their skins. Max turned to see that the Custodian had returned and was leaning over them with a broad, broken smile, smacking his lips. "Oh, I do so *love* a good scare." He chuckled to himself and winked at Max. Max glared back at him.

A few minutes later, it was time to move out.

"It'd be nice if we had mules or something to carry all of this junk," Ernie commented, adjusting the large pack that was slung on his back. He might have super-speed, but what good was it when it was buried under a mountain of kitchenware?

"Would you stop your whining?" asked Harley. "It's not like you're the only one who has to walk." Harley's pack was easily twice the size of Ernie's.

On they marched, as the Griffins witnessed a strangely comical soap opera unfold over the grueling day. Several times during the march, the Custodian would offer Athena some suspicious sort of rotting sewer flower that reeked like flatulence. Athena would just smile and then discard it when the Custodian wasn't looking. He'd always return, batting his scabby lids at her and offering what he felt was a charming smile, but really looked more like the grimace of a demented dog. Athena was always kind but businesslike in her response.

The companions continued to march like this for several more days, deeper and deeper into the Roots of the Underworld. They'd trekked up uncountable stairs and down an infinite number more. All the while they had been twisting and turning through an endless maze of tunnels. One cheerless meal led into another, until the entire journey was a blur. Luckily, the Custodian had turned out to be a more reliable guide than Max had imagined.

Finally, after emerging from a particularly smelly and monotonous tunnel, the group found themselves standing at the end of the path. Beyond lay a canal filled with swirling water that looked even creepier than the slime that had covered the walls behind them. What lay beneath was anyone's guess, but they were about to find out. On the surface of the fetid pool, a flat barge of questionable construction was moored. Its wood was rotten and choked with gunk.

Turning to face his brood of adventurers, the Custodian offered a broken smile. "This is the end of the terrestrial road," his voice slithered. "I hope you've enjoyed your tour. I know I have. . . ." He smiled at Athena. "All aboard now, and whatever you do" — he paused as he leered closely at the Griffins — "*don't* touch the water!" He then giggled to himself and adjusted his sweaty goggles upon his crooked nose.

"I bet he'd just love to see one of us sucked into the water," Natalia complained as she stepped onto the boat. Max had to agree as he followed.

"I don't like it. We're too exposed." Max heard Logan confer with Baron Lundgren. "You know as well as I do that this isn't a defensible position. All of us floating along on a dinner plate with no place to go?"

"There is no other way," Cain returned.

"If you'd told me about this," Logan maintained in disapproval, "we might have come better prepared."

Cain turned to Logan and narrowed his eyes. "With jet packs and force shields? Don't be foolish. This place has its own set of rules. All you'd manage to do with your weapons is draw the Watchers."

Logan set his jaw. "Better to prepare for the worst than sit here like carrion waiting for the vultures. Anyway, you told me the Watchers aren't in this section of the Underworld."

"I said that was my belief, not fact," Baron Lundgren corrected. "In the meantime, you have my word that I am doing everything in my power to assure our safety. Now, please, we all have jobs to do." With that, Cain moved to the back of the vessel and spoke in hushed tones with the Custodian, who had taken up a pole and was beginning to push them away from the pier.

225

Tensions were mounting. Something was in the air. Everyone could feel it.

Later that evening, Max was awakened by a splash and a flurry of shouts. Rubbing his eyes and leaping to his feet, he was greeted by Logan pushing him to the ground. "Stay down!" he commanded. "And keep away from the edge."

"What's going on?" Brooke called, unable to see past the tangle of rushing knights.

"Someone went over the edge," Harley whispered. "It looked like he was pulled in, too."

"Who was it?" asked Natalia, horrified. "Is he okay?"

Harley shook his head. "One of the T.H.O.R. agents."

And at that moment, Logan came striding back across the barge and took a quick head count. The Griffins watched the Scotsman's eyes meet Cain's. Logan shook his head, signalling that they hadn't been able to save the knight. A somber silence fell over the craft as it moved along.

"Maybe it was an accident?" Brooke ventured in a cautious whisper.

"Down here?" Natalia shook her head skeptically. "I don't think anything is an accident." Natalia was about to add to her hypothesis, when she looked up to find Cain standing there with a disapproving frown. Natalia closed her mouth and glared back up at him.

The rest of the night was fairly quiet. There were no more accidents, but the conversation was notably sour. When Max arose the next morning, he grabbed a granola bar and walked over to the rail of the barge, staring ahead into the oblivion of night as they continued to crawl through the labyrinth of the Underworld.

"Did he drown?" Max asked of the fallen T.H.O.R. agent, as Logan walked over and squatted down next to him.

"Eventually," the Scotsman replied coldly. Max felt a shiver race across his skin. "But if you're asking if that's why we couldn't save him, then no."

"What happened?"

Logan paused, chewed on a piece of beef jerky, then checked Max's shoelaces. "Keep those tied. We don't need you going over the side, too." Max quickly laced his boots, and as he did, Logan leaned over to whisper in the Guardian's ear. "There's something following us," he explained. "I want you all to stay toward the center of the boat at all times. Got it?"

"Is it in the water?"

"Maybe. It could be on the ceiling, invisible. After all the Doppelgänger business above, it could even be one of us for all I know. . . ." His voice trailed off in foreboding. "Don't speak of it, though. Only to me, and only when I speak to you first. Understand?" Max nodded. "Good." Logan smiled briefly, patting Max's shoes. "And good work on the knots. Keep 'em tight. I'll check in on you in a bit."

Max looked over at his friends, who were hunched in a hushed conversation while they ate their meager breakfast. With dubious eyes, the Guardian scanned the walls and ceiling, looking for the threat. Yet his eyes always ended up at the back of the boat, where the Custodian stood, looking right back at him.

Max tried not to shiver.

The barge bumped against a wall of stone, waking Max from his fitful sleep. Looking up, he could see they were leaving the tunnel works and sliding across the black water into a cavernous chamber. Ahead, perhaps the distance of a football field, was another pier where they'd likely moor. It was what lay beyond the pier that caught Max's eye, though.

"Check that out," Harley marveled.

"Behold the Dam of the Underworld," began Cain Lundgren, waving his hand at a massive wall of iron and wood that rose up in front of them at least a thousand feet from the surface of the lake. It was made of hulking timbers taken from skyscraper-sized trees, which were strengthened by miles of chains. As they drew near, the fellowship could see that the Dam was actually a kind of vertical metropolis, complete with wide ramping roads, clustered dwellings heaped one atop the other, and a dizzying matrix of elevators that crept up and down. Everywhere, thousands of short men with beards, barrel chests, and massive shoulders marched to and fro. Dwarves.

The bottom of the Dam was obscured by steam, but Max could clearly discern the tops of seven toothy gears rising up out of the murk, towering over their heads. The gears weren't moving, and it didn't look like they'd budged in centuries.

"On the other side of this wall lie the violent waters of the Gjoll, the river that surrounds Hell itself," continued Baron Lundgren as he stepped off the barge and onto the stone pier. "Touch nothing. And though you may be tempted, do not speak to the dwarves...." He then turned and pointed a warning finger at Ernie, who shook his helmeted head vigorously in return. "Not a peep."

"And why is that exactly?" Natalia ventured, fueled by both curiosity and the desire to get under Baron Lundgren's skin.

"Trust me, it's better you don't know."

24

Never Trust a Cannibal

UNFORTUNATELY, THERE was no way to avoid the dwarves. They were everywhere, running along the Dam like an army of mice on a giant slice of cheese. Some welded links of chain; others were busy whetting axes or hauling wheelbarrows along the pier. As far as Max could tell, they were all male, though rumor had it that female dwarves had beards, too. Whatever the case, their whiskers were long. Some were braided, others frizzy, and more than a few were neatly tucked into their belts. Not a single dwarf offered eye contact, either, even when the Griffins were close enough to sneeze on.

Max looked over at Natalia. She was gaping as she drank in the amazing Dam of the Underworld. The sheer immensity of the structure pulled at the corners of her vision. It felt like she was trying to focus on an impossibly blurry picture at close range. It didn't matter how many times she turned her head, or how far she backed up. Natalia couldn't possibly fit the entire landscape into one picture.

"This is totally freaky," Ernie said, gulping. "What do you think they're doing?"

"I have no clue," answered Harley. "But it can't be good."

"Lucky thing for you guys that Agent Thunderbolt is . . ."

"It's beautiful, isn't it, my children?" the Custodian asked, cutting Ernie off and startling the kids. He always seemed to appear out of nowhere, no matter how near or far he'd been the moment before.

"Not particularly," argued Natalia. "And stop sneaking up on us like that!"

The Custodian looked at her closely, leering with his tongue lolling out. "Oh, I thought little children liked to be scared . . . isn't that right?"

Harley frowned. "You're a creep," he said, twisting the ring of iron on his finger.

"You don't know the half of it, boy," the Custodian said with a devilish smile, but just when Harley thought the strange man was going to do something really despicable, the Custodian slipped back to the front of the ranks. For countless hours, he led the exhausted fellowship across the Dam, until they finally reached a door that was cut into a stony outcropping.

"Now what?" Agent Thunderbolt asked, zipping ahead. "There's no doorknob."

"Silly child," the Custodian said, pushing passed Ernie. "There is always a way."

Set in the center of the door was a keyhole. With a silver key twirling around his index finger, the Custodian turned to the others like a tour guide ushering tourists through a museum.

"Welcome to the Canticle," the Custodian proclaimed, gazing over the crowd before settling his creepy eyes on Athena, where they lingered. "This is the Great Stair that will lead us to Garm himself."

"Garm?" wondered Ernie aloud.

"The Hel Hound that guards the Eye of Odin," reminded Natalia.

The Custodian pushed a stray roach leg back into his mouth, smacking his lips in appreciation. Then, latching on to the silver key, the strange man unlocked the door. As it swung open, he sang, "Last one in's a rotten egg!" before skittering through the archway on his spidery legs.

As they crowded through the door and onto a stone landing, Max watched the door close behind them, and a series of clicks sounded soon after. They were locked in.

A cold wind howled through the web of darkness as Søren and the other T.H.O.R. agents raised Ever-Burning lamps. With the meager light, there wasn't much they could see. The fellowship was now standing at the top of a stone staircase that led dizzyingly downward into the unknown. The stairwell was broad, but it was bereft of railings to keep them from falling over the edge. It didn't seem mathematically possible, but whoever the architect was, he must have been a wizard — at least that's what Ernie surmised. If there was anything supporting the stair, none of them could see it.

"Can you hear that?" the Custodian's disembodied voice could be heard whispering. "It's the wailing wind. We've finally made it to the lungs of the Underworld."

"That's nonsense," Natalia countered, as she and the other

Griffins tried to stay as far away from the ledge as they could. "Caves don't breathe."

"Oh, but they do, my succulent little friend," the Custodian rattled. "Everything must breathe ... and feed!" The Griffins jumped as the Custodian rushed through their midst, smacking his lips before he skittered down the stairs, giggling to himself.

Down they followed the madman, deep into the bowels of the Underworld. Stair after stair, and flight after flight, the descent was arduous. He allowed them to stop, though only on rare occasions. It was just enough time to pass around a canteen and catch their breath, but they'd move on quickly, despite aching knees and feet.

"Check this out," Ernie whispered to Harley, holding a penny over the ledge. "Think it'll hit bottom?"

"Foolish child," the Custodian hissed, his face pulled back in horror as a bony hand shot out and ripped the coin out of Ernie's hand. Afraid to protest, Ernie watched in disgust as a small roach skittered across the man's cheek and disappeared. "You'll wake the Watchers, and that would be *very* bad. . . ."

"I've never heard of *Watchers*," Natalia said, her eyes narrowed.

"This is their home," the Custodian explained, glowering at Natalia. "And the last thing you want is to have them angry."

"You're just trying to scare us," charged Natalia. "I've had enough of your ridiculous ghost stories."

"He isn't lying," interrupted Cain, his voice taut with concern. "I'd been hoping to avoid the Watchers, but we no longer have a choice. However, as long as we obey the rules, we should be fine."

"What rules?" Natalia asked, pulling out her *Book of Clues* as she wrote RULES OF THE UNDERWORLD, NUMBER ONE directly across from a sketch of a Skreecher that she'd drawn earlier — Lord Saxon's diary would be nothing compared with her book when she was finished.

"There are many rules, but if you remember only these, it will be enough," Baron Lundgren explained. "First, do not stray from the path."

"We already knew that one," Ernie said, tightening the strap on his Agent Thunderbolt helmet.

"Next, touch nothing! Including the void beyond these stairs . . . It is not as empty as you may think."

Ernie's confident smile faded.

"The final rule applies most to the Guardian," Cain explained, turning to Max. "You must not, under any circumstances, use the *Codex*. Do you understand?" Max nodded. "That weapon of yours will draw the Watchers like hungry bears to a campfire."

"What if somebody breaks a rule?" asked Harley.

The Custodian laughed, and the fumes of his rancid breath rolled out of his disgusting mouth. "Snacktime!" he proclaimed. The Custodian adjusted his goggles, pulling them away from his pale skin with a sick slurping sound. He smiled broadly, exposing those rotting teeth.

"Why is it that everything down here eats people?" Max asked offhandedly.

"Because, down here, there is so very little to eat," the Custodian replied, sizing up Max with his eyes. "In the Underworld, hunger is your only companion, gnawing at you, chewing at you. And the longer you're down here, the hungrier you'll become until..." His voice started to dissolve into a gasp. "...Until you'll eat almost anything just to make the hunger go away."

"You're disgusting," Natalia accused. "And I wouldn't be surprised if you tried to eat one of us."

The Custodian's rolling eyes suddenly locked onto Harley, and narrowed. "Is that so?" The creepy guide then turned his goggled eyes toward Max. "Am I so very evil that you think I'd eat poor defenseless children like you even after bringing you all this way?"

Max nodded and folded his arms. "In a second."

The Custodian's wicked smile dropped and his lips seemed to quiver. "Oh, you are such a bright boy, aren't you? Too bad the game has to be over so soon. I was just starting to enjoy it!" Suddenly, the Custodian's spiderlike appendages swung around and snatched Max up into the air. Max only barely managed to shout before realizing he was in the Custodian's clutches. There were shouts, and the next thing Max knew, he was plummeting to the ground. When he recovered his senses and looked back up, he saw the Custodian slumped against the stairs, his broken jaw lolling to the side, and Logan standing over him with clenched fists.

"Hold!" shouted Cain, placing a warning hand on Logan's chest. "Whether we like it or not, the Custodian is our only hope for reaching the Eye. Without him, our lives are forfeit." The

Custodian cringed as Søren and a handful of knights surrounded him.

"I disagree," Athena's voice called. "From here our path is clear."

"What are you talking about?" argued Cain.

"This monster told me as much earlier," she countered. "At the bottom of these bloody stairs, we'll find both Garm and the amulet. We don't need him any longer." The Custodian looked at Athena, his face crestfallen by her betrayal.

"So what would you have us do?" Cain asked,

"Our job is to protect the Guardian," she answered flatly. "We can't fulfill our duty under the current conditions. Keeping the Custodian in our fellowship is an unacceptable risk."

"You want to let him go?" Natalia complained. "He'd just sneak back and eat us one by one! Or worse, bring some of his pets!"

Athena shook her head. "No. I would not let him go free." Her voice grew cold as she looked into the darkness beyond the ledge. "Let the Watchers have him."

"But . . . ," protested Natalia. She hated the Custodian, but throwing anything to the Watchers seemed impossibly cruel.

Athena turned to Natalia and nodded reassuring. "Life brings harsh decisions, Natalia. One day you'll understand. You said it yourself. If we let him go, he'd just slink back and finish off Max later."

The Custodian shrank, pulling himself into a pitiful ball. "You've my word," he sniveled, eyes darting from one pitiless face to the next. "I never would have hurt the boy! I was just going to teach him a little lesson. . . . "

Natalia stepped behind Logan, shielding her eyes. But even as the knights moved in, the Custodian sprang to life. His legs shot out in all directions like loaded springs, flinging the T.H.O.R. agents into the air. One of the knights slid over the edge, clinging to life by the strength of his desperate fingertips. As the soldier tried to claw his way to safety, the Custodian let out a horrible shriek and raced over the edge, pulling the Templar down into the darkness, where the Watchers waited.

Any thought of the Custodian suffering a similar fate was quickly dashed with the faint click of his legs echoing in the darkness. Just like a spider, that madman was somehow able to cling to the walls, as he raced across the underbelly of the staircase.

The companions looked at one another, trying not to think about the fate of their fallen friend. Now that the Watchers had been wakened and the Custodian certain to return in vengeance, it was time to fly. Throckmorton grabbed Brooke, hefting her over his shoulder as he fled down the steps. Ernie ran after the gargoyle in a blur of motion, as the remainder of the fellowship followed close behind.

With each step, the air grew steadily colder. "We're getting close!" Athena shouted, pointing toward a pale light a few hundred feet below. "Garm's Gateway! Dead ahead!"

Even as their hopes rekindled, a clear, howling cry rang out from above. The companions turned to one another anxiously.

The Black Wolves had found them.

SOON THE Canticle was filled with dog soldiers racing down lines of cable. Like a flood, leather-clad fiends from the Black Wolf Society swarmed. The fellowship fled down the stair before them, but it was no use. More dog soldiers were landing by the moment, cutting off any path of escape. The party was trapped, caught between hammer and anvil, as Black Wolves pressed in from above *and* below. Then the air was filled with the cawing of a cloud of ravens.

Weapons clashed as the torrent of werewolves caught the Templar in their trap. Logan's men may have been better soldiers, but werewolves had a nasty habit of not dying when they were supposed to. After falling to the ground, they'd jump back up, meaner and nastier than before. Without silver, the knights couldn't stop them. There simply wasn't enough room on the staircase, and already several Templar and Wolves alike had fallen over the edge. The swarm of ravens, thick as a pestilence, played their part as well. The birds pecked at eyes and pulled out hair until the stair became a cloud of confusion.

Feeling helpless against the onslaught, Max was about to activate the gauntlet when he felt a strong hand on his shoulder. "Take this, Guardian," Baron Lundgren spoke, forcing a small, shining object into Max's hands. "It's called a portal prism, and if the worst should happen, activate it, and it will take you to the Tree." Without further explanation, Cain turned to engage the dog soldiers as they poured over the stair.

Then the Guardian felt someone come up from behind. He spun to see Athena standing there, breathing heavily.

"Hold on to my hand and don't let go!" she commanded.

"What?"

"No time," she snapped, as the werewolves pressed ever closer. "Do it now. We have to get out of here!"

Though hesitant, Max did as he was told. The next thing he knew, Athena leapt off the edge, dragging Max with her. They fell for several frightful seconds, when all of a sudden Max felt a sharp jerk. She'd been holding on to a rope of her own. Like a trained acrobat, she swung onto a landing several flights below the enemy.

Max barely had enough time to crawl to safety when a brilliant flash of light burst above them, followed by screams as the staircase crumbled away. Athena grabbed on to the Guardian, ducking under the next flight of stair for cover as the debris slammed down. Max looked up after a moment. The explosion had ripped a hole in the staircase, severing the distance between Max and his friends. "Come on!" she commanded, unhitching the rope. "We have to keep moving."

"But we can't leave them behind! What if . . . ?"

"You have to trust me," Athena said, looking deeply into Max's eyes. "You can't always believe with your eyes. Sometimes you have to trust your gut."

Athena pulled Max through an opening, just as a stream of ravens rushed after them. As though by magic, a door swung shut, and the ravens beat and clawed on the other side. Nothing was getting through — in *or* out.

The explosion on the staircase had nearly sucked the fellowship into the void. Only with quick thinking and even faster reflexes were Logan and the T.H.O.R. agents able to keep the Griffins from being flung out over the ledge. The good news was that many of the Black Wolves hadn't been as lucky. The bad news was that there was no longer any way to get down to the door. The divide between staircases was simply too broad. Throckmorton might have been able to fly them across, one by one, but at the moment, however, there was still a swarm of Black Wolves on their side of the gap to deal with. After the explosion, however, the fighting ceased, and the leader of the Black Wolves stepped forward.

As one, the Griffins gasped when a dog soldier removed his mask of leather.

"Dr. Blackstone?" Ernie asked. "What the . . . ?"

The chief disciplinarian of King's Elementary School scanned the stairwell. "Where's the boy?" he asked, seething.

"Beyond your reach, Diamonte," spoke Cain Lundgren, who stood unmoved though their ranks were outnumbered three to one. Yet fire burned in his eyes as he regarded Dr. Blackstone. "The Guardian is beyond even your reach."

Blackstone's eyes raced down the stair to the light of the door below. "We shall see," he growled. Then Diamonte

Blackstone turned and barked orders at his Wolves. Without another glance, they disappeared up the stairs as the ravens followed without a sound. Their mission had been a failure.

"Okay, that was freaky," Natalia said as Brooke nodded in agreement.

"At least they're gone," added Harley. "Those would have been tough odds in this tight space."

"Perhaps," Cain said, placing his hand on Harley's shoulder. "But I'm afraid they'll be back before long. There is more than one entrance to Garm's Gateway."

"Is Max really safe?" Brooke asked, concerned eyes regarding her father.

"For now," Cain replied. "The passage below has been sealed with such force that even I would be hard pressed to open it." Brooke looked visibly relieved. "And he is not alone, which is a boon. Yet I sense something amiss . . . ," Baron Lundgren's voice trailed off as he stared into the darkness.

"Do we follow the dogs?" Logan asked, eager to get his hands on Blackstone.

"I think not," the Baron responded after another moment of reflection. "We can better serve the Guardian on a different path."

"Where?" asked Ernie.

"The Iron Forest." With that, the Baron reached into his pocket and pulled out a shining object. Regarding it for the briefest moment, he slammed the portal prism to the ground. Light flashed as a chasm of pitch blackness erupted at his feet.

A Rather Handy Lump of Clay

ERNIE, AGENT Thunderbolt, took an uncertain step onto the sward of silvery grass that lay on either side of the path where they now stood. "Ouch!" he shouted as some of the blades stabbed through the thick tread of his racing shoes. Bending down, Ernie gingerly ran his finger across the tops of the blades, quickly yanking his hand back and sucking at his finger. "This isn't grass," he complained, turning to Cain. "It's more like a field of knives!"

The companions had emerged from the Canticle unscathed, thanks to Cain's portal prism, but it had been close. Even as the portal closed, they could just make out the spectral forms of the Watchers racing toward them with claws outstretched. It was a ghastly vision. For the moment, though, their surroundings had improved. Instead of narrow stairs leading into oblivion, the companions had taken a winding path that led down a short hill, disappearing into a tangle of woods. Yet this was like no forest they'd ever seen before. Everywhere they looked the color seemed to be drained away, leaving behind a coppery stain. And it smelled a bit like a rusty junkyard.

"What'd you expect?" replied Logan, pulling Ernie back to his feet. "It's called the Iron Forest for a reason. Just be careful. One fall on this turf, and your face will never be the same."

Harley picked up a stone and threw it across the grass. It skipped once, then twice, before it disappeared with the horrible sound of fingernails on a chalkboard. When he picked up another rock, Natalia pinched his arm. "Do you mind?" Harley shrugged and dropped it.

"How long do you reckon we have before Max gets to the World Tree?" asked Logan.

"Minutes, hours, never ... It's impossible to tell, really," Cain replied. "I've lived long enough to believe in miracles. Let's hope today is a good day to be granted favor."

With Throckmorton at his side, Baron Lundgren led the remaining troops down into the strange stretch of trees. There was no rolling canopy of leaves over their heads, only the twisting iron boughs, where a pale shadow stretched in all directions. As they marched along, the three Griffins looked upon the passing flora. Every piece of vegetation was made of iron. Harley bent down and ran his finger along a vine that crossed over the path. "This looks more like old rusty barbed wire than anything else," he noted.

"It used to be a natural forest," commented the Baron, as they moved deeper into the wood. "But something terrible happened, and the land has been cursed ever since."

"So faeries can't come here?" wondered Natalia. "I mean, they'd be allergic to the iron, right?"

"Generally, that would be true," Cain replied. "But somehow during the time of the curse, the faeries who called this wood home managed to adapt. They remain here, though they have been changed. They are a dangerous lot, so be on the ready."

"Tell me about it," Ernie commented. Everywhere he looked, the trees and vegetation alike seemed to be looming at him with iron fingers. "We're being watched."

"By whom?" asked Brooke as she moved closer to Throckmorton.

"Monsters," Ernie said, taking a large bite from an apple he'd pulled out of his coat pocket. "Can't you see 'em?"

"No, we most certainly cannot, Agent Thunderwear," Natalia replied tersely. "I suspect you're hallucinating. Maybe you need another Delirium Worm or something."

At that moment, a dark cloud of wings came into sight, and the air was split by a terrible cacophony of sound.

"Skreechers!" Harley cried.

"Again?" complained Natalia, covering her ears. "Don't they have something better to do?"

"*They* aren't the problem," Cain answered, as the winged creatures fled back into the recesses of the forest.

"Seriously?" asked Ernie, knocking on his helmet to feel if it was securely fastened. "Then what *is*?"

Suddenly, the ground began to shake.

"The Iron Maidens." Cain's voice fell upon the Griffins like a hammer. The last time they'd encountered these horrible trolls, the Griffins had nearly been smashed into smithereens.

"Form a line!" Logan roared above the roll of pounding drums that accompanied the approaching monsters. Immediately,

Throckmorton and the T.H.O.R. agents formed a protective circle around the children.

That's when every speck of light in the bleak Iron Forest was snuffed out, enshrouding their fellowship in a blanket of pitch. Hideous roars filled the air, the ground shook, and the clang of metal echoed all around the Griffins.

It was over before it had even begun. . . .

As soon as Max stepped through the door, the gateway closed behind him, sealing them inside a world of utter darkness. There would be no going back now.

"Over here," he heard Athena call as she lit a spark. Soon, an Ever-Burning lamp illuminated their surroundings. Max and Athena were standing inside a yawning cave. Above, beads of fluorescent dew dripped down stalactites hanging from the arched ceiling. Below, on the floor among the towers of stalagmites, lay a carpet of bones. The cavern stank like roadkill and Max had the feeling they must have taken a wrong turn — that was, until his eyes spotted a pedestal standing high on a hill of crimson in the center of the cavern. Above it hung a glittering metal object, hovering in the air as though by magic. Max couldn't believe it. The Eye of Odin!

Filled with excitement, Max stepped toward it, but Athena held him back. "Wait," she whispered. "Nothing's that easy."

The Guardian of the *Codex* nodded as he watched Athena meticulously study the strange room. "Where's the Hel Hound?" he asked. "I don't see Garm anywhere."

"That's because you're not looking correctly," Athena replied. She waved her hand at their surroundings. "He's everywhere, you might say. In fact, you're standing in his mouth."

Max's eyes popped as he raised his boot. A thick glob of goop stuck to the sole, just as he started to notice how spongy the ground was — just like a tongue. And the forest of yellowed outcroppings? Yes, he saw it now. Those were Garm's teeth.

"Welcome to the final leg of our quest," Athena offered. "Either we pass this test and save the world, or we're dog food."

Max swallowed hard.

Slowly, they made their way to the pedestal, Athena calculating the risk of every step while Max watched the scattered bones with foreboding, hoping they'd find greater success than the poor souls who'd tried before them.

Standing within an arm's length of the amulet, the treasure hunters paused, both lost in their own thoughts. Then Athena reached into a satchel and pulled out a magnifying glass that appeared to be the twin of the instrument Iver had given to Natalia. Like utensils on a Swiss Army knife, she unfolded a series of lenses and started studying the amulet. "Just as I thought," she murmured, flicking through the lenses to study the amulet from different angles. "It's booby-trapped. Level nine, probably. This won't be easy."

"What do you think will happen if we trip the trap?"

"I'm not sure," she answered, pulling the lenses away from her eye. "If it were me, I'd guess I'd flood the chamber with the acid. Cheap, simple, and deadly efficient."

Max shivered as he looked warily at a set of bleached bones nearby.

"Still." Athena paused as she moved around the pedestal and examined the hovering Eye of Odin, "despite its strength, the spell appears to be pretty straightforward. It has two layers. The first piece constantly checks to see if the Eye of Odin is still there. As long as it is, no worries. But if it's missing, that's when the trouble starts."

"Can you defuse a level nine trap?" asked Max hopefully.

Athena nodded. "Given the time and the tools . . . neither of which we have."

"So that's it?" Max asked. He couldn't believe they had come so far just to fail at the last moment.

Athena shook her head, never taking her eyes from the amulet as it hovered in the air. "Maybe if I had a Modeler Muse or a Time Stopper. Those just might work."

"What's a Modeler Muse?"

"It's a shape-shifting gas that can mimic anything it touches — for a while, anyway. Long enough for us to escape."

"Would Eden's Clay work the same way?"

"Sure," said Athena with a sigh, but when she caught the look in Max's eye, she cocked her head. "Why do you ask?"

"Cain had some in his vault," Max began sheepishly. "I sort of accidentally put it in my pocket after I knocked it off the shelf." With that, Max pulled it out and handed it to Athena.

"Why, you wonderful little thief," she proclaimed, smiling from ear to ear. "I could kiss you."

Max blushed. "I was gonna give it back," he explained.

"Oh no, you're not." Athena smiled, but her brows soon furrowed. "There's still a risk. Eden's Clay can replicate the Eye right down to the molecular level, but it can't copy its magical properties. If the trap is tuned in to the magic of the amulet as well, we're in trouble."

"Do we have another option?" Max asked.

"Doesn't look like it," she replied, shaking her head. "It'll have to work, because if it doesn't, it won't matter, anyway. Your father and that monster of his are about to stab the World Tree, and if they do, we're all goners. Might as well go out in a blaze of glory." With that, she set the lump of clay back in Max's hands, who wrapped his finger tightly around it. "Now, I want you to take a good hard look at the Eye. Once it's burned into your memory — and I mean *every* detail — close your eyes and focus on that image."

"I'm an awful sculptor, though. I got a terrible grade in art. In pottery my vase blew up in the kiln."

"Don't worry about it," she said. "The clay will do the work. You just show it what to become." With that, Max took in a deep breath and did as he was instructed. His stormy eyes devoured the hovering amulet, drinking in every curve and delving into each shadow. Then Max closed his eyes. He was afraid that nothing was going to happen. That was, until he heard Athena gasp. Max opened his eyes. Slowly. There, in the palm of his hands, sat the Eye of Odin — or at least a perfect replica, right down to the minute scratches.

"Okay, we're going to have to work as a team," Athena

instructed, as she pulled the strange magnifying glass back to her eye. "We have to replace the Eye with the replica with no hesitation. Not for a second, okay?" Max nodded. "Good. Now when I give the word, I'm going to grab the Eye. As soon as I do, you put the replica right where the Eye was — in the air."

Time seemed to stop as Athena watched the amulet and its protective spell. "Now!" she shouted, dropping the magnifying glass and reaching for the Eye of Odin. Moving faster than the wind, Athena had pulled the Eye free. Max's heart jumped, realizing it was his turn before he'd even had a chance to breathe.

"Max . . . now!" Athena yelled. Max nodded and shoved the Eden's Clay replicate amulet into the air. It hung there, just like the original. Max looked around breathing heavily, as he fully expected the Hound of Hell to wake up and swallow them. But that didn't happen. . . .

"Uh-oh," Max murmured, as his eyes caught shadows moving in the periphery, and the soft glow of an emerald light played through the cavern. Max and Athena watched in horror as the scattered bones strewn throughout the darkness drew together to form a spectral army of skeletons. There were hundreds of them, moaning as they swayed from side to side, empty sockets glowing spookily.

Max reached to activate the *Codex Spiritus*, as blue flames danced in his eyes.

"No!" Athena pulled his arm back to his side. "Stay calm. Your fire won't work on the undead."

At that moment, a large skeleton covered in jewelry approached, raising his bony finger at Max.

"Who dares to strive with the Dead?" Max said nothing as the cold, lifeless words creaked from the dead man's jaw.

"Who dares to strive with the Dead?" he repeated, this time nearly shaking Max's teeth out of his mouth.

"I . . . my name's Max Sumner."

"Beware, Lord of the Dead, you speak to the Guardian of the *Codex*," Athena spoke, stepping in front of Max with her twin swords drawn.

The skeletal leader let out a long, empty laugh that sounded like rocks sliding down a hill. *"Guardian? What care we for the titles of the living? You're a thief, and that is the title that you'll bear 'til the day of Ragnarok, when the world is lost."*

The jeweled leader roared, raising a rusted scimitar overhead and charging forward, his army just behind him.

Athena managed to block the blow of the enchanted scimitar, but sparks flew and her sword was cloven in two. "Activate the prism!" she shouted to Max, as the army of the undead soldiers rushed in from all sides. Max fumbled for the object in his pocket, hands sweating as it slipped in his grasp. More weapons clashed as the female Templar parried and dodged. Max continued to fumble with the prism. "Smash that bloody thing on the ground. Now!"

Max finally managed to grab a hold of it. As soon as the prism hit the floor of the cavern, a black pit rimmed in green fire opened beneath them. Without a word, Athena grabbed Max and dropped into the portal.

AGENT THUNDERBOLT awoke with a start. He was alive, which was a beginning. The only problem now was that his aviator goggles were frosted over, and he couldn't see a thing. Luckily, his chin strap had kept his helmet where it belonged. With one free hand, Ernie lifted his eyewear and peered out. Gasping, Agent Thunderbolt quickly discovered that he was wound in a cocoon of iron vines, covered in hoarfrost. Even worse, he was suspended upside down from one of the iron trees. Nearby, he could see Harley, Natalia, and Brooke, all dangling like Christmas ornaments as well.

Ernie seemed to be the only one who was awake. The air was freezing, though a grunt from below made him forget about any discomfort. Back on solid ground, something disgusting was bubbling in a cauldron atop an enormous campfire. The smell was enough to make him barf, but Ernie figured that might be a bad idea. It would have ended up on the heads of the Iron Maidens, who were crowding around the fire like impatient chefs. Their lugubrious bodies were barely contained beneath a mottled assortment of bone and metal armor. Matted hair fell from their tiny heads and rolled over enormous shoulders, and their black teeth looked like rocky shards of death. He'd seen images of these trolls before, in the SIM Chamber, but this was worse.

The Maidens were talking in a guttural language that seemed to feature a lot of grunts, roars, and for some reason, hitting. As Ernie looked around, he didn't see any sign of the adults nearby. He struggled a bit with the vine that was wrapped about him. With a little burst of speed, he'd probably slide right through the bonds. Then again, if he left his friends, he'd have to live with his cowardice for the rest of his life. Ernie sighed and continued to fret, hoping someone with a better idea would wake up soon.

"Psst . . ."

Ernie turned to see Brooke looking back at him. "Where are the others?" Her tiny voice floated through the air. Ernie shrugged. All he could see was Natalia and Harley. He had no idea where Cain and the T.H.O.R. agents were. Then Brooke closed her eyes to concentrate. After a short time she opened them, looking very relieved. "I think everyone's okay," she assured. "I can sense it, but we won't be for long if Agent Thunderbolt doesn't get us out of this mess." Ernie paused at the mention of his moniker, but immediately grew suspicious as Brooke pointed to a spot near the base of the tree. Ernie's eyes locked on the compass Iver had given him. It must have fallen out when the Maidens strung him up. "If you can reach it, I bet that'll lead you to my dad," she explained. "Find him, and bring him back as soon as you can."

Ernie wasn't convinced, but he didn't really want to sit

around waiting to be an ingredient in the Iron Maiden stew. Agent Thunderbolt nodded reluctantly.

"Good luck," Brooke breathed, smiling faintly.

Ernie gave her a shaky thumbs-up. He knew that he'd have to use his powers and that with each use, there'd be less of him and more of whatever he was turning into. But if there was ever a time to risk it, this seemed to be it. Anything was better than being eaten by those disgusting monsters. Ernie waited for the nearest Iron Maiden to turn her back. When he thought the coast was clear, he took a deep breath and blurred into action. With only a whisper of sound, Agent Thunderbolt practically melted out of his bonds before zipping over to Brooke and untying hers as well. Then he raced down the tree. In less than a second, he'd scooped up the compass, checked the bearings, and disappeared into the darkness.

It didn't take long for the Iron Maidens to discover one of their captives was missing — and a second was untied! The nearest Maiden rushed to the tree, but Brooke had already climbed out of reach. The beast let out a frustrated roar, alerting her sisters that their meal was getting away. As one, the Maidens began to pound their rocky fists against the bark, shaking the tree to its roots. Brooke clung to the branch with all her might, trying not to fall as the tree shook violently.

Then something very odd happened. From the edges of her consciousness, Brooke could hear someone crying for help. She could sense that the tree was somehow alive, but it wouldn't be for long. Brooke could feel its soul cry out as the Iron

Maidens tried to pull it to the ground. As the screaming in her mind grew louder, Brooke decided she had to do something.

Grasping more tightly to the bough, she closed her eyes and concentrated deeply, allowing her healing power to seep through her body and into the branch. At once the tree began to shiver, and Brooke wondered if she hadn't done more harm than good. Then a strange warmth started to flow through the tree, and suddenly Brooke found herself looking into two deep eyes lodged in the thick metallic bark. "Hello," Brooke said as the tree regarded her with fascination, as though trying to decipher whether the girl was friend or foe.

Then the tree's eyes narrowed, filling with fury as it turned to regard the monsters that were tearing away at its flesh below. That's when it went berserk. Taking one of its mighty branches, the tree creature slammed into the nearest Iron Maiden like a wrecking ball. The monster flew through the air, squealing like an oversized pig before it disappeared into the horizon.

The portal opened in a flash of light. Gone was the skeleton army and rank cavern. Now beneath them lay an expanse of lush grass, and above, the golden sun warmed a soft blue sky. The fresh breeze was scented and cool, and as Max turned his head, he could see the towering World Tree wrapped in a radiant bark of gold as it swayed in the center of the plain.

"You all right?" asked Athena as she helped him to his feet.

"Yeah," Max said, nodding. "Think Logan and everyone are going to meet us here?"

"That's my hope," she answered. "But I'm not sure. If anyone could maneuver the Underworld without a guide, it's Cain. Keep your fingers crossed."

Max looked over his shoulder for any sign of the enemy, praying that Watchers — or some other gruesome monster — hadn't devoured his friends. "So where's my dad?" Max wondered. "I thought the Black Wolves would be here by now."

"Looks like we're early."

That's when Max felt a chill race up the back of his neck, as a cold shadow passed overhead. He looked up, but there wasn't a cloud in the sky. Something told him things were about to get messy.

"Duck!" Athena commanded. The shadow returned, passing only inches from their scalps before a blast of debris exploded around them. Max was sure a meteor had struck. He wished it were that mundane. Unfortunately, what stood before them was worse: a winged monster of stone. Its stony brows were bristling with spikes; its tongue was forked and its horns swept forward, chipped and jagged. A gargoyle. It had talons, a sweeping tail, and jaws lined with a forest of teeth, yet this monster was at least five times the size of Throckmorton and could have bitten Max in half.

"Going somewhere, boy?" the gargoyle spoke in a craggy voice as Max shrank under the long shadow of its batlike wings. As the beast spoke, a massive army of Black Wolves marched toward the base of the World Tree. The dog soldiers had finally arrived.

The hulking gargoyle growled as it took a step toward Max. "I've been waiting a long time to eat a Guardian," it snarled. "Almost got your grandfather one time, but it looks like today's finally my lucky day."

Max reached for his *Codex* ring as his eyes swept the grassy plain, now filling with a countless army of Black Wolves. In a blink, the gauntlet raced up his arm, and Max could feel the rush of power building. Then a familiar voice echoed over their heads. "Stand down, Azrael!"

The gargoyle reluctantly obeyed. At the same time, the Black Wolves parted as a tall horse approached. Its coat was black and smoke rose from its nostrils. Max met the eyes of the rider and gasped. It was his father!

"I was starting to doubt that you'd join us," Lord Sumner said, smiling warmly at his son before stepping down from the saddle. "You're a Sumner, though, through and through." Max bristled as his father walked over to embrace him, wondering why the traitor was bothering with the pretense of affection. It was clear enough, at least to Max, that it was all for show.

"And Athena," Lord Sumner began, walking over before extending his hand. "I'm a bit surprised to see you, though. Where's the Scotsman? Tell me the rest of your merry band of adventurers wasn't killed?"

"You wish."

Lord Sumner smiled as he studied the female Templar thoughtfully for several long moments. "I see. So you abandoned them in the Underworld then, did you? Terribly convenient, no?"

"I don't know what you are talking about," she spat, though her eyes betrayed frayed nerves.

"I think you *do*," he said with a smile. Athena reached for her sword, but dog soldiers quickly pinned her arms. "Come now. We both know that would be foolish. You've come so far . . . your plan is almost within reach. " Athena glowered.

"Does it surprise you that I've discovered your little secret, my dear?" Lord Sumner asked, his voice laced with condescension. "Though I have to admit your efforts have been truly admirable. I only wish you'd taken my offer months ago. Working for me would have worked out far better for you — in the end." He smiled coldly.

Max looked at Athena, then at his father, trying to understand what was going on.

"Max, remember our little talks about trust?" Lord Sumner continued, placing a heavy hand on Athena's shoulder. "This is your first lesson. Oh yes. She may be pretty enough, but this little babysitter of yours was a snake in your garden all along. . . ."

"You're lying," Max challenged.

"Am I?" his father answered coolly. "Why don't you ask her yourself?" Max looked to Athena, but she wouldn't return his gaze.

"I don't care," Max said, frustration rising as blue fire sparked in his eyes. He'd waited a long time to confront his father. "I just want to know why you killed Iver."

Lord Sumner shook his head, kneeling down to look his son in the eyes. "I don't know what these Templar monsters have told you, but I didn't have anything to do with Iver's death. Though I see they've managed to turn you against me. Typical," he said with a sniff. "No, Maximus. It wouldn't be the first time they've killed each other for political gain. It doesn't surprise me. Not a bit. Thankfully, though, their day is at an end. The last of their ragtag forces have finally abandoned their posts, retreating into their holes like rats. They are finished. The Templar have fallen."

"I wouldn't be so sure," Max spat back. "There's still a lot you don't know. . . ."

Lord Sumner smiled in self-satisfaction. "Trust me, there is nothing they know or plan that I haven't already discovered. And when you finally see the light, you'll be proud of what I've accomplished — for *us*! I'm giving you another chance, Max. Join me now."

Max glowered, but remained silent. "Very well," his father acquiesced. "I'll leave Azrael to look after you until it's time to depart. You'll have plenty of time to reconsider.

"And, son, please turn off that ridiculous gauntlet. You're making the werewolves nervous, and they tend to bite first and ask questions later." With that, Lord Sumner mounted his nightmarish horse and disappeared into the massive army of werewolves.

"This way," his father's gargoyle spoke, shoving Max toward the World Tree. Reluctantly, he'd obeyed and changed his gauntlet back to a ring. They'd bound only Athena, so Max figured he could turn it back when he needed it.

The once-beautiful glade had been trampled beneath the heavy boots of the dog soldiers, and the clear skies above had been swallowed by gray as the temperature steadily dropped. As Azrael led their march, Max looked over his shoulder to where he could see frost creeping toward them, devouring the beauty that had surrounded them. It was as if the whole world were getting ready for the End.

"Where are you taking us?" Athena demanded, as she was towed along.

"You're in no position to ask questions," the gargoyle growled. On they marched, Athena dragging behind, until they reached the eaves of the World Tree. Azrael took a spear and slammed it into the earth, before chaining Max to it. "What are you doing?" the Guardian demanded, struggling to get free as panic welled. The bonds were so tight that he could no longer reach his ring.

"My job," was all that Azrael would say. Then the gargoyle led Athena away. Max had no idea what her fate would be, but he wasn't optimistic. Worse yet, without the *Codex*, there was nothing he could do to save her.

"Heya, Max," a snarling voice slithered from nearby. The Guardian spun around, and when he caught site of Ray Fisher, Max growled like a rabid dog.

"What's wrong? Ain'tchya happy to see me?" Ray asked, walking over to pat Max on the head.

Even uglier than before, Ray was still covered in a sea of blue scales, with spiraled horns sprouting from his head and yellowed fangs hanging in that grotesque mouth. He was larger than the last time Max had seen him, though. The transformation from human to monster was accelerating.

Through Morgan LaFey's dark magic, Ray had been infused with Max's blood — the DNA from the Guardian of the *Codex*. Because of that, Ray could now use the Spear of Ragnarok, just as Max was supposed to be able to do — if he could ever get it back.

"Get lost, creep!" Max spat.

Without hesitation, Ray punched him as nearby werewolves started to laugh. Anger welled as Max felt his eye begin to swell shut. "Doesn't surprise me that you waited 'til I was tied up," Max said, pulling at the chains. "No matter what kind of a monster you turn into, you're still the same coward that you always were."

"What's this?" Ray asked. With a snarl, he grabbed Max's backpack, ripping the straps apart as he wrested it away. "You got that little book of yours in here?" Ray dumped out the contents on the ground, but he didn't find the *Codex*. "Where is it, Silver Spoon?"

"Let me go and I'll show you," Max muttered, his eye squinting in pain.

"Wait a minute . . . what's this?" Ray asked, as he pulled out a link of chain connected to a strange amulet.

Like the coming night, Lord Sumner returned, Azrael at his side. He looked stern as anger boiled in his eyes. "It's called the Eye of Odin," he said. "Give it to me, boy." Ray scowled but didn't resist as his master took the object away. "I had a suspicion that I'd get my hands on this before all was said and done, despite Blackstone's incompetence."

"Congratulations." Max's voice dripped with sarcasm.

Lord Sumner shook his head. "No, son. The congratulations are yours. This is a most welcomed gift. Thank you."

Max searched for words, but none came.

"You see, Maximus, if the legends are true, with this little trinket, I'll be able to harness the power of the World Tree. Then nobody will be able to stand before us. Together we will lead a glorious revolution. And with the Spear of Ragnarok, we will cleanse this foul planet and start anew."

"Dad . . . you can't," Max said, his voice weakened with the weight of failure.

"For too long, mankind has slowly killed this planet, poisoning the waters and destroying its habitat. Petty wars rage all around us, and for what? Zealots? Corporate greed? It has to stop."

Max was listening to the rants of a madman. The words rang hollow in his ears, as though the encounter were a surreal nightmare that just couldn't be true. "But you can't kill everybody on the planet. What about Hannah? What about . . ."

"Certain arrangements have been made, son," Lord Sumner replied, his voice calculating. "Yet there are always regrettable casualties. One day you will understand." With that, his father turned and walked over to the World Tree.

Max's stomach sank.

The reaction was slow at first, but soon the ground started to tremble, and the World Tree, large as it was, began to shake, then combust in an inferno. The flames streamed over Lord Sumner, and into the Eye of Odin.

A Bit of an Odd Twist

LORD SUMNER'S eyes sparked as his body shook under the strain. Yet the funnel of fire didn't slacken as the Eye of Odin stole the essence of the World Tree, locking it away. However powerful the Eye was, the wearer had to be capable of handling it. Lord Sumner looked like he was on overload.

Max watched in horror as his father was brought to his knees, sweat streaming down his pained face. Azrael moved to intervene, ready to knock his master away from the swell of flame. *"No!"* Lord Sumner screamed, his voice growing like the ocean tide. It no longer sounded human. *"Do not interfere!"*

Pulling against his chains, Max felt sure he was about to be devoured in a fiery explosion. If only he could break free somehow. Then something drew Max's attention from overhead. A small silhouette darted through the firestorm above, and it was coming right at him. A falcon! Its wings were on fire and it was screaming. Then it fell.

The bird slammed into the ground, rolling in an explosion of fiery feathers. Then, in a puff of smoke, the bird disappeared completely, only to be replaced by the spiky form of a mischievous faerie.

"Sprig!" Max shouted, looking over his shoulder to see if anyone was watching.

"Yes, Max Sumner. Sprig has come to free you," she said, batting her eyes against the waves of heat that rolled off the dying World Tree. "We promised to help you get your revenge, and revenge you shall have." Within seconds, she released Max from his chains.

A moment later, a terrible explosion erupted inside the World Tree. Max saw his father fall to the ground as the flames burned higher, licking the sky. The Spear of Ragnarok was blown out of Ray's hands as he hurtled through the air, landing with a thud near Max. Rising up, he turned to see the Guardian had somehow broken free from his chains, and then shook his fist as he saw Sprig, now in the form of a small dragon, race off with the Spear in her talons. Ray roared.

"Lose something?" Max asked with a satisfied smile, as a blue fire flickered up and down his gauntlet. Though his face throbbed in pain — now free of his chains — this fight was going to get a lot more interesting.

With a roar, Ray lunged after Max, leaping through the air. Max smiled. It was too easy. With a single thought, the Skyfire slammed into Ray's chest, sending him to the ground. Blue skin crackled and Ray writhed on the ground.

Even as the enemies battled, Lord Sumner dropped his weary hands from the World Tree and the transfusion of magic was snuffed out. Staggering under the weight of his new power, Lord Sumner moved slowly and the Eye of Odin blazed around his neck. He was smiling faintly. A second later, the ground beneath his feet shattered like glass, crumbling into a fiery abyss, taking Lord Sumner with it.

"Dad!" Max cried out, but his father was gone. And so was the werewolf army, which had vanished into another pit. The air felt like a furnace and ash choked Max's vision. As Max spun around, looking for Ray, he heard a deep, growling hiss vibrate up through the fiery fissures that crisscrossed the plain. Max's blood froze in sudden realization.

As Cain Lundgren had warned, Max's father had awakened Malice Striker, the Great Dragon, and paid with his life.

A bone-shaking roar rang out as a monstrous dragon clawed its way out of the abyss, spreading its wings and blotting out the sky. Wrapped in an impenetrable coat of red scales, the dragon's eyes flashed, volcanic fire dripped from its jaws, and its tail broke upon the ground like an earthquake. Raising its armored head, the beast turned its gaze toward the World Tree. Its eyes widened and its mouth salivated in hunger. With another roar, the monster laid its wings back upon its thorny hide and began to heave its great bulk toward the World Tree. Max stumbled backward as his last drop of hope fled.

Yet even as Malice Striker drew near, Max glimpsed a blazing light shoot up from the abyss and hover just behind the Great Dragon. It was Lord Sumner, the Eye of Odin shining around his neck! Max's father remained there in the sky, watching the dragon as if he were about to make some terrible decision. Then, he drew himself close to the beast, hungry hands outstretched toward the unsuspecting dragon.

In horror, Max realized what his father intended. After having drained unimaginable power from the World Tree, Lord Sumner wanted more!

Yet even before he could lay a finger on its hide, the Great Dragon was aware of the threat. With a rush of jaws, the Great Dragon snapped at Lord Sumner, who barely evaded the strike. The battle was on!

Raising his arms, a barrage of golden flares leapt from Lord Sumner's fingertips and exploded into the armored beast, which shrugged off the attack. Opening its jaws, Malice Striker unleashed a stream of fire that filled the sky, smashing into Lord Sumner. But when the fire dissipated, Max found his father unharmed and defiant, surrounded by a golden shield of energy. Lord Sumner had indeed become powerful if he could withstand the dragon fire. If he survived the dragon, Max knew there was no force on earth that would be able to stop him. Max found himself wondering whom he wanted to win: the man who had betrayed him or the dragon. Either way, the world would be the loser and Max was powerless to do anything about it.

As the two titanic powers waged their battle, the sky was torn and the ground was broken. Rocks were hurled into the air, ice whizzed overhead, and dragon fire rained down from the sky. Taking shelter, Max could see that his father's shield was beginning to falter as the Great Dragon pressed its attack. For all the power Lord Sumner had stolen from the World Tree, it simply wasn't going to be enough. When he managed to surprise the dragon from behind, unleashing an attack that singed the face of Malice Striker, the beast let out a terrible roar, spread its wings, and launched into the air with the force of a hurricane. Once again, Lord Sumner was on the defensive, fighting for his life as an endless onslaught of dragon fire tore away what remained of his protective shield.

Realizing the game was up, Lord Sumner summoned a portal to escape, but no sooner had the rift opened, than it was slammed shut. He looked around in confusion, and then opened three more portals. All closed just as quickly. When he turned, he found the dragon regarding him like a cat playing with a mouse. The beast would not be letting Lord Sumner get away that easy.

Then, from his hiding place in the shadow of a large outcropping of ruined earth, Max felt something tugging at his pant leg. It was Sprig, and at her feet was the Spear of Ragnarok.

"Sprig is back," Max's Bounder offered with a weary smile. "And she has brought Max his *revenge*."

Cautiously, Max took up the Spear, and the *Codex* ring transformed into the gauntlet as Skyfire enveloped the weapon. Exhilaration swept over Max. He was now holding the one thing that could change the course of the battle.

"What do I do, Sprig?" Max asked, looking back toward the Great Dragon and his father.

Sprig narrowed her eyes. *"Revenge . . ."* she repeated in a hiss. "Max's father is the enemy. He is the betrayer, the slayer of Max's friends, and soon the slayer of the world!"

A chill swept over Max. Despite the horrors, he couldn't use the Spear against his father, could he? "But the dragon . . ."

"The beast will return to its burrow," Sprig assured. "You must trust us."

A fiery explosion flashed across the sky, and as Max turned, he could see his father fall through the air and crash to the ground, his golden energy barely a flicker. The fight was over. A moment later, Malice Striker landed nearby to examine the fallen form of Max's father. Curiosity and hunger drove it to bend its head ever closer to Lord Sumner until it was within arm's reach. But even as it did, Lord Sumner's eyes shot open. With his last strength, his fingers grasped hold of the dragon. The Eye of Odin flared to life and the trap was sprung.

Unable to break away, the dragon howled, trapped in a fiery transfusion as Max's father stole its power. Yet, beneath the monster, Lord Sumner was shaking so violently that he looked as if he might explode. The struggle between the Eye of Odin and the Great Dragon might very well tear both combatants apart.

While the two fighters were locked in combat, Max knew he had to make his decision. He realized instinctively that he had only one shot with the Spear, and it would have to count. For the first time in his life, though, Max knew exactly what he should do. Clenching his jaw, Max raised the Spear of Ragnarok and fired.

A blast of blue energy rocketed over the battlefield and smashed into the side of the Great Dragon. A flash of blinding light erupted, followed by a terrible earthquake. Soon, Max could see a shock wave of cobalt fire racing toward him, ripping up everything in its path. Max threw himself into a nearby pit, hanging over the side as the wave crashed overhead, then smashed into the World Tree, which erupted in an inferno. The Great Dragon howled and clawed at the ground, belching fire and smoke into the sky. Then, with a terrible whine, it raised its scarred face in one last look at the World Tree, which was now beyond its power, and disappeared back down into the pit from which it had crawled.

On the ledge, though, lay a small and motionless form.

It was Lord Sumner.

Max staggered to his feet, and without thinking, found himself making his way across the devastated landscape toward his father. But even as he drew near, he could see the Eye of Odin, lying broken upon the ground. Smoke rose from its surface as sparks of magic leapt into the air. When Max reached the amulet, he could see it begin to shimmer, then dissolve into nothingness, releasing a river of amber energy that was drawn back into the World Tree. Exhausted, Max stumbled and fell, but not before seeing that the burned-out wreck of the World Tree had already repaired itself, and was now sending its life force across the plain. Even as Max sat upon the earth, he could see the ash and smoke begin to fade, and the holes in the earth mend. The skies cleared, the sun emerged, and swaying grass swept over the ground. With a weary sigh, Max let the Spear of Ragnarok drop to the ground. Everything was as it should be.

Everything except Max's father, who still lay unmoving upon the ground. Max didn't know what to hope or expect. Part of his heart wanted his father to be all right. Another part hoped his father's reign of terror had finally come to an end.

"We did it," Max breathed, wiping away the ash from his brow. As if in a dream, Max felt a shadow pass overhead, and soon saw Azrael, his father's gargoyle, drop out of the sky, scoop Lord Sumner into his arms, and disappear through a portal.

Sprig wrung her hands anxiously. "No," her voice quavered. "Max had revenge in his hands, but Max chose mercy. Max will be sorry."

Max shook his head as the spriggan sat down next to him. "I don't think I'll ever be sorry, Sprig. I did the right thing. And I proved I am not like my father." Max yawned and lay back on the grass.

Sprig purred as Max stroked her ear. "Perhaps . . ."

Soon Max fell asleep.

Max slowly opened his eyes. For a moment, he'd forgotten where he was, but when he looked up and saw the World Tree swaying in a warm breeze, he let out an enormous sigh of relief. Ragnarok had been averted. Either that, or he was in heaven.

Blinking, the Guardian of the *Codex* found Logan staring down at him. "Easy, Grasshopper," the Scotsman said. "It's been quite a day." Max smiled faintly as his exhausted eyes gazed across a field of lush green spotted with wildflowers. The paradise had been restored, and the land made new again.

"Yes. Well done," Cain Lundgren proclaimed with a rare smile. He offered his hand and carefully helped Max to his feet.

"What happened?"

"Are you serious?" Ernie scoffed as he stood there in his Agent Thunderbolt helmet, goggles, and lightning-bolt T-shirt. "You defeated a dragon and saved the world, that's what!"

Max looked around and saw the other Griffins there as well, along with Brooke, Cain, Throckmorton, Søren, and the remaining agents of T.H.O.R. who had survived the terrors of the Underworld. Then Max's scattered memories started piecing back together, and his face fell. "Athena . . . ?"

"I'm sorry," Logan said. "She . . ."

"Here!" Athena's voice called out from behind them. All heads turned to face the female Templar, stunned that she'd somehow escaped the clutches of death. Athena wasn't alone, though. One arm was wrapped tightly around an unconscious Ray's neck. In her other hand, she held the Spear of Ragnarok, and a green portal flickered behind them.

"I don't understand," Max exclaimed. "What's going on?"

Athena offered a weary smile. "Just completing my mission," she replied, taking a step back toward the portal, dragging Ray's limp form with her.

Natalia rushed forward, her face crestfallen. "Is this some kind of joke?"

Athena shook her head, though she smiled weakly before slamming the head of the Spear into the ground and pulling back a portion of her sleeve. Inked into her shoulder was the familiar mark of Vlad Dracula's Order of the Dragon.

"No!" Natalia protested. "You can't do this."

"I'm sorry," Athena answered softly. "We'll meet again, and maybe then you will understand." With a last step, Athena grabbed the Spear and dragged Ray through the portal before it slammed shut.

"She's a double agent?" Harley exclaimed. Natalia looked as if she were about to burst into tears as the ugly weight of betrayal struck her. Ernie just stood there with his mouth wide open, unable to say a thing.

"Why didn't you try to stop her?" Max exclaimed, turning to the Baron.

"Athena was under Lord Dracula's protection. None of us could have stopped her from taking the weapon. Not even me. Let's all pray he'll simply hold the Spear and Ray for safe-keeping, rather than for something more sinister. He would be a formidable adversary, should it come to that. But for now, the day is won and we can rest from our worries."

"What about Blackstone, though?" reminded Ernie. "He's still out there, right? Isn't he going to come after Max again?"

"I do not think you'll be seeing much of your old teacher," Cain replied. "We now know that he is a Doppelgänger, and we will be prepared for him should there be a next time."

Then Baron Lundgren's face clouded. "It's your father who gives me concern," he continued, turning to Max. "Lord Sumner may never recover from the wounds he received today, but if he does, his Black Wolves are far from defeated. One army has been destroyed, of course, but your father has many armies. They will be ready when he calls."

"Will the Templar be ready?" asked Max.

Cain sighed. "We can hope. It may take years to recover, though. Many have fallen, and their fortresses are destroyed." He stared silently ahead, as if peering into the future. "Yet, even now, hope arises. From all over the world, Templar families are gathering together. Side by side, they will rebuild from the ashes. Who can say but that the Templar may very well grow more powerful than ever before."

Cain turned back to Max and offered an approving smile. "You did very well today, Max. I couldn't be more proud. And if Iver were here, he'd tell you the same." He paused as he set a hand on Max's shoulder. "Despite your feelings to the contrary, Max, none of this has ever been your fault. You must know that your father would have acquired the Spear one way or the other. And you certainly did not hand it over to him knowing that this is how he would use it. No. What you did, you did for love. None blame you."

Max said nothing, but inside he felt like a dark shadow had been lifted from his heart.

"Further," Cain continued, "you risked your life to protect your father today — even after all he had done. Extraordinary. I would not have believed it possible. In that moment, you proved that mercy is greater than vengeance — and this is what gave you power over the Dragon; indeed, it is what saved us all. The Spear did not fall into your hands by chance, my young friend. No, you were meant to save the world, as you told me not so long ago. But not because of your power; rather, because your heart, despite all that you've been through, is truly good. All of us here, every Templar, and each and every soul on Earth owes their life to what you did today."

No one said anything for a long moment, then Ernie took off his helmet and scratched at his ear as he looked around the grassy plain. "So what now?"

Cain smiled wearily, and patted Ernie on the shoulder. "What now, Mr. Tweeny? Well, I think it's time for us to end this chapter of our lives, don't you? I for one could use a vacation. And I can only imagine how far behind you Griffins are in your studies. But there is one last thing that we must do first. . . ."

29

GRAYSON MAXIMILLIAN Sumner III stood uncomfortably in the ceremonial garb that the Templar Chamberlain had insisted he wear. Dressing for church in slacks and a button-down shirt every Sunday was bad enough, but Max would have gladly added a jacket and tie if he could escape this current ensemble. As far as he was concerned, he was being forced to wear a dress. Imagining what Harley was going to say, Max sighed as the Chamberlain fixed his collar, then made sure Max's hose was on correctly. *Hose.* Max couldn't believe it. He felt like a ballerina. Luckily, the hideous leggings were hidden under a burgundy tunic embroidered with a silver griffin on the chest. That was about the only part of the ridiculous getup that Max liked.

The Chamberlain was an older gentleman with a balding pate thinly covered by wisps of white hair. His brow was beaded in perspiration as he fussed over Max's appearance. Halting for a moment, the old man let out a grumble and rummaged through his sewing case as he looked for something in vain. With a final growl, the Chamberlain left the room, promising to return momentarily.

Max looked around at the Gothic features of the room. Stained glass windows filtered in a kaleidoscope of color. Only a few days before, Max and his friends had been escorted to a sprawling castle hidden deep in the mountains of Scandinavia. Logan had neglected to mention the exact location, but Max had overheard Cain saying that this was one of the last surviving Templar strongholds, a secret place, where survivors from all over the world had come to rebuild their lives.

"You look right smart," the Scotsman said as he entered the room. Max turned to see an amused smirk on Logan's face, which was, for the first time in Max's memory, devoid of even a single whisker.

"You shaved?"

"So I did," Logan acknowledged as he walked into the room. Max's bodyguard was dressed in his familiar black leather, however, there was a cluster of stars about the Scotsman's collar that Max had never seen before. Iron studs lined his sleeves and a sword hung at his side. "Don't tell anyone." He grinned mischievously. "It'd hurt my reputation." Then he walked over and investigated Max's ensemble. "Anyway, look at *you.* Why I bet that pretty little Lundgren lass won't be able to take her eyes off you now."

"Very funny," snorted Max. "Besides, I'm probably wearing the same dress she is. How come I have to dress like a princess and you get to wear that?"

"I'm not the guest of honor. That'd be you, Grasshopper. Tradition is tradition. Even your grandfather wore an outfit like that, long ago," Logan replied. "Welcome to the world of statesmanship."

"Are you finally going to tell me why we're really here?" Max pressed, as the Chamberlain bustled in to finish up his work and hurriedly bustled out.

Logan smiled. "You just saved the world, Max. There are some people out there who'd like to thank you proper-like."

"But do I have to be dressed like *this*?" Max complained.

"You do if you expect to receive the Order of Arthur."

Max paused, his eyes caught in mid-roll. "The what?"

"The Order of Arthur," Logan repeated. "And when you do, I expect you to behave yourself. Act like a gentleman. No rolling your eyes or sighing."

"What does any of this have to do with King Arthur?"

"The Templar have been around for over eight hundred years," Logan explained. "But even before that we existed under a different name. We've always had the same purpose though — to fight evil. King Arthur was among our order, once upon a time. The Order of Arthur is given only to knights who've performed the highest service," the Scotsman continued. "I guess defeating a dragon qualifies these days," he said with a smile, catching Max's eye. "I'm proud of you, Grasshopper. We all are."

"Thanks," Max said, averting his eyes. He didn't like people fussing over him, yet Max had to admit it that it felt pretty good.

"It all fits, you know?" Logan began. "Arthur's descendant receiving his medal? But I think that's enough of the history lesson. From here on out, I'm ordering you to have fun."

"It's kind of hard when every time I look at Ernie, I keep thinking that whatever he's becoming is my fault."

"There are worse things than being a Changeling."

"Like what?"

"Like he could be dead, that's what," Logan argued. "You

saved his life — gave him a second chance. Remember that the next time you start beating yourself up over it. Besides, there hasn't been a downside to his new powers yet, has there?" Max shook his head after a long pause. "Who knows, but maybe he's the lucky one, after all. Finally a superhero."

Max sighed and straightened the front of his tunic, just as someone knocked at the door. "Are you ready, young master?" the Chamberlain inquired, poking his white head back into the changing quarters.

"Let's go," Logan said, as he gently pulled his reluctant charge along.

"But I look like a . . . ," Max maintained.

"Zip it," Logan commanded with a smile. Max sighed and followed, watching the floor the entire way. He didn't want to see the expression on everyone's face as he entered.

"Nice dress, Sumner," Harley's voice called out. Max knew it. His face turning red, the Guardian of the *Codex* raised his eyes to see both Harley and Ernie in basically the same outfits. All three began to laugh. Brooke and Natalia were standing there, too, both wearing flowing dresses of white, with elaborate embroidery sewn all over. Their hair cascaded in rolling curls down their shoulders and onto their backs. Natalia, for the first time in their lives, actually looked like a girl, rather than just, well, Natalia. In fact, she was actually *pretty*, right down to her French manicure. All three boys looked at her, stunned.

"Stop staring at me!" she complained, punching Harley in the arm. "I'm not a zoo animal."

The Chamberlain cleared his throat. "Places, please. The ceremony has already begun."

With that, Ernie raced over and whispered something into the old man's ear, and the Chamberlain's face grew pale. "Absolutely not! You should have thought of that before now. You'll just have to wait."

Ernie groaned. "But I have a nervous bladder. It's hereditary! I can't help it."

"You had most certainly better help it," the Chamberlain responded.

Brooke and the remainder of the Griffins took their places at the door behind Ernie, who by now was standing dramatically cross-legged. They were ready for what lay ahead — whatever that may be. As long as it wasn't an army of werewolves or a fire-breathing dragon, they figured it couldn't be that bad.

Then, from out of nowhere, Honeysuckle appeared, flying through the hall with a trail of stardust streaming in her wake. The pixie was clad in a miniature version of Brooke's dress, and she looked every bit as healthy as the day Max had first seen her. Honeysuckle settled on Brooke's shoulder, but not before stopping in midair and sticking out her tongue at Max, who just rolled his eyes. Then he turned to look for Sprig, but he couldn't see her anywhere. Maybe Bounders weren't required to attend. Or maybe Sprig was just shy. But if it hadn't been for that little bundle of spiky fur, Max would never have survived back at the World Tree.

"Come now," the Chamberlain's voice quavered, waving Max over. "Stand here, please. Right behind the girl, if you don't mind." Reluctantly, Max took his place near Brooke and tried not to look at her. Just then, a blare of trumpets sounded, and the doors swung open, letting a rush of light spill over the kids, nearly blinding them. Max couldn't see anything on the other side, but he held his breath anyway as he followed Brooke through the doorway. Wild cheers greeted his ears and his heart began to pound.

As his eyes adjusted, Max saw that they were in the wide hall of a cathedral lined with colorful banners. A river of red carpet cut through the middle, and on either side, row after row of Templar stood cheering. Max hadn't expected to see so many knights, especially after what had just happened. They must have been the survivors from the Black Wolf offensive, come to start the journey of rebuilding their lives. Then he looked ahead and saw a raised platform in the front of the hall, several figures in white robes waited.

"On with you," the Chamberlain insisted, and the five of them started making the long journey to the stage. Most of the attendees were strangers, though Max began to notice some familiar, albeit unexpected, faces. Augustus, his father's corpulent head butler, was there. Max hadn't seen him since the night his father's castle had burned to the ground. Dressed in a tight-fitting tuxedo, polished off with a monocle, spats, and a red sash, he looked positively debonair. What's more, he was smiling. Augustus never smiled.

There were others whom Max found just as curious. The Librarian from the Templar Library stood next to Mrs. Bone, their elderly homeroom teacher. Just a few paces away, Monti from the

Spider's Web clapped animatedly. There were others from the town of Avalon as well, none of whom Max would've associated with the Templar in a thousand years. Yet there they stood.

Max wasn't so pleased to see all the guests, though. For instance, as he neared the dais, Max could see the familiar figure of the Grand Inquisitor, Ulysses Belisarius. Unlike Augustus, he looked as bitter as ever, with his quick eyes narrowed in skepticism. Luckily, Ulysses was quickly forgotten when Max saw Grandma Caliburn. Beaming, she was dressed in a satin gown, with a diamond griffin pendant upon it. On either side, Wellington and Mortimer flanked her. The hobgoblins had evidently been forced to bathe before coming to the ceremony, but their clothes were just as shabby as ever. One was complaining about not being able to see the celebration, while the other kept cupping his ear and asking his friend to speak louder. Max smiled.

Then, just as Max was about to step on the stairs, he caught a sight that shocked him more than any other. Standing in the front row in a shimmering gown of deep burgundy, Annika Sumner looked like an empress, her dark eyes lined with tears and her lips parted in the warmest smile Max had ever seen. She was beautiful beyond measure as she stood holding Hannah, in a matching dress, in her arms. His sister was laughing and clapping, having the time of her life.

Not realizing he'd completely stopped, Max came to his senses when Brooke gently pulled on his sleeve. Nodding, he climbed the stairs, where Logan, Baron Lundgren, Throckmorton, Søren, and the remaining T.H.O.R. agents waited. Hanging from each of their necks was a ribbon with a shining silver medal. All eyes, however, were on Max.

Another trumpet sounded, as the five friends lined up across the dais from their companions. A tall man Max didn't recognize stood in the center of the platform. He was dressed in a tunic of white emblazoned with a red cross, and a matching cape cascading from his broad shoulders. Obviously a Templar, he was older, though clearly he was still very powerful. This regal knight had a strong jaw that ended in a neatly trimmed beard of silver, with a waxed mustache. His cheekbones were sharp, his eyes bright. In fact, he reminded Max a little of Iver, but at the thought of his old friend, Max felt the pang of loss.

One by one, the children's names were called out, and the lordly knight placed a matching silver medal over each of their heads and around their necks. First Brooke, then Ernie, Natalia, and Harley. Max was left for last, and as his name was announced, the crowd erupted with even greater fervor, if that was possible. Max's face flushed as he stepped forward. After a bit, the master of ceremonies raised his hand and the crowd quieted. Turning away from Max, he addressed the audience.

"As acting Grandmaster of the Templar Order, I have the privilege and honor to introduce the heir to the House of Caliburn, and the chief hero in the terrible events that have now passed." Another outburst of applause until the Grand Master raised his hand again. Max felt like his heart was going to explode out of his chest. Even his fingers had grown numb.

The Grandmaster raised a gold medal, holding it above Max's

head. "This, the Order of Arthur, is bestowed upon you, Grayson Maximillian Sumner III, Guardian of the *Codex*, heir to the House of Caliburn, and protector of the Order the Templar. Indeed, through your acts of extraordinary bravery, the fall of the Templar was averted and a new day has dawned. Like a phoenix from the ashes, we will rise again, more powerful than ever before." He then placed the medal around Max's neck.

The Guardian was instructed to turn toward the audience. Another trumpet blasted. "All hail the House of Caliburn!" The hall erupted in a roar of cheers. Max waited for the ovations to fade, but they didn't. Instead, the roar was strengthened by an army of trumpets and the rising measures of a hymn sung by an invisible choir. Then, just when Max thought the cathedral would explode, a blinding light erupted high above. The throng looked as one upon a strange figure that hovered overhead. Immersed in a veil of purest light, at first Max thought it might be an angel. Then he smiled. Looking back down at him with eyes of kindness was his beloved teacher Rhiannon Heen. She winked, as if to let him know that she'd been watching over him the entire time.

Lost in a daydream, Max was brought back to reality when Brooke slipped her hand into his. Then Harley threw his arm over Max's shoulder, and Natalia put her arm around Ernie, who started to laugh. Then the five friends collapsed into a giant bear hug, as Sprig appeared in their mist. For the first time in ages, Max's heart no longer hurt. As he looked at his friends, remembering all that they had gone through together, Max smiled to himself. Yes, it was good to be a hero, but it was still better to have friends.

ᴀPPENDIX

Round Table, a Brief History

Iᴛ ᴀʟʟ began seven hundred years ago when the Templar Knights were brutally betrayed. Overnight, the once mighty armies that had selflessly protected the world were labeled traitors and forced to become fugitives. Those knights who escaped death went deep into hiding, fleeing into the mountains or across the seas. The Golden Age of knighthood and chivalry was over.

The survivors were either locked up behind the doors of unassailable fortresses or sent walking among us in disguise. They remained in secret contact with one another, communicating in signs and symbols placed upon an ordinary deck of cards. These were the distant ancestors of Round Table.

As years passed, the Templar once again became powerful, but never again did they reveal their existence to the rest of the world, preferring instead to act in secrecy, where they could deal with evil on their own terms. Their fortresses were hidden, and staffed by squadrons of noble knights. Libraries were established. Centers of power were laid down, and schools began to emerge.

Within some of the most prestigious schools, which the children of the Great Houses attended, entire courses were devoted to the study of Round Table, which had now become a means of passing on the secrets of the Order. It didn't take long before the strategies of Round Table training began to take on a life of their own. Competitions quickly formed among students, though these contests were first held in secret, frowned upon by the Instructors. Yet, after the very Round Table players who had trained for just such an event successfully defended one of the schools against an enemy, the schools eased their policies and the popularity of the games exploded. It was at this time that schools began to introduce Round Table Tournaments. At first only a few schools participated, but over the course of a century, most of these unique schools invested heavily in their Round Table teams.

The history of knucklebones dice is linked closely to that of the Round Table cards. The same students who turned Round Table into a game also imported the use of knucklebones.

Knucklebones had always been considered mysterious, but their popularity accelerated when they were linked to the game of Round Table.

Just as some players tend to prefer certain decks, there is also great attention paid to the dice. Some Houses, such as Belisarius, prefer iron knucklebones, with the numbers blasted out of the surface by dragon fire. Others, like the Caliburns, prefer translucent dice, signifying that they have nothing to hide. There are enchanted knucklebones, such as the Dice of Damascus, as well as cursed knucklebones, which have a habit of betraying their owner at the worse possible moment.

Together, Round Table and knucklebones have shaped the competitive world of the Templar students, where true mastery could only be proven by tournaments hosted by the Wise and the Powerful.

A Round Table Glossary

Black Wolf Society ⊢ A mysterious and powerful secret society. Mingling technology with magic, the Black Wolves have become one of the most terrifying armies on the earth.

Bounder: ⊢ Bounders are faeries that are bound to a human, whom they serve and protect for the rest of that person's life. Generally, the "binding" process occurs when the human saves the faerie's life or, in some instances, completes a quest.

Changeling: ⊢ Changelings are usually thought to be the off-spring of faeries that have been left in place of a human child, with the human parents often not realizing that the change has occurred until much later. However, changelings can also be created from humans that are transfused with faerie blood. As soon as this is completed, the human will begin exhibiting certain symptoms and changes in their appearance, tendencies, and talents that are in common with the creature from which the faerie blood was taken. This can range from anything from the appearance of wings and pointed ears, to superhuman powers such as flight, speed, or enhanced eyesight. The changes are not immediate, yet as the human uses more and more of their newfound faerie talents, more and more of their humanity will fade away until there's nothing left except the faerie itself.

Crypt Sentinel: ⊢ Crypt Sentinels are undead monsters that guard the burial chambers of royalty and the wealthy, wherein may lie valuable relics, treasure, and enchanted weapons. Crypt Sentinels are bound to their tombs by an unbreakable oath, often in penance for criminal activity in their earthly lives, and are merciless in their wrath against grave robbers.

Doppelgänger: ⊢ Doppelgängers are the most dangerous and cunning of the shape-shifting faeries, employed most often as assassins. Unlike most shape-shifters, the transformation of a Doppelgänger is almost undetectable even by the most wise. They can appear as a perfect facsimile of almost any creature they choose: animal, human, or faerie.

Dragon: ⊢ The dragon is indisputably one the most terrifying monsters on Earth. While most are capable of flight, all of them are armor-plated, with rows of sharp teeth, long claws, piercing eyes, and alarming intelligence. They can range dramatically in size (from arm's length to the size of a battleship). As far as the faerie food chain goes, dragons are on top. Griffins are the dragon's only natural enemies. But to take down a large serpent, the griffins must hunt in packs.

Eye of Odin: ⊢ The Eye is an ancient artifact with a single, magical purpose: to give its wearer the ability to absorb the power from anything he or she touches. Considered too dangerous to remain on Earth, the Eye of Odin was hidden deep in the Underworld.

Fireball Pixie: ⊢ Like most pixies of Faerie, the fireball pixies are most often described as beautiful adolescent girls with wings of gossamer and are no taller than a leaf. They are known for their red hair and tempestuous passions. Fireball pixies, however, are among the most dangerous members of their family tree: If their ire is stirred, they can wield fire and flame as explosively as any dragon. And can fly twice as fast.

Frost Giant: ⊢ Frost giants are an ancient race. Enormous both in strength and stature, they are known for both their lofty wisdom and bottomless hunger. Heroes beware!

Gallow Goblin: ⊢ Gallow goblins lurk in dungeons, labyrinths, and torture chambers, where they wait for hapless adventurers to fall into their slimy fingers.

Gargoyle: ⊢ Gruesome statues carved from stone, gargoyles stand guard upon cathedral rooftops, warding off evil spirits that would threaten both the church and the surrounding village. Legend claims gargoyles would come to life at night when the villagers were most vulnerable, only to return to their resting places before the sun rose.

Goblin: ⊢ Twisted faeries, black of heart with sinister intentions, goblins make up the bulk of the dark armies of Oberon, the Shadow King. Though there are many subspecies of goblins, most are about the height of the average eleven-year-old, with long apelike arms, scaly hides, jagged teeth, and crooked noses that ooze with disgusting, slimy snot. Limited in faerie magic, goblins rely on crude weapons and their overwhelming numbers to defeat their foes.

Grand Council: ⊢ Made up of the heads of the Thirteen Great Houses of the Templar families, the Grand Council is convened annually or in times of extreme emergency when important decisions must be made.

Hobgoblin: ⊢ Hobgoblins are toadlike faeries standing about three feet tall. Despite their name, they are far removed from their goblin relations and tend to be rather good-natured, relishing practical jokes.

Ice Imp: ⊢ Ice Imps are small crystalline faeries made of snow and ice. They fly on bony wings and are as vicious and ravenous as a pack of piranhas.

Inferno Imp: ⊢ Inferno Imps are skinny bat-winged faeries with large eyes and red skin. Sadly for them, their only talent lies in blowing themselves to pieces. When not exploding, they tend to be rather miserable and not the least bit fun at parties.

Iron Maiden: ⊢ Huge troll-like monsters with coal-black skin and rotting teeth, the Iron Maidens are what become of the souls of mothers who betray their children. They are doomed to walk the earth in this hideous form, loathed and feared by all.

Leviathan: ⊢ Leviathan is the most ancient of all sea serpents, as well as being the largest and most feared. No ship, no matter how large, has survived the wrath of Leviathan once the serpent's fury has been awoken.

Lord Saxon: ⊢ Lord Saxon was known throughout the world as the finest treasure hunter and adventurer of his day. Traveling across vast, unexplored ice fields and through blinding sandstorms, nothing seemed capable of standing in the way of Lord Saxon. It was once thought that all of this man's missions had been chronicled until rumor surfaced of a final and secret journey into the Underworld itself. The story of this adventure can be found in his diary.

Malice Striker: ⊢ Also known as the Great Dragon, Malice Striker is a monstrous serpent that lives just beneath the roots of the World Tree, lying in wait to protect the World Tree from others until the prophecies are fulfilled, at which time it will destroy the World Tree itself.

Morgan LaFey: ⊢ Morgan LaFey is the half-sister of King Arthur of Camelot. Sorceress. Immortal. Beautiful. Rich. Her dark motives are known only to herself.

Order of the Dragon: ⊢ Led by Vlad Dracula, the Order of the Dragon was once a brother order to the Templar Knights. However, while they fought on the same side, and often shared members, the Templars accused the Dragons more than once of using harsh and gruesome tactics to defeat their enemies. The Dragons, on the other hand, accused the Templars of being indecisive and pursuing peace at any price. The bitterness between the two orders continues to divide them in times when the world needs them the most.

Order of the Grey Griffins: ⊢ A secret society with four official members: Grayson Maximillian Sumner III; Natalia Felicia Anastasia Romanov; Harley Davidson Eisenstein; and Ernest Bartholomew Tweeny. The Order of the Grey Griffins formed shortly after the members banded together to rescue Ernie from the kindergarten bully.

Portal: ⊢ Portals are magical doorways that permit instantaneous transportation from one place to another, usually in a very unpredictable and sometimes dangerous fashion.

Quivering Quillback: ⊢ The size of hedgehogs, Quivering Quillbacks are nearly impossible to spot with the naked eye. They have long, curious noses and twitching whiskers. They blend in perfectly with tall grasses, as their backs are covered in bristling blades. They are relatively harmless and perfect for gardens, and they delight in feasting on bugs of all kinds.

Round Table: ⊷ An ancient game of high adventure, heart-thumping battles, and careful strategy, Round Table is played with a deck of trading cards and a pair of dice called knucklebones.

Skreecher: ⊷ Leathery-winged monsters, Skreechers lurk in the Underworld, swarming over their prey in packs. Due to their smaller size, they are not usually a threat to humans.

Snatcher: ⊷ Snatchers are sinister faeries best known for lurking in your closet and creeping beneath your bed. That cold shiver down your spine could very well be a Snatcher's icy breath.

Spriggan: ⊷ Spriggans are small but surprisingly dangerous faeries left with the thankless task of guarding the treasures of the faerie hills. Easily bored, spriggans are notorious thieves and troublemakers. As shape-shifters, they can take the form of any living creature.

Stone Troll: ⊷ Massive monsters, standing nearly twelve feet high, Stone Trolls have hulking shoulders, beady eyes, and rocky hides that are as strong as plate armor. They are quick-tempered and will eat almost anything unlucky enough to get in their way.

Templar Knight: ⊷ An ancient order of knights, once the most beloved and respected soldiers in the Old World, the Templar Knights were betrayed and attacked on Friday, October 13, 1307. Those who survived went into hiding — taking with them their mysterious secrets and legendary gold.

T.H.O.R.: ⊷ An elite Special Forces division within the Templar, T.H.O.R. stands for Tactical Headquarters for Operations and Research. Its agents deal with the most dangerous and ominous paranormal threats to humanity. While all Templar Knights are dangerous warriors, the T.H.O.R. agents are the best of the best.

Tundra Troll: ⊷ Lumbering beasts covered in snowy white fur, Tundra Trolls roam the arctic plains, searching for lonely stragglers.

Underworld: ⊢ Commonly thought to be only a myth, the Underworld is filled with all sorts of unpleasant and creepy things that find their way into human nightmares. There are many halls and many levels going down into the infinite dark, where larger and more horrible things lurk, gnawing on the bones of the earth.

Vlad Dracula: ⊢ The historical Prince of Walachia (born 1431), Vlad "The Impaler" has been wrapped in a dark mythology, arguably linking him to the birth of vampires. A respected warlord and ruler, Vlad is one of the most powerful members of the knightly Order of the Dragon.

Werewolf: ⊢ Werewolves are cursed mortals who take the shape of giant wolves during the full moon. It is said that some men, whose will is strong, have been able to master the art of morphing between man and wolf, even in the daylight, but such power is extremely rare. Though holy water may slow them down, the only way to defeat a werewolf is to pierce its heart with silver.

World Tree: ⊢ The World Tree is the central force in the universe that ties everything together. As long as it stands, the world will flourish. However, when it is struck by the Spear of Ragnarok, as foretold in the prophecies, life will end in a terrible cataclysm of fire and ice.

About the Authors

BEST OF friends since diapers, Derek Benz and J. S. Lewis grew up sharing birthday parties, Saturday morning cartoons, comic books, and baseball cards. Together the boys spent much of their childhood exploring the sprawling woodland behind Derek's family farm, which they secretly suspected was enchanted. Beneath a vast canopy of ancient oak trees they would battle blood-thirsty goblins, and hunt vicious dragons.

Adventure lurked behind every shadow in a forest full of magical stories and tales waiting to be told. There was nothing within those woods that was impossible, and the thrill of chronicling their adventures has stayed with them to this day.

Mr. Benz has always been interested in archaeology, linguistics, mythology, and cosmology, and currently he works for a Fortune 100 company.

Mr. Lewis enjoys spending time with his wife and daughters, watching the Minnesota Vikings, reading comic books, studying theology, and eating ice cream.

Mr. Benz and Mr. Lewis are the authors of *The Revenge of the Shadow King* and *The Rise of the Black Wolf.* Both live in Arizona with their families.

Visit *www.greygriffins.com*
to learn more
about the magical world of
the Grey Griffins.